RUPERT'S
LAND

RUPERT'S LAND

a novel

MEREDITH QUARTERMAIN

NeWest Press

Library and Archives Canada Cataloguing in Publication
Quartermain, Meredith, 1950–
    Rupert's land / Meredith Quartermain.
Issued also in an electronic format. ISBN 978-1-927063-36-1
    1. Title.
PS8583.U335R87 2013   C813'.6   C2013-901536-1

Editor for the Board: Douglas Barbour
Cover and interior design: Natalie Olsen, Kisscut Design
Landscape photo © cw-design/photocase.com, Map © I. Pilon/Shutterstock.com
Author photo: © Imaging by Marlis

NeWest Press acknowledges the financial support of the Alberta Multimedia
Development Fund and the Edmonton Arts Council for our publishing program. We further acknowledge the financial support of the Government of
Canada through the Canada Book Fund (CBF) for our publishing activities. We
acknowledge the support of the Canada Council for the Arts which last year
invested $24.3 million in writing and publishing throughout Canada.

#201, 8540–109 Street
Edmonton, Alberta T6G 1E6
780.432.9427
www.newestpress.com

NEWEST PRESS

No bison were harmed in the making of this book.

printed and bound in Canada 1 2 3 4 5 14 13

For

Ellen & Lois

An attempt has been made to analyze the aims and
functions of secondary education....

1. To prepare the individual for efficient participation in the duties
   of social, civic, political, and family life.

2. To prepare the student to become an efficient economic factor.

3. To prepare the student for the activities whose primary purposes
   are personal development and personal happiness, through the
   correct use of his leisure time.

———————

Handbook for Secondary Schools,
Alberta Dept. of Education 1930

CONTENTS

PROLOGUE

They're following a line of willow trees beside a field of plants with yellowing tops. He stops, pulls some carrots. Wipes dirt off on his pants, bites into a crisp root.

She carries on ahead toward the sheds. Then stands looking back at him with her arms crossed.

He grabs a few more carrots and stows them in his sack. She wants to know which one he thinks is the chicken-house.

Maybe the one with the stove pipe.

Or maybe the one with the flat roof.

She wants to go where *she* thinks they are, farther away from the house — says, Let's get some eggs, as though for sure they'll be there, the way for sure yesterday she was gonna shoot a duck.

Chickens'll wake everyone up.

Inside the chicken-house. No-one'll hear them.

She lifts a wooden latch on the flat-roof hut. The walls inside are dirty wood painted white, a metal trough runs down the middle. It smells worse than the school toilets.

Where are the chickens?

Something grunting and hairy runs at them.

Out, out quick.

A blotchy pig butts into them and noses into their legs and into his sack after the carrots.

Can't get the door open. (He yanks it against the pig.)

Don't let it out.

They push the door shut on the grunting animal.

Across the yard, he lifts a rusty hook holding the door on the stove-pipe hut.

Black and brown birds crouch on shit-coated poles. He tries not to breathe through his nose. A row of boxes hangs on one wall, a metal can with pockets dangles by the muddy window. He slides on fresh chicken shit, and grabs onto the cold iron of a rusty stove. She's already at the boxes, stinky dust clouds rising from her steps.

He edges over to the boxes, and puts an egg in his sack.

Don't put them in there, they'll get broken. Put them in our pockets.

A black-and-white hen and a gold one hop down from the roost. They shake their red flappy skin at the dangling can, croaking and bucking, eyes this way, eyes that way. Shaking the red skin hanging from their beaks.

Something puffed and spiky red with fat legs and a tail like a clump of bulrushes flaps from behind the stove.

Ouch. What's it doing?

The rooster squawks and claws at their legs — blood-red face around its fat beak. She tells it to back off and they kick it away, making it run around filling the room with dust and feathers till it lands on the stove top and shrieks its morning call.

His pockets are full of eggs.

She grabs at a chicken; it flaps away.

We should get out of here before someone comes.

We can put it in your sack.

She reaches for a speckled hen on the perch. The rooster lands on the girl's back, beating its wings and pecking at her head.

Get that thing off me.

He grabs the hanging bucket and pushes it at the rooster.

The hens crowd in behind the stove. He lets go of the bucket and heads for the door—ready to go.

She's going for a black one — the last on the perch — snatching at its back and then catching hold of its wing as it flaps away. Hunching over it, she traps it on the shit-specked pole. Stuck there now, looking over at him.

Get it by the leg.

She lets go with one hand and digs for a leg. The bird kicks and scrabbles beating its wings against her face till she gets its feet and holds it upside down away from her, brushing her face against her sleeve and spitting out feathers.

I guess we should kill it.

Kill it later.

He pulls the sack over the bird.

The rooster runs at them, nicking his legs.

Okay—go.

He bangs open the door and they run past the well pump to the wagon track along the row of trees.

The rooster lands on the well-roof and screeches.

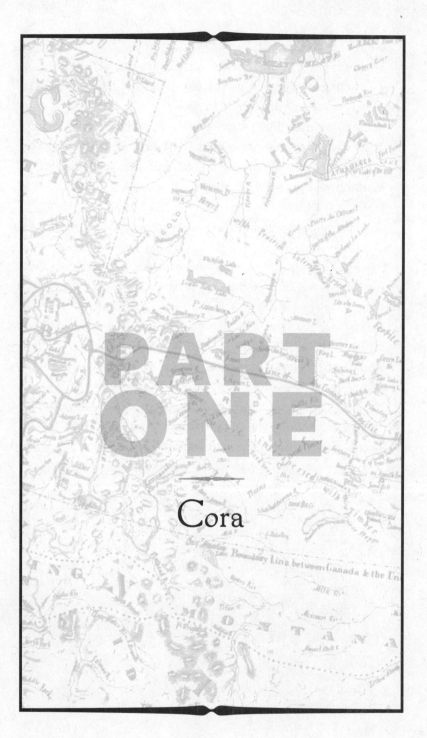

PART ONE

Cora

CHAPTER 1

Not to Judge Rupert's house again. Hot feet in hot oxfords on hot sidewalk in hot dust out to the edge of town. Hey, all a ya, let's get a move on, give yr mother some rest. Gus and Dougie. Hands off my sling-shot. Shut-up or I'll tell. Tell what, baby. That cat.

Cora takes her time unbuttoning her Sunday-best dress, sliding its sleeves off her arms, looking over her shoulder into the propped-up hand-mirror to see a brown island floating on her shoulder-blade. Once you had angel wings and that's where they were attached, Mom said when Cora was little. Did you have angel wings on your arm? No, darling—mine's just a birthmark. A mark of birth. Someone wrote on you when you were born. Maybe it was the hospital. Or maybe it was an angel. Maybe it was just being born. You were damaged. You were marked. You were chosen.

Once I was Indian, Cora thinks, all that's left is my brown island.

Get a move on girls, yr not going to Buckingh'm Palace.

Elaine sits cross-legged on their bed, carving a scrap of lumber into a bird.

You're getting wood chips all over the bed.

So! I'll brush them up.

Well don't get them on my side.

Don't worry, Miss Moods.

I got a sliver in my arm last night.

Must've been the kindling.

No. It wasn't.

Hot bloomers cling to Cora's legs under her school skirt. She holds her wavy hair away from her neck, and twists from side to side, then, squeezing between apple-crate shelves and the bed, lies on the floor. If only they could go to Buffalo Lake. She props her feet on the wall, making the skirt and bloomers puff out and slide up her legs. She'd dive under water away from the upside-down trees. She'd swim far out from shore till the others became pebbles on the beach.

What're you two doing in there? I'm coming in.

We're changing.

Well hurry up.

Lying on the floor, Cora buttons up her clean-for-the-week blouse. Pearl buttons, picked out in Edmonton, made out of glass, not real pearl like the seed pearls on Mom's wedding dress. Even those not real pearls—just something that might grow into pearls if you planted them and watered them and weeded them.

———◆———

How come we're going to Judge Rupert's again; we went last Sunday.

Elaine runs up the street and turns a cartwheel in front of the Bonds' house—such a little show-off, Cora thinks. I'm doing one too. Dougie charges after her, holding chubby arms over his head. No Douglas. Dad grabs. Dougie bounces past, dives down onto his hands, pushes his short legs up in the air, and flops onto the ground. Ow. Ow.

I told ya not to do that. Elaine, young ladies do not show their bloomers to the whole street.

Dougie lies on his back, scrunching his eyes shut and loudly saying Ow.

Let's go. Next time remember how much it hurts.

Dad slaps clouds of dust off Dougie. Look at ya. Know how much time yr mother spends washing and ironing yr clothes?

Aw Dad. Gus bumps a stick along the top of the Bonds' wire fence. Let's go out to the coal mine and shoot gophers.

Judge Rupert's a smart man. He's from England, he's read whole libraries of encyclopedias and books, and yr darn lucky he shows his collections to ordinary folks like us.

She follows her father, moving her leg as though it's leashed to his, placing her feet where he puts his, on a tuft of weed or a crack in the sidewalk. Step on a crack, break your *father's* back. Keeping pace with his flapping pant leg, she hopscotches along, only on cracks, breaking his vertebrae from neck to tailbone.

His suit's the same kind as Judge Rupert's — a wool tweed, his shoes the same kind of brogues, polished every day except Sunday. No work on Sunday. Except cooking. Last time, Judge Rupert showed them his raccoon cage. Bandit masks crouching on a shelf, staring at humans. She put her fingers through the chicken-wire and stretched its holes. That fella was the first in Alberta to be born in captivity, the Judge said, pointing at a porcupine chewing its way along a rail holding the wire.

Claiming her father's footprints, her toe catches the back of his heel. He tells her to quit walking right behind him, what does she think she's doing, walk properly, and get your sister and brothers back here. Half a block ahead, Elaine, the smart-aleck, walks nimbly along the top rail of a fence; Gus and Dougie pelt each other with spruce cones. Hey, wait up, she calls. Her voice disappears into porches and windows of bungalows with pyramid roofs, chimneys poking up from their squared-off peaks.

He's taking bigger, faster steps. Focusing on the grain elevator at the end of the street. He wears the same banded hat as the Judge. But Judge Rupert has a natty panama with black band, whereas her father's is a straw boater with a red and blue one. She wants to snatch it off and clap it on her head. She'd be like him. Go out to work with the men, instead of washing clothes and canning beans and sewing.

He's on a *trajectory* — she learned this in Physics. An object moving through space like a bullet from a rifle. His path toward the elevator has *velocity* and *acceleration,* such that his hat, if it met with an *inert object,* such as her hand, would stop, while he continued, hurtling along his *vector. Energy* transferred from one body, a hand, to another body, a hat. *Force* times *displacement* of hat from its line of action equals *work.*

Is cooking the roast *work,* she asks him.

He doesn't answer.

Why don't we eat just raw things on Sunday?

Yr mother mostly gets it done Saturday.

What about doing dishes, what about eating — is that work?

He looks at his watch.

Or walking — why don't we just stay in bed and sleep on Sundays?

He keeps his eyes fixed ahead. Giving her the silent treatment. His tie squeezes shirt-collar into neck, his back like a fence-post. She puffs up her chest like his, juts her jaw forward (she must find *her trajectory* — her way to be).

At the Telephone Exchange and the Church of the Nazarene Gus wants to know when they're getting a telephone.

We're not.

The Wellmans have one.

They can afford it.

Why do they have to exchange telephones?

Ah, don't ask such silly questions.

It's to do with switching between wires, Cora answers. Someone calls on one wire but they want to talk to someone with a telephone on another wire, so they have to get the Exchange to connect the wires.

Why isn't everyone on the same wire?

Dougie wants to know if the Nazarene people have flesh in their church — like Pastor Crawford talks about in ours? Dad, what is flesh?

Flesh is meat, silly. Gus stuffs a cone down Dougie's shirt.

Flesh of the Lord, Elaine says, you eat that at communion, and you drink his blood.

It's just bread and grape juice.

God's flesh is sky.

Yr all talkin nonsense. Don't talk about what ya don't know.

So what is it?

Pay attention in Sunday School and you'll learn.

No. She wanted another way to be than church and Sunday walks along Alberta Avenue past the hospital — a white two-storey clapboard building with green shutters that reminds her of Anne of Green Gables. Mom went there, when Cora was in Grade One, and came home with Dougie. Afterwards she was sick in bed for months. She couldn't sit up. Mrs. McKickly propped Mom's head on a pillow and fed her soup. She couldn't walk. Cora had to carry her chamber pots out to the backhouse.

Another way to be. Not a girl way. Not bothering about babies and sewing and cooking. Not thinking about dresses and month-lies. Another way, like the way men built streets, ran churches, ran schools, drove trains and everyone listened to them. Another way to be, like the way Indians were not town people, they could read tracks and signs that town people never see.

She had to find another way to be than Cora Wagoner of Green Pastures Baptist Church, Stettler, Alberta.

On Original Road, they walk toward the railway tracks and the edge of town. Graded gravel spills into dust-coated weeds and dried earth, then the edges of stubble fields. Her feet raise puffs of dust. The air tastes dusty and the tracks smell of creosote. She brushes off her white blouse, lifts her hair off her neck. Far far away, the road stretches, dipping and rising, cutting through field after field of tawny prairie dotted with clumps of trees, a road like a bullet hitting nothing till it reaches the sky.

With the others she stops at Judge Rupert's gate to look at his bear tethered in the field in front of his house.

Is it a boy bear or a girl bear? Dougie squints at the animal. Dad says he doesn't know.

How dya tell?

I couldn't tell ya that either.

But there must be a way to tell. She studies it to see if it has breasts. What was that story in a brown library book with gold letters—about a princess who dressed in a bearskin to escape her father the king? She rode in a magic wheelbarrow.

A stout leather collar runs around the bear's neck with a heavy chain linking it to a post. A prince out on a hunt chased the princess-bear with his dogs. Was Judge Rupert out on a hunt when he caught this one? Please don't shoot, the princess-bear called out. The prince was so surprised at the talking bear, he took her home, she did all the housework for the prince's mother.

Judge Rupert's bear has worn a circular path into the ground, and torn up all the grass within reach. Near a chipped basin of dusty water, it sits on its haunches working a paw at the chain, snapping its jaws hopelessly at the flies landing on its nose.

Yr lucky to git this close to a bear. Dad wipes a handkerchief across his forehead. He slides his tie knot away from his neck and tries to undo the top button of his shirt.

Bear bear over there, Elaine chants, would you like a pear.

It shakes its heavy head and claws the links. Gus throws a spruce cone at it. The bear yanks its head back against the chain, letting the cone slide off its oily thick fur. Gus runs up to the animal and pokes it with his stick. This time it growls and lurches up. What'rya doing! Dad yanks Gus away, snatching the stick and whacking Gus's legs and backside. He walks out the gate back toward town. You get back here. Dad pushes him up the driveway. The Judge is expecting us. Gus stomps ahead, kicking pebbles.

Quit raisin dust!

There's bears in the Bible, Dougie says, falling in beside his father.

Dad slides his tie knot back into place, doing up his jacket.

They ate forty-two children.

Do ya know why they did that?

Why?

Because the children were making fun of the Lord.

Oh…Dad?…Dad, was Elisha the Lord?

No he was a man of the Lord. Ya don't make fun of a man of the Lord.

What if the prince didn't capture the bear and find out she was a princess and marry her? What if the bear made the prince follow her into the forest?

— ◆ —

They enter the front hall with its wide staircase and balustrade to bedrooms on the upper floor.

Mr. Wagoner. (The judge holds a white napkin.)

If you remember you were gonna show your collection to my youngsters here. (Her father turns his hat brim round and round in his hands. With it on he looked like all the other men in town, driving automobiles, going to church, to a bank or the courthouse. With it off, his hair sproings out like Gus's and he's ordinary again.) Sorry to come at the wrong time.

No no it's fine now. Just put your hat on the stand.

The judge leads them down the hall, past a sitting room and a parlour with dark shiny tables and upholstered chairs with doilies. Instead of bulbs on cords, the Rupert house has proper lamp-shades like white flower bells growing out of its ceilings. It has sofas and whatnots and bookcases and tables and pictures in picture frames and armchairs and rugs and a piano.

He shows them into a room, under the jowls and nostrils of a moose lurching from the wall. Across from Cora, an elk head with spiky antlers lunges out above a row of china plates. As though, if she went into the next room, she'd see its rump and tail. Do they have glass eyes or real eyes? Animals watching her from every corner, mouths shut, except for the bear ready to bite a glass case of prairie chickens. Cora starts a staring contest with the owls. Were they really looking at her or were their black pupils little pockets of night sky looking everywhere? In a photograph, she counts 60 ducks hanging from ropes beside the judge with his rifle.

And this is my albino collection. A white gopher, a white crow and a robin entirely white except for its red breast. The judge is on a *trajectory* too, like Dad, but what was hers? This one's French artillery. He opens a case of World War I badges, and holds up a red-white-and-blue ribbon attached to a metal cross. This one's from the Belgian military police. Cora presses wet palms into her thick cotton skirt. She's inside a canning jar on a shelf in the cellar. Elaine's in the next jar carving her bird. A spider is building a web around the jars.

From under a glass case containing a model sailing ship, Mr. Rupert pulls out four trays of coins. What was a *trajectory* anyway? Was it like a comet? Would she burn up? He's going on about a man on a coin — Louis XV of France. Or could *she* be a judge — staring over her court, above it all, like the moose? That's five francs in 1728. A gunner sent me that in March of '15. A month later he was dead. Gus gazes out the window. Dad turns Gus's head. Pay attention, the judge is showing ya something.

A brass figurine of a fat laughing man with no shirt that came from China, a pair of Chinese sandals and an opium pipe. Then a boa constrictor skin, a sisal skirt and a walrus tusk. What would it be like to shoot a really big animal, instead of gophers on Maynard's farm? Cora hides a yawn behind her hand. She lifts her right foot and balances it on its toe, then wiggles her heel back and forth in her hot shoe. Oh could we please sit down? But no chairs. Just cases of bird's eggs, seashells and arrowheads—each specimen carefully labeled: robin, wren, magpie, oriole, pheasant, golden eagle, barn owl. Scallop, abalone, nautilus, oyster, cockle, sundial, sand dollar—there's barely room to stand.

She stoops over a box of rock samples. Wavy patterned like the striped cliffs at Drumheller on a long-ago school trip, Dad grumbling, What do they want to teach nonsense about dinosaurs for? Paleon—ancient being. Ology—the study of. Another way to be, like the lady with a magnifying glass sticking out of her cowboy hat, pounding her chisel into rock. She's wearing dungarees—she's got a whisk dangling from her belt, Netty laughed and ran off. The lady put down her chisel, and strode over, kicking a bucket out of the way. Cora shook hands. Hello, I'm Mary Tyrell. Come with me. Past a man measuring a bone as big as an axe handle. Cora ran her hand over skeletal fingers half buried in a slab of stone.

Did you know the founder of paleontology was a woman? Mary Tyrell's eyes bulged through her spectacles.

No ma'am.

Her name was Mary Anning and she discovered the first complete skeleton ever found of an ichthyosaur, in 1811 when she was the same age as you are.

Cora pulled a chunk of stone printed with fern leaves out of Mary Tyrell's wheelbarrow. Take it, dear. That's pecopteris. It grew here 300 million years ago.

Have you got any fossils, Cora asks the Judge. But he doesn't collect fossils, just petrified wood. She fingers the yellow sulphur, pink quartz, black papery mica, grey shiny molybdenite in his box of samples. Where does he get such things? Her box under the bed holds shale, conglomerate, and sandstone she found at the lake or along the tracks. When the Wellmans brought in stone for their rock wall, she snared some granite. Cora picks up the judge's soapstone and turquoise. Would he notice if she just took one of the smaller pieces? He's holding up a pair of spurs once owned by Gabriel Dumont, Louis Riel's man with his camp three or four hundred strong on Buffalo Lake.

A scuffling sounds in the hall and the door opens part way. Oh, the judge frowns, where are we going to put that? He shuts the coin drawers, Well I guess you better come in. A Cree woman sets a tray of milk and cookies on top of the coin cabinet, the smell of chocolate mingling with the smell of fur, antlers, beaks and feathers. This is my wife Martha. She stands next to a flock of arrowheads, flying like geese across their mounting board. Cora smiles imagining Judge Rupert going to an Indian reserve to select Mrs. Rupert, a chief wearing a crown of feathers like the picture in her History book giving him his daughter. She pictures Judge Rupert laying a deer at his feet like Hiawatha did for Minnehaha. But of course that isn't what happened.

Some of my ancestors shot these at buffalo, Mrs. Rupert smiles, pointing at the arrowheads, but I myself prefer a rifle. No one says anything. Then Dad—pleased to meet you ma'am —straightens his shoulders, and pinches Cora's arm. She shakes hands, wanting to ask Mrs. Rupert if she was the one who shot the stuffed deer and her fawn grazing near the glass-fronted bookcase, and did she know how to tan hides and make moccasins.

Such a pretty blouse, did you sew that yourself, dear?

Oh—uh—thanks—no—my Mom did it. I'm terrible at sewing.

Dad glares at Cora behind Mrs. Rupert's back as she passes around the plate of cookies. What do you say, Douglas?!

Well, I'm terrible at dusting, Mrs. Rupert offers Gus the cookies, How do you dust a moosehead, anyway?

You do a passable job, the Judge runs his finger along a deer antler coating it with dust, then blowing it off. No, not for me thanks, he waves away the plate.

I like your animals, Elaine pats the fawn, they're perfect Mrs. Rupert.

She's just like Mom, Cora thinks, except Mom doesn't shoot rifles—she's like Mom used to be when she lived in the mansion with all her sisters in Toronto, with lots of bedrooms and dressers and china and crystal sets and lace tablecloths, and round and oval photographs on the wall, china dogs, overstuffed chairs, and curly-legged tables.

Red men, it said in History. Canada was a wilderness with a few tribes of red men. But Mrs. Rupert isn't red, she isn't even brown, and she wears the same print dresses Mom does, not blankets or buckskin and moccasins. Not a bed-sheet wrapped around her middle like the medicine man holding a pipe at the front of her History book. Torture captives—that's what Indian women and children most liked to do, the book said. Why would they want to do that? In English they had a poem about a *tragic savage* Onondaga woman. The poem called her a *madonna,* as though she were in the Catholic Church with a halo floating over her head. Maybe Mr. Rupert was captured by Indians. They were going to kill him and then Martha stopped them, like Pocahontas. Don't scalp him, she said, he's a good man. She saved his life, so he married her. And they lived happily ever after, like the princess bear and her prince.

What was it like, anyway, to be savage? Nothing comes to Cora except darkness, the pit of a well, a sense of choking or dull emptiness. Or coyotes tearing up a dead steer, a wild horse bucking and kicking at the Exhibition, buffalo stampeding over a cliff. Savages didn't have a great father god, it said in History, they relied on dreams about spirits. Medicine men rolled on the ground, it said, foaming at the mouth. But maybe her History book is telling stories, like the princess-bear, that aren't really true.

Spirit dreams—another way to be—did Mrs. Rupert think of these?

In the hall on the way out, Dad asks Judge Rupert what he thinks of the not guilty verdict in the arsenic case in England. Her sister and her aunt died of it! Well, she had the best barrister in the country. Dougie grabs Cora's arm and points into the shadows under the stairs. A suit of armour moves toward them. A sharp spike juts up from its helmet. Its eyes, big as jarlids, are empty and dark, its mouth, a metal snout, spews a rubbery ringed hose like a fat snake. It snuffles and wheezes toward them, grasping at them with heavy leather gloves. Fee fi fo fum, it rasps, rattling a rusty tin box on the end of its snout. Cora and Dougie back away. Elaine and Gus rush out the front door ahead of Dad. Gerard, the judge says, that's enough.

Gerard's different at home, tomorrow he'll sit in front of Cora in History class, silent as the mooseheads, drawing airplanes in his notebook. Or deer and crows and owls — so real she could almost see them breathing.

When they get to the gate, Dougie wants to know whether the bear has died. Lying in its dusty circle, its fur hangs loose from its body, its paws outstretched as though it'd been standing and suddenly fell over sideways. Flies land on its nose and walk around. Maybe the princess ran away with its body, and left only the fur.

Dad loosens his tie again, marching steadily south on Original Road. Where's he going? Cora matches her steps to his, straight south as though they'd keep on going through the rows of bungalows, then past the golf course, and out the other side of town into the wheat fields, south till they hit the Drumheller canyon, south till they crossed the United States, then South America, south till they hit the South Pole.

What would they do when they got to the South Pole — turn around and march north again? What did poles look like — knitting needle through a ball of yarn. A telegraph pole, a flagpole. And a flag saying South or North. Indians didn't have poles; they could tell directions by the sun. They could find animals and humans by signs white people never notice. Another way to be.

Dad yanks off his jacket, carries it over his arm. Damp patches show on the armholes of his waistcoat.

Dad, is Gerard a halfbreed? Dougie walks between Cora and her father.

Who's Gerard?

He's Mr. Rupert's son. He had this scary mask on.

Oh.

Dad what is that — halfbreed?

Means you're half Indian.

So why doesn't he go to Indian school?

Cuz he's half white and he's Judge Rupert's son.

Dad strides along Alberta Avenue, jaw shut, tramping past fenced yards containing a tree or a bicycle or dry grass — rows of bungalows and fences — tramping steadily toward Taylor Street. Then Main Street with Wellman & Bond's store, the bank, the Buffalo Hotel.

Why did they call it a massacre at Frog Lake when only a few died? Cora draws an imaginary arrow on an imaginary bow.

They killed about a hundred.

My English teacher says they only killed a few. The Indians were starving and the Agent refused to give them food.

What does he know about it?

She.

It was the whole town, they took them hostage.

Didn't anyone in the town have guns? (Gus and Dougie — If you're gonna be anindian ya gotta yell and go like this — singing out whooo-oo-oo-oo and batting hands on their mouths. She ran after them, galloping her horse-legs and making Indian whoops.)

They snuck in at night, people didn't have time to load their weapons.

My English teacher says it happened in the daytime — Big Bear tried to stop it — it was only when the agent wouldn't go to the Indian camp that they shot him.

It was part of Louis Riel's ambush — they were a bunch of hooligans.

I wonder if Mrs. Rupert misses living with her people?

Why would she want to go around barefoot in a blanket?

He shifts his jacket to the other arm. They pass the hospital again. Gus throws a cone up in the air and whacks it with a poplar switch. Gus was still a baby when Mom came home from the hospital with Dougie, Gus still sleeping in a crib. Her father slept in a bed next to the crib. He came home way after supper. He fell down in the front room. Mrs. McKickly said he should just go straight to bed. She hung up his coat and hat. You go on in there Mr. Wagoner; don't wake little Gus. But Gus woke up anyway, calling mama, mama, louder and louder. Her father came out in his pajamas and grabbed the switch from behind the stove.

Mr. Wagoner, don't you bother with that, let me take him.

I'm gonna to teach him a lesson.

Mr. Wagoner.

Outa my way.

Gus and Dougie captured Cora, tied rope around her and barred her into their firewood fort. Her head poked over the top. You guard, Gus told Dougie. Dougie pointed his stick-gun at Cora. Gus went into the house and came back with Dad's .22. You put that back, Cora knocked over her firewood jail, struggling with the rope. There's no shells in it. I don't care; you never point it at anyone. But it's just a game. I'm not playing this game; you put that back, right now.

Cora wonders whether the Indians put the prisoners in a teepee, or tied them up with ropes on the ground. Did they make the Frog Lake settlers eat dried buffalo and berries or did they starve them? What if a settler wanted to become Indian — did they let him, and if they did let him, did they make him smoke a peace pipe, or bring in a deer, or prove he could dream of spirits. Could a girl become Indian?

I think Mrs. Rupert was captured by settlers.

She's lucky the Judge married her or she'd still be covered in dirt, carryin a baby on her back — like the riffraff comin through town.

Maybe I'm part Indian too, maybe *I've* been captured by settlers.

He shakes his head, gives a curt tsk, pressing his lips together. You smarten up or I'll give ya back to the Indians.

———◆———

Sunday afternoon. Mom lying down in her room. Dad in his armchair reading his Bible. Nothing to do but hang about on the back stoop, wait till dinner. Sunday afternoon waiting for Monday wash day, Monday school. Monday workday. She crosses Lake Avenue and the CPR tracks, takes the path through the fields to Cold Lake. A killdeer cries, swooping past her and away — taking you away from her nest, Dad said. She wanders along the beach, picking daisies and purple vetch, then slips into the trees. An old rowboat with the stubs of oars points out toward the lake, growing an aspen through its bottom. She leans against the trunk, props her feet on the bow seat and looks through bulrushes at the sungleamy water. She'll drift in her boat, like Moses, to a faraway land — far away from Dad and his Bible lessons for her baptism. Her rowboat'll become a canoe and she'll become an Indian in buckskin and moccasins, like Pauline Johnson. She'll take her canoe through crashing waves, find the calm waters on the other side. She'll dip her paddle and her paddle will sing a brave song.

CHAPTER 2

Cora pushes aside some cloth and dumps her books on the table — where's she going to study with patterns and white fabric, piles of sheets and pieces of blouse littered everywhere, Mom sewing sewing sewing? She opens her chem book: boron's the only nonmetal that has fewer than four electrons in its outer shell, it says under the periodic table.

I'm working on your dress.

What dress?

For your baptism, dear, what do you think?

She holds up the white cotton garment. So definitely not like the dresses in *Good Housekeeping*.

Oh Mom, does it have to have puffed arms and full gathered skirt? Netty's had a straight skirt and slim sleeves.

Her mother slumps her shoulders, pushes a strand of hair back into place. Gives her that look that says she's worked on it all afternoon and doesn't want to hear about it.

You don't want something too revealing when it gets wet.

Why don't we just wear swim suits?

In church?!

When we go to the beach, swim suits aren't too revealing.

Oh for Pete's sake—you know perfectly well why. Mom fans herself, then starts cutting a long white strip of cotton.

What's that for?

Ruffles for the front of your dress; if you could just get them gathered for me...

Oh Mom, I'm trying to study Chemistry.

I've got these sheets to turn and Elaine's blouse.

Cora slams the book shut, threads a needle and starts running the thread through the cloth, planning a chemistry experiment on Mom's silver teapot and her aluminum candy dish. Her book says she can get the silver tarnish off without even rubbing it if she puts them in a pot with hot water and baking soda.

You'll need a longer thread than that; measure it against the bodice.

She's got the needle half way. She snips it off, yanks out the thread, gets a huge long one and starts working the cotton into puckers and ripples. Her fingers rub and chafe at it, bunching it too much this way, then flattening it too much that way.

Mom, I can't really see myself in this dress.

Why ever not?

It looks like something people wore back in the '90s.

Well I'm not going to start over and make you another one.

I'll wear my school clothes.

You need something white.

Boys don't wear white.

Well you're not a boy are you?

I can't even see myself getting into that baptism pool.

It's just a ceremony, dear, just something everyone goes through —it'll make your father so pleased.

In the weed-tangled lot next door, an Indian man in denim like the farmhands wear stands with a horse. The animal is dusty and gaunt. Its saddlebags flat and empty. Two more Indian men stop beside him, one holding a fishing rod. They wear flat caps and jackets that were once part of a suit. A woman carries a baby in a shawl tied around her shoulders.

Mom, they've come again.

Give them the potatoes and carrots on the kitchen table.

The ones for supper?

We'll dig more from the garden.

Cora gathers the vegetables into a towel and carries them out to the woman. The faded pattern on her flour-sack dress is the same as one Cora had a few years back. Thank you ma'am, the woman says. Her thin hands nest each potato and carrot into a cloth bag. She wears a crown of braids pinned tightly across the top of her head. The lines on her face make Cora think of the weathered rocks at Drumheller.

A little distance away, the men wait with the animal, keeping their backs to Cora and the woman. The baby, holding a piece of beaded thong, silently stares at Cora over the woman's shoulder. Cora wants to ask the woman how she'll cook the vegetables — where is she camped? The nearest reserve is more than thirty miles.

Thank you ma'am. The woman meets her eyes, seems to gaze into her in a way she doesn't understand. Then a line comes to her from a poem they studied in English, the one the teacher said wasn't in the provincial course outline: *Starved with a hollow hunger, we owe to you and your race* — about a Cree chief who was hunted down like a cattle thief by settlers.

Cora feels red creeping into her cheeks, and looks down at the woman's feet poking through her shoes. The woman turns back to the men, and they walk away.

Where will they go? Somewhere roaming across the prairie — no town — no school — no church. No house even, just a teepee you could set up anywhere but they don't even seem to have that. Cora follows them down Taylor Street to Prairie Avenue. They're a block ahead going towards Red Deer. Towards the sunset. She follows them past the school. Past shacktown, where a man sitting on a crate watches her as he takes a puff. A baby cries behind the old blanket that makes the door of another shack. The Indians turn north on the road to the coal mine. The road that goes on forever in a straight line.

She turns back to town toward Mr. Maynard's grain elevator, its white clapboard now a dusty orange under the reddening sun. Such a jolly man — Hilda's dad. Always telling jokes. He taught Cora how to drive a team, and let all the Maynard kids ride up and down the elevator man-lift. He let them play cards and go to dances, even though they were in the same church as Dad. He's my best friend, Hilda said. And Hilda's Cora's best friend.

Troon brothers' team passes her, pulling its Model T — covered with dust. Cora's fingernails are black again, and dust fills her nose. A knot of men in flat caps waits around the dole office, their trousers and jackets same as the ones Dad wears or the school principal, too stained and faded now for church or a job. One is sewing a patch on a sleeve. Another is tying a string around his shoe, holding on the flapping sole.

She stops to read the town notice board:

For Sale: Int'l Cream Separator.
Troon Farm.

Girl wishes position for general
housework in town. Phone 41.

Maybe she should put up a notice for a job, Cora thinks, but then she doesn't have a phone.

For Rent: furnished room for
a lady roomer. Phone 34.

Will sacrifice for $600 cash. Quit farming.
Used very little Sawyer-Massey Engine.
Phone 27.

Be Aware! Indian children are required by law
to be in Residential Schools. Report runaways to police.

At the Buffalo Lake church picnic, Mr. Maynard said Stettler Green Pastures Baptist should be doing more for them. Our native brothers, he said. The church should gather food and rummage, try to help out in hard times. Ah gwan — Mr. Lawson spat watermelon seeds into the bushes, they've got all that land.

A lot a them are starving.

A lot a ours are starving too. The mayor took another forkful of chocolate cake — United Church hands out bread to sixty men a week.

They kin hunt and fish on all that land — Mr. Lawson threw his rind after the pits, Whata they need us for.

There's sickness — bad sickness. Mr. Maynard pushed back his straw hat and ran a handkerchief over his brow.

What kinda sickness.

TB.

Ah, balderdash.

I'm serious. My brother in Ottawa knows the man who studied it. The kids in those Indian schools are getting it, bringing it back to the reserves. The schools're too hard on them.

Mr. Lawson helped himself to a piece of Mrs. McKickly's apple pie. The mayor crossed his arms, looked out toward the lake. Can't be all that serious — otherwise the government would do something about it, I guess.

———

Where were you?

I followed them.

Who?

The Indians.

Whatever for?

Mom, Mr. Maynard says our church should be doing more for them.

Doing what, dear?

Helping them — I don't know. Giving them food.

Her mother rips a worn bed-sheet in half to stitch edges to middle.

Do you think our church should do that?

Do what?

Help the Indians.

Her mother runs the raw edges of sheet steadily through the jumping needle on the machine. The government looks after them quite a bit.

What does it do?

Gives their children schooling. Gives them rations.

Then why are they starving?

I don't know — I guess some of them can't do very well for themselves.

Mr. Maynard says the Indian schools are bad.

How would he know that?

He says his brother knows someone who did a study of it.

Really.

Mom, we're doing a pageant about the Indians for the fall fair.

Her mother trims one side of the seam in the sheet, folds the other side over it, pins it flat.

It's about Louis Riel and Gabriel Dumont and the war of 1885.

Her mother puts the sheet back in the machine; pumps the treadle. The metal foot flattens the seam edges onto the sheet.

Mme Lumière's made it up for us.

What part are you going to have?

I'm going to be Gabriel Dumont.

Couldn't one of the boys play that?

No one wanted to.

Who's acting as Riel?

Madame Lumière was going to make Bunk do it, but Gerard Rupert wanted to.

Well you won't be very popular around here.

Why not?

Because those two men stirred up a ruckus that got a lot of people killed. Good working people. And people trying to help Indians—like farm instructors. I'll bet Judge Rupert isn't pleased.

Mme Lumière says the Indians were starving, and the agents weren't giving them any food.

They could farm like the rest of us.

Mme Lumière says they weren't giving them any farm equipment either.

Well I don't know what history book she was reading.

Her mother stops the machine, attaches the empty bobbin to its top spindle and loads it with thread from the spool.

Mme Lumière says I should go to university.

Well Mme Lumière isn't the only person who has a say in this.

Doesn't it matter that I can get a scholarship?

There's still your living expenses. She bends over the machine fitting the bobbin back into its round hole.

Why didn't you go to university like Aunt Beulah and Aunt Faith?

How could I go, when I hadn't finished high school? Mom stops, gives her that look again, the you-know-perfectly-well look, meaning Cora knew perfectly well that she had to go out to work after her father died and left the family penniless. Anyway I went to business college and got a steno job.

Didn't you *want* to go to university?

Your father's the one who should've gone to university. He can rhyme off dates of all the wars in history, do long division in his head. He wanted to become a teacher or a minister. He should've really.

But don't you wish you'd done something exciting like Aunt Beulah and the Red Cross?

Well there's no Red Cross out here is there? Mom pulls the sheet out of the machine, snips the needle and bobbin threads, holds the sheet up inspecting it.

Anyway, we all did pretty much the same; got married, had

children—like women do everywhere. Except that Beulah didn't bother with hers much—too busy running off to the League of Nations.

Who looked after them?

Oh she hired people.

But it wasn't the same, and Mom knows that. Because Aunt Faith married the premier of Alberta and Aunt Judith married an engineer who ran all of the hydro power for Ontario. And Marie Curie wasn't the same as a housewife either. Marie Curie tested things in a laboratory. She discovered things that helped people. Things that changed the world for everyone. Like Aunt Beulah does with her food programs.

Mom, did you like your father?

I know what you're asking.

Well did you?

He used to let me inside his darkroom to watch the pictures come up under water.

Did he strap you?

Don't make comparisons.

I'm not, I just want to know. Did he ever?

You be thankful you've got a father.

So did he?

He got mad when I picked up his camera.

So did he use his belt?

No he had a switch. I wanted to take a picture of Mama in her nightgown, holding a tulip I had brought to her.

She pins collar pieces together inside out, runs the machine around the edges.

It was just before she died.

Just before Mom got a stepmother and baby sisters—Beulah, Faith and Judith. Cora thinks of witch-faced women making Mom wear rags and sweep cinders, locking her in towers, abandoning her in forests, poisoning her with combs and apples. After awhile her father died too of typhoid and then she was an orphan.

But Mom just kept going like now matching the collar to the back of Elaine's blouse, putting the collar and back into the sewing machine, lowering the needle into the cloth. Only then she had a real job, going out to work every day and earning her own money.

She stops the machine, looks at Cora like she did that time she tried on Netty's lipstick. You don't ever want your father to die, Cora.

What did he look like in the coffin?

That's not the point.

She pumps the machine with her foot and stitches the fabric together. Your whole world falls apart. The photography business went to his brother—our house and furniture sold to pay off mortgages and loans—the eight of us moved to a Polish rooming house way out on the edge of Toronto. I was at Havergal College. I was your age. I had to quit. Uncle was kind enough to pay for my typing and stenography training.

Dad lying in a coffin dressed in his new white business shirt and a black tie. She adds his rope and willow switch to the wooden box and tries to stuff in his Bible but it's too big. She takes the Bible to the woodshed and chops it up. But the pieces bleed all over the white satin lining of the coffin. She slams the lid shut.

Cora!

What?

I'm talking to you.

Mom, what if Dad died—would you go back to work?

Heaven save us from—I wouldn't know what—after eighteen years.

Mom, what if I got a job and earned some money to pay for university?

I don't know where you'd get a job with so many men out of work now.

Netty says I can help her clean at the Hotel.

Well you know what your father thinks of Mr. Lawson and that hotel.

So don't tell him.

I'm not going to lie if he asks.

Why's he so against it anyway, people have to have hotels to stay in.

Mom drops the scissors on the floor. She gets down under the table, comes up flushed, claps them down, then starts lifting sheets and dress parts looking for something.

Girls in hotels can make mistakes they regret.

What kind of mistakes?

Get into trouble with drinking men, and gambling men. And those aren't the kind you want to marry either.

She cuts sharply along a sleeve pattern pinned to its cloth, accidentally cutting off a marker point.

I don't know what I'd have done if our pastor hadn't got your father to give it up.

Dad?!

With the Lord's help and our pastor's, he turned himself around.

Dad playing cards and drinking?!

It's all in the past so don't go mentioning it to him.

Where did he do it?

Do what?

Drink and gamble?

Oh...here sometimes — or — not a word of it to him, understand!?

Aunt Beulah thinks Dad goes to church too much.

Don't criticize; he changed his ways and he provides well for us.

Well I don't think he cares what I do after high school.

Of course he does, he's very proud of your good marks.

Then why does he say only highfalutin people like Aunt Beulah go to university, not ordinary folk like us?

Did he say that?

Yes.

When?

Last Sunday walk. He doesn't even believe in fossils; he thinks God made them 4000 years ago.

Well it doesn't really matter does it?

Do you think God made all the plants and animals 4000 years ago?

I don't know. I suppose not.

Do you believe people evolved from apes?

No, I don't. And I don't think it matters. It's more important to do unto others...

But science is important, Mom. Marie Curie taught herself chemistry. She started out in the basement of a Polish chemist called Napoleon Milicer, and taught herself chemistry by reading treatises.

What happened to those ruffles you're gathering?

I'm not doing them.

For Pete's sake why not?

I'm going to make a laboratory in the attic where I can study and do chemistry experiments; and keep my rock collection and my library books.

But she isn't because Dad's between her and her room, home early for some reason and wanting to know where she's going.

When your mother asks you to do something, you do it.

I'm going up to the attic and then I'll do it.

You'll do it right now. He hangs his coat and hat on the hooks by the door and sits down at the head of the dining table. Just sits there with his arms crossed, staring at the silver teapot on the sideboard. Then at Mom. And then at nothing. Like he did when he found out he had to do clerking at the store as well as bookkeeping.

You're home early. She's unpinning the pattern from the sleeve.

Clayton closed the store early.

Why?

No customers the whole day, no one yesterday neither.

He keeps looking at Mom, like Cora doesn't know what, like he's waiting for her to do something instead of stabbing pins into her cushion and then folding the sleeve over and starting to pin it together. But what can Mom do about the store? Maybe he just wants her to look at him but she doesn't.

Get on with your sewing then, he mutters. Is he talking to Mom or her? Cora drags a chair out and sits at the table. He heads into his room, pulling his tie off.

Where's my gardening clothes. Now he's glaring at Mom from the bedroom door.

I put them where I told you.

And I told you I want them in here so I don't have to get them from somewhere else.

There's no room in there with all the boys' things.

Then move some of their stuff out.

Hodge, we've got to work out a better arrangement.

He clomps into the bathroom, then back to the bedroom banging the door shut. He comes out in his dungarees, but he doesn't go out to the garden; he just sits in his leather arm chair, doesn't even read the newspaper, just sits watching Mom sew.

Okay I'm done, can I go fix up the attic?

I need four more ruffles.

It's going to look like a wedding dress or a baby bassinette.

You watch your attitude, Dad growls. Your mother's gone to a lot of trouble over that dress. Your baptism's two weeks from this Sunday. You better be ready.

What if Pastor Crawford says I don't know my lessons well enough?

You better know them in two weeks.

Mom, Mme Lumière wears dungarees.

At school?!

No, but she wears them walking around town sometimes.

Honestly, I don't know why she's at that school, taking away men's jobs.

She's my favourite teacher—I get her for French, English and Art. Mom, can I have a pair of Dad's old ones for riding?

Stop pestering your mother, no daughter of mine's going around in dungarees.

Mme Lumière wears dungarees when she goes out painting watercolours; we've met her at Cold Lake on our Sunday walks, haven't we Dad?

Will you stop talking about that Lumière woman. What kind of name is that anyway?!

Hodge?

What?!

Are you going out to the garden?

I can't even sit in my own chair?

We need some potatoes and carrots for supper.

But he doesn't move; he just sits there.

CHAPTER 3

She hates her monthly. Safety-pinning rags in her bloomers. Everyone knowing when she carries a bag to school. Carrying
the stinking rags home. Rinsing their red clots down the bathroom sinkhole and chucking them in the bucket under the sink.
Monthlies make you cross and smelly. You've become a woman,
Mom said, like it was so special fooling around with reeking
cloths. Monthlies are so women can have babies, Mom said. Well
she does not want babies. Babies make you sick like Mom was
after Dougie. Babies make you stuck at home all day sewing. She
scrunches another rag over the seam in her bloomers. Babies are
a woman's life, Mom said. But Aunt Loretta didn't have babies.
Aunt Loretta was the head of nursing at Calgary General.

She slides past line-ups of grade threes and fours—up the school
steps. Up the stairs inside—walk, don't run in the halls, walk on the
right side, stay in your lines—stepping into the hollows on the stair
treads, scuffed by all those shoes before hers—up to grade twelve
—holding the wooden banister on its brass arms. Just get to the
second flight of stairs, before the principal. Good morning Cora.
Good morning Mr. Black. Why must she turn red as though she

were still in grade four and Miss Pierce had glared, Go to the principal's office. (Bunk smirked. Bunk in his slicked-back hair and never-patched pants, because Bunk's father owned a store and her Dad only worked for his Dad.) But it wasn't my fault. We'll let Mr. Black decide that. But he pushed me. You were running. (A shiny two-handled cup lay on the floor knocked off its stand.) Mr. Black's desk had eight legs. Its top, bigger than two beds, came up to her chest — it was piled with stacks of papers higher than her head except for a big open patch right in front of her where he kept the black leather strap. What do you have to say? Someone pushed me. Who was that? Bunk. Is that so? Miss Pierce says you were running in the hall. Were you? She kept her eyes down. Yes, she mumbled to the dints and scratches on the edge of the desk.

Bugger, bugger bugger, under her breath on the stair landing, to the grey and balding heads of Canada's prime ministers. Dad said it when he sawed a pole too short. It didn't reach to the next garden stake. Bugger it. Through the porch rails. To her shadow in the shadows.

In grade four Miss Pierce made her stay after school. Miss Pierce's desk was bare except for a vase holding a dried tansy. She sat down, opened a drawer, took out a pencil and started on a pile of tests. Cora sat in the empty rows in front of her. Miss Pierce made X's and ticks. Cora slid out a book. Stand up, Miss Pierce said without even looking up. Miss Pierce had a gold tooth. Cora looked out the window at the water tower, shiny white above the roofs of the houses. What would it be like to climb it, like Bunk and Wheeler and Mugsy? Way up above the town — what would it be like? To climb up there and paint BUGGER in big black letters? Nice girls don't say words like. Miss Pierce wrote b----r on the board. Gold was soft, Cora learned in Science. If Miss Pierce bit a carrot, would the tooth bend? Take this foolscap and write on every line, I will not say...Over and over. Saying it every time she would not say it. I will not say, she wrote on the yellow sheet, bad words.

The woman in the photograph on Mme Lumière's desk is wrapped in fur. She rests her chin on one hand, and gazes inquisitively with a slight smile, as though waiting for you to speak. Like Mme Lumière does, smiling right into Cora, with her bright red lips, and arched eyebrows—like Cora's answer is the most wonderful thing to hear. Smiling like she knows all sorts of secrets just for Cora—stories from faraway Montreal—the land of Jacques Cartier and *coureurs de bois,* where they drink *café* and eat *croissants* and *escargots.*

Who's her girlfriend, Bunk wants to know.

Why—you jealous—wanta date, Mugsy snorts.

Wheeler draws a lightbulb on the blackboard. He adds legs and arms, then high heels and a purse.

Dad says, Bunk scoffs, how can she afford living in a hotel on a teacher's salary?

Monsieur Bonk, Mme Lumière would say, if she were here, like she said yesterday in French class. *Bonk,* like a dullard hitting a log. *Monsieur Bonk qu'est-ce que c'est cela?*

Cela, cela—Bunk straightened up, looked at his textbook, then grinned at Mme Lumière like French was his favourite subject. Like she had secrets even for him.

Qu'est-ce que c'est cela—

*C'est...c'est...*Bunk shifted something from his right hand to his left and grabbed a pencil. He flipped pages, and grinned back at her, I'm sorry Ma'am what page are we on?

Cet objet rouge et jaune dans votre main? Qu'est-ce que c'est?

Oh...that's a yo-yo, Ma'am. He brought out the red and yellow disks from under the desk.

C'est magnifique, c'est fascinante. Her hair was so crisp and *court.* Her eyes so funny, strange—so laughing back like that word *drôle* in the story of Monsieur Lepoupin. Like that time she taught Cora, after school, just Cora, no one else, a swear word in French: *maudit.*

Yes, I mean *oui. C'est...c'est.* Bunk pulled the loop off his finger and held out the yo-yo to Mme Lumière.

Montrez-moi le yo yo.

You mean…show you how?

Ici avec moi.

Bunk walked to the front of the room. Everyone laughed as he tried to find the French word for *finger* and *string* and *like that*—*roulez,* she prompted and he followed *vous roulez* like that. *Comme ça.* Yes, I mean *oui, comme ça.* He placed the loop on her finger and the disk in her hand, grinning—he was her star—he shadowed her hand with his hand—down, up. She rolled it and caught it. Good, I mean *bon.* Very I mean *très bon.*

Cora walks to the blackboard and erases Bunk's cartoon. Suck. SSSSSSSSSS.

They're supposed to be practicing a pageant about Gabriel Dumont and Louis Riel and the war of 1885. But instead, while she's out of the room, they're talking about how come Mme Lumière doesn't go to church, who her girlfriend is and what happened to her husband—probably didn't know how to cook, so he left—she probably poisoned him with arsenic like that lady in England.

Cora's supposed to be Gabriel Dumont. Gerard is Louis Riel. *Your people need a leader. The English are taking their farms and ranches,* she'll say. *Come back and lead them. Like you did in Rupert's Land.*

This church at Batoche will be my headquarters, he'll say. *I hereby declare a provisional government of Saskatchewan. You'll be my adjutant general.*

Bunk will be Major Crozier of the Northwest Mounted Police. Wheeler will be General Middleton with 5000 Canadians. Mugsy will be Sir John A Macdonald.

Hey Gopher Chief, we're gonna hang you for treason. Bunk draws a gallows and noose on the blackboard. Hang you for treason, halfbreed. But they're not because Mme Lumière made the scene end before that, showing Riel as a heroic leader. *Exovedate,* Mme Lumière said, Louis Riel's name for his council means sheep leaving the flock.

Cora wishes she could draw horses and birds like Gerard's doing in his sketchbook, just like real ones.

Mugsy stands on his chair and wags his finger. *Let him hang though every dog in Quebec bark in his favour.*

Hey four-eyes, when're you and Gopher Chief getting married?

Leave her alone, fatso, Gerard mutters.

Mugsy jumps down from his chair, grabs Gerard's book, rips out a drawing of an airplane and tosses it across the room. Call me fatso huh. Halfbreed. Shouldn't you be in Indian School. He rips out a horse.

Well what have we here if it isn't Four-eyes herself. Mugsy rips out the page.

Quit callin' her four-eyes. Gerard snatches back the sketch-book.

Netty and Hilda look at her with big O mouths. *Maudit.* Bugger. They're always seeing things. They're as bad as Bunk and Mugsy. She studies her pageant speeches. *Let me chase these invaders back to Manitoba.*

Then Gerard/Riel will say, *Stop this violence, we must negotiate for peace.*

We need time for that; let me rout them.

You've killed too many already.

This is war; they're the enemy.

We must negotiate for peace; or they'll kill us all.

Let me fight the Indian way — pick off a few, then disappear. I can stop General Middleton.

Riel/Gerard stares out the window, his arms crossed on top of the sketchbook.

Cora picks up the airplane drawing and puts it on his desk. He keeps his arms crossed, ignoring it.

Gopher's mad.

Would you babies grow up, Hilda picks up the sketch of Cora, puts it in her textbook.

Yes, Ma'am, anything you say Ma'am, Wheeler salutes her.

Did he really draw her picture, really her—like his planes and horses? But she won't ask Hilda. Then they'd never let up.

General Middleton/Wheeler will say, *Surrender, Riel, in the name of king and country.*

And Gerard/Riel will say, *I give myself up to fulfill God's will and for the freedom of my people. I surrender to defend the people's cause.*

I Gabriel Dumont/Cora do not surrender. I gather small bands of warriors and attack Middleton's troops. But they are too many and we flee. Never do I surrender.

Louis Riel, Bunk/Judge Richardson will say, *You are charged with treason — seduced by the devil, you maliciously and traitorously made war against our Lady the Queen at Batoche.*

British civilization, Gerard/Riel will reply, *has defined such government as this which rules the Northwest Territories as irresponsible government. What I have done I was called to do for my country.*

———

In Mr. Gale's room, maps of Canada show Rupert's Land and Unknown Regions. Bunk and Wheeler perch on desktops flipping packs of cards. Lemme see, Netty elbows the huddle. Not for girls. Yeah, we can guess what the pictures are.

What if she wore the Canadian Shield? She could put Hudson's Bay around her neck, upper Canada over her chest, Labrador and the Northwest Territories over her shoulders.

Watch out, Four-eyed mole's here.

She passes the boy-patch smell of tobacco smoke and sweaty P.E. clothes. To Unknown Territories — the Indian ones.

Hey, Mole, dog gotcher tongue?

Why does Bunk call her Four-eyed Mole but Hilda gets The Buffalo? *Quiet, The Buffalo's studying.* Or *make way for The Buffalo.* He even holds the door for her sometimes. Queen buffalo. How does she do it — smiling and reigning? He even talks to her like she's a normal person.

Cora places a feather in her pen groove.

What's that—yr quill—ha ha Mrs. Einstein writes with a quill.

Bunk grabs the feather and breaks it into pieces.

She takes the yo-yo off Bunk's desk, slips the loop over her finger, snugs the wooden disks into her palm.

Hands off, you'll wreck it.

Keeping a row of desks between them, she spins its yellow and red wheels, bouncing it back to her hand and tossing it out again.

You're ruining my string—stupid four-eyed cow. He knocks the thing sideways. It dangles and twists on its cord. She chucks it under Mr. Gale's desk.

———◆———

Mr. Gale's chalk taps: 1605 Champlain founds Quebec; 1609 Champlain defeats the Iroquois; 1632 Treaty of St Germain; 1649 Iroquois destroy Hurons. She pours ink into the cup in the corner of her desk, dips her pen. Bunk's reading Tarzan on his lap. Wheeler knocks her elbow as she copies down the board. Ink blots. Bugger.

What else happened in 1649?

A statue on Mr. Gale's desk holds the globe on his shoulders. Arms and legs bulging in ripples and rolls. Is that what Mr. Gale looks like under his red tie and the black and white checked jacket? His moustache is sharp, Netty says. The boys' door open a crack —Dad's undershirt tucked in the belt of his trousers—his arms pasty smooth, saggy—not like Mr. Gale's statue.

Gerard!

Yes sir?

What happened.

Sir could I leave the room please.

Not until we finish this point.

No. 1 or No. 2, Bunk snickers at Gerard.

What happened?

I think it's no. 2.

Wheeler.

The Hurons went west, Gerard shrugs.

Cora flips pages in her history text. The arrival of the Ursulines, 1639 — a crowd of women in black robes, faces closed in huge white tents. Why did the King give special gifts to any girl who married under the age of sixteen? She'd rather run through the woods like a *coureur de bois* — moccasins and coonskin hat, birchbark canoe on her rippling muscled shoulders. She'd shoot through dark branches, dig her paddle into rocky rapids. Run in fringed buckskin through trunks of forest to the trading posts. Run back — gleaming with red and white beads — her canoe packed thick and soft with fox and beaver pelts. She'd run them through the *bois*. Run to the ships at Montreal.

What else Gerard?

Can ya hold it, Gopher.

Enough, Bunk.

They got smallpox from the priests.

Do we know that?

It says...

It says the Indians *thought* it came from the priests.

Wheeler, what did the savages do to Father Daniel, Father Brébeuf and Father Lalemant?

Killed them.

How did they do that?

(Does Gerard think his mother's a savage?)

Bunk, how did they kill the priests?

Put red-hot irons in their throats; poured boiling water on them.

I don't believe they were that cruel. (Let them look at Miss Red-face.) They must have had a reason for what they did.

You're the new professor of Canadian history, I suppose, whose opinion matters more than our textbook.

So are Indians still savage? (In for a penny in for a pound, Mom said.)

My, we are talkative today.

Dad hires Indians on the farm sometimes, Hilda says, they wear clothes and go to church just like us.

Well, everyone's in a flap today, Netty are you going to lecture us too?

No sir.

Indians don't build ships and trains and cities, Bunk crosses his arms and leans back in his seat. That means they're savages.

After school, Cora drifts with Netty toward Main Street and her dad's hotel, Hilda heading to her dad at the grain elevators along the tracks.

You were great Hilda, with Mr. Gale, Cora says, What's Gerard supposed to think?

She's sweet on Gerard Rupert, Netty squeals. We're gonna get you a date honey.

Now they'll be cooking up ideas about her and Gerard. A date where you put your hair in curlers which she doesn't even have nor does Mom, then you dress all special, paint on Clara Bow lips, and go sit in a booth at the Palace, and then what? What would they even talk about?

◆

Behind the counter at the Buffalo Hotel is a wall of keys and mail slots. Away from the counter an archway to a room hazy with smoke, laughter and men's voices — men sitting on stools, drinks in front of them. This is the thing Dad says you must never do, even though Mom said he used to, till the Pastor got him to stop.

Never drink. Never smoke. Only wicked people drink and smoke. Behind the bar, shelves hold all sorts of bottles — green and brown and clear, square, squat, sleek and frosted. The men have newspapers, or chat with Mr. Lawson in front of the shelves of bottles. A man with a cigar asks, How many mother-in-laws does it take to change a light-bulb? Mr. Lawson shrugs. None, the man says, It's fine, I'll sit here in the dark, I'll be ok, don't worry about me. Another man laughs.

A sin before God. What only the most horrible people do. The foulest and awfulest. You go to hell. Your skin on fire. You drown in thick ugly blood. For ever. While Dad and Mom and Hilda and Netty watch you from Heaven.

Netty unlocks a cupboard at the end of the second-floor hall. How much does it cost to stay in your hotel? A dollar a night, unless it's long term, then it's cheaper. They get out a rolling mop-bucket, some rags and borax, Netty humming that song about putting on the ritz. If it costs a dollar a night to live at university, it'll take a lot of cleaning to pay for it.

Number 32 smells moist and clammy, like coughed-up phlegm. Towels droop from the chair and the curtain rod. The blankets and top sheet tangle in a knot next to pillows stained with red marks. Someone's drawn soap hearts all over the mirror.

What a mess, Cora buries her nose in her pile of crisp Clorox-smelling towels.

Guess they were having fun. Netty untangles the sheet, spreads it on the floor. Cora grabs a pillow, strips it, drops the slip into the sheet. Under the second one her fingers touch something rubbery and jelly-feeling, like fish-skin off one of Dad's boiled kippers.

Ick.

It's a rubber.

I know it's rubber.

It's a sheath — a French letter!

Funny thing to use for mail.

Netty grabs it. Hey it's new, I'm going to keep it.

She holds it up to the light.

It's just a sock.

Know how you tell?

Netty fingers the knobbly bit sticking out of the end.

There's nothing in it, that's how.

Cora strips another pillow. Quit looking at me like that.

Netty wraps up the rubber in her handkerchief and snaps it into her purse.

I wasn't born yesterday.

They're illegal you know — they're not that easy to get.

So! Are you going to mail someone a note?

Cora spreads a fresh sheet. Netty bundles the laundry out in the hall, then runs the carpet sweeper over the floor, pulling something lacy and black from under the bed. Bet she's sorry she lost these.

What?

The most gorgeous lace knickers and bra, that's what — I mean look at them. They cost at least $20, and the bra's got underwire! Netty closes the door, starts unbuttoning her blouse.

What're you doing?

I'm trying them on.

What for — they're not even yours.

Finders keepers.

What's so interesting about them anyway — it's just underwear!

Do you dare to try them on, or are you going to be a school-girl all your life?

Cora tucks the sheet and blanket around the foot of the bed, yanks the side edge over her hand in a neat crease, tucks it in.

I'm going to buy my own, Cora smears the soap hearts with a wet cloth.

Yeah, when?

When I earn enough money.

I thought you were saving it all for university.

Netty fits the black lace bra cups over her breasts, and struggles to make the black satin band connect at the back.

Hey, do me up.

How?

Fit the hooks into the eyes.

Not like at home, Cora dressing under her nightgown in front of the heater, pulling on combinations, suspenders bloomers, wriggling into her blouse. No one ever saw anything at home. Like what Netty had — bare naked.

Netty's breasts, all bread-dough soft, bulge out of the too-small, strapless brassiere. She slips on the skimpy knickers, and kicks her legs in the air.

You going to wear schoolgirl bloomers all your life? Netty leans against the door frame dropping one hip. A deep dimple creases soft white flesh overhanging the knickers. Golden fuzz coats her sturdy legs.

Rather do that than end up married to Bunk.

Rate you're going, you'll end up an old maid.

A fussy frump then. In her blue lisle stockings. Her face like a last-year apple, a witch's nose touching her witch's chin. End up a schoolmarm with a stick body and claws for hands — children running away from her, boys making stink bombs and shooting spit balls at her A is for apple over and over on the blackboard until she died. But she's not going to make herself all fluffy and cushy like Netty does.

Netty takes off the lingerie, gets back into her bloomers and camisole, puts on her black school skirt and V-neck sweater. In the next room, Cora opens the window. Two stories below, an empty dusty yard stretches away through vacant lots to the railroad tracks. Bunk leans against the wall near the lounge door. He brings his hand to his mouth and blows out a long stream of smoke, then takes a swig from a brown bottle. He lifts one leg and clamps his boot to the wall, drops his head to his chest, hangs it there. Nothing moves in the yard except the smoke from his cigarette, then he leans his head back on the wall again, takes another puff. His boot comes unclamped from the wall. He puts it down, raises the other one up.

Netty comes in behind her. Your boyfriend's waiting for you Cora says, not turning round. Netty's hands encircle her chest, slip the black bra over her white blouse and fasten it in back. Fits perfectly; you should keep it.

Get this thing off.

It's just right—gives you real shape.

Footsteps sound in the hall. Mr. Lawson calls out wanting to know if you girls are going to get these rooms done before midnight—he's got guests waiting. Cora pulls the brassiere over her head and chucks it at Netty. After eight rooms, Mr. Lawson pays her twenty-five cents.

CHAPTER 4

Dad, I found an arrowhead like Judge Rupert's. Cora holds the flint out and sights along the line of her arm to a hut at the far end of the coal mine.

That's just a piece of rock.

Dad, do you know how to skin a deer?

First ya hafta shoot the deer. So let's practice your shot.

I *am* a good shot, I've killed hundreds of gophers out at Maynard's farm.

Okay let's see ya hit that tin over there.

When's it gonna be my turn, Gus interrupts.

Soon enough.

Cora takes the rifle, scrunches one eye and lines up the can in the V of the sight. No no, get the butt right on your shoulder. It'll kick. No it won't, it just pushes you back a bit. Dad, I've tried it hundreds of times and it always bangs into me. Just do it right for a change — you'll see. She places the hard edge of the butt on her collarbone; it's going to hurt for sure when she fires. She sights again. Get your cheek right against the stock — good — sight the tin — no, don't raise your elbow so high. He comes around behind — the wool of his jacket grazing her arms, his chest heat on her back, his breath on the back of her neck. Hold it into your shoulder — he pulls her hands so the butt snugs against her cheek and shoulder. Okay now hit the can.

Of course she misses it.

My turn okay Dad. Gus tries to grab the rifle.

Never grab like that. Sit down and learn by watching your sister.

Cora raises the rifle again.

Hold it farther out with your left hand.

Dad I can't do it when you're standing over me like that!

Okay okay have it your way.

He stands off, crossing his arms.

She knocks off the can.

See what I told you. Just keep practicing.

———◆———

Her feet creak the oiled floorboards of Wellman and Bond's, down the aisles of licorice allsorts and chocolates, flour sacks, lard pails, crates of apples, then round the corner to Dry Goods where Dad works. She's supposed to be getting two spools of white cotton thread for Mom — Coates mercerized super sheen, not the cheap kind. But she dawdles through the shelves of Eddy matches, Lucky Strike tobacco, pipes, pipe cleaners, rifle oil, shotguns, Lux soap bars, laundry bluing, sewing patterns, lace, ribbons, barrettes, tooth powder — fingering some thigh-high knickers with little bows stitched onto them. The ad in the paper said Brevity knickers had *smart French appliqué*. The ad called them *rather doggie*. A terrier in her bloomers. What would he bark at? What would he fetch? Would he roll over with his legs in the air so you could scratch his tummy?

Cora catches a whiff of cigar from the back of the store. In the office window five steps above the aisles, Mr. Wellman's talking to Dad, the window a kind of movie screen where the two men face each other, Mr. Wellman in trenchcoat and fedora, waving his hand with the cigar, her father with his jacket off, shirtsleeves held up by stretchy metal bands on his upper arms, his head barely above his boss's shoulder.

Your granddad was a banker, Aunt Ida said, and that doesn't mean putting money in safes and working ten till three, neither.

Aunt Ida waved her knitting needle at them. It means he was settin longlines out on the Grand Banks a Newfoundland. Two men and a dory on the open sea. And proud of it. He wanted me brother to be one too. You get on out and jig fish in the bay, b'y, Father said. No Father, I can't handle the boat, he said. Ya won't learn by sittin on your arse, Father said, get on out there. I don't want ta fish, your dad said, I want ta get my highschooling. Then earn the money ta pay for it. Get out, and don't come back till you got fish. It was terrible times then. Fishermen couldn't sell fish for more than about $2 a hundred pound. No one could afford flour even.

Your dad tried every darned thing ta get around it. He hid the dory and told Father the boat was gone, somebody'd taken it. Father found out the boat was over in the next cove, he beat your dad till his ears bled. Your dad tried sneakin fish off the stage. Since when, Father wanted ta know, did cod come without guts. Me brother got another hiding for that one.

Your Dad aint no scaredy cat; he's got adventure in him. He finally got into the boat and rowed as far as he could, dropped the jigger, tied it ta the gunwale, lay down when he got tired a jiggin the line. When he looked up, he saw he'd drifted right outa the bay. He tried ta row but he couldn't make no headway. Shore got farther and farther away. Night came. He was too feeble after the diphtheria ta row, see. He huddled down in the bottom of the boat outa the wind. Morning came. He saw a schooner not far off, all its sails up. He waved and called. He could hear the spray off its bow. Her men waved back like he was out for an afternoon stroll. Meanwhile Mother's beside herself, telling Father,

Your son's lost at sea — get some men together and look for him. Ah he's just run off, somewheres, he'll come back when he's hungry enough. No he's not — the dory's gone, he's out on the water. Finally Father and another man went out. What're ya doin way out here, Father yelled. Your dad lay in the bottom of the boat. They hauled him back in. What's the use a ya — can't even row a boat. He took a cane ta him. Good for nothing angyshore. Made his back all red and purple.

But your dad had adventure in him. He ran away t'our brother Frank in Halifax. He was in the chandlery business, had a lovely house, servants. One day my favourite brother was gone, and he never came back. Cuz he had adventure in him — aint that so Hodge?

Don't talk nonsense Ida, Dad muttered, and hoed the ground till every weed in sight was chopped to bits.

Mr. Wellman's head pushes at the top of the office-window movie-screen, he leans toward Dad, opens his hands and shrugs. Dad leans back a little, looks up, nods. Mr. Wellman waves out toward the aisles. Dad shakes his head.

There's no one in the dry goods section apart from Cora. Around the corner Mr. Bond's grocery section had three customers when she came in. A small notice above the doggie knickers says, Mrs. I. L. Clark of H. W. Gossard Co. will be at our store from Friday Noon Sept 26th until Saturday Noon, Sept 27th for special service regarding Corset Fittings.

Mr. Wellman strides through the aisles and out the front door. Her father stands in his movie, hands dangling at his sides, scowling after his boss. Cora drifts past racks of low-waisted frocks with wide lapels and elaborate drapery tied with bows. Strapslippers with Cuban heels. Silk hose made of mercury threads.

She'd rather wear the men's gumboots and work gloves, flannel shirts and overalls — she fingers the double seams and rivets in Red-back Denim. Then hats like Dad's and Mr. Wellman's, under a sign saying, Quality Brock and Biltmore. Netty can stuff her brassiere, making herself all showcase and curvy, like a vase on a shelf for Bunk to poke and prod.

She tries on a fawn fedora with chocolate-coloured band. Or how about a black one with rolled edges? Not a flat cap—like the men wear who smoke and talk around Percy's Forge while Percy waves his hot irons at them and lectures—Dad never wears those.

What do you think you're doing?

He's standing on the little platform at the top of the steps outside the office.

Keeping the hat on, she strides down the aisle, digging her heels into the floor and swinging her arms. I wanna be in your movie.

What movie?

You and Mr. Wellman in your window.

Get that hat off before Clayton comes back.

She leans against the overalls counter studying herself in a mirror. I'm a customer—I'm trying it on—I might buy it.

He pounds down the steps toward her. You, take that hat off now and put it back, his black eyes like one of Judge Rupert's owls ready to strike.

Why can't I be a customer?

Do you know where you are?!

His teeth are clenched. Mr. Bond or another customer might hear if he yells like he does at home.

Put it back.

He grabs her arm, snatches the hat and plunks it down on the stack. Black, brown, grey, each with exactly the same band. Each one transforming her into their movie.

She follows him into the office.

Have you ever smoked a cigar—I wonder what it tastes like.

Believe me, you wouldn't want to.

Mom says you used to smoke.

Mr. Wellman's large oak desk and her dad's small metal one fill the room. She plunks down in Mr. Wellman's chair and spins it around to the blotting paper held in its frame by four leather corners. Ink bottle. Pen in a brass tray. Fat pen makes a slim cigar. She holds it between her fingers, takes a puff. Tips the chair back.

Did you like smoking cigars?

I'll getcha a chocolate one.

How come you don't smoke them anymore.

Same reason I don't drink or play cards — it's sinful.

A cash pouch comes in on the zip line from the grocery department. Dad pushes past her chair, unclips the pouch and clatters it down on his desk. Oh for darn sakes. Did they haveta use a twenty?

It's not lying, or stealing or killing. It's not coveting or graven images.

It's a sin against the Lord.

But which one — it doesn't break a commandment.

Anything not done for the glory of God is a sin!

But how do you know when it isn't for the glory of God?

Okay, outa here — I haveta open the safe.

He pushes her out the door, then bangs it shut. She opens the top half — a horse in a stable — except he's on the inside. Chicken-coop, he called it once, telling Mom he was sick of tripping over Clayton in that chicken-coop.

Across from the desks, the big black safe rules the room, gold letters flashing Wellman & Bond above double black doors with nickel-plated handles and a combination dial. Real as a bank. Important as a church. Built out of thick slabs of black steel by the men of J & J *Taylor* LIMITED, TORONTO *Safe* WORKS. Where could *she* get a real job? Netty's mom used to work here but not anymore.

No one's allowed in there when he opens The Safe, hunching down over the dial and opening its dark cavern that reminds her of the oven in the kitchen range. On its racks, it's roasting ledgers and bundles of bills, grey cash boxes, brown paper rolls of coins. He opens a tall green book and records some figures in the columns, then opens another book and records figures in that.

Is this where you lay eggs? She takes another puff from her pen cigar.

You. Shut up. And show respect!

He reaches past her and snaps the pouch onto the zip line.

What're ya doin here anyway? Didn't your mother send ya over for something?

Dad can I get a job here — like Netty's mom?

No you can't.

Why not?

Ya don't know enough for that sorta thing; anyway I do all the clerkin now and its little enough.

How does your pen work — it's different than the ones at school. Cora opens the gate and grabs one of his pens. You don't have to dip it, you can just write.

She scrawls Cora Wagoner across the back of an envelope on Mr. Wellman's desk. How do you get the ink into it? Can I have one of these?

When you can afford to buy one.

How'm I going to afford one if I don't have a job?

He pulls some receipts off the spike and mutters figures to himself as he enters them in a red account book.

Let me add those up, like you let me with the church accounts.

Put that back and get outa here.

Is this how you do it? She opens a bottle of ink, plunges in the pen, and pulls the lever, testing it out on another envelope. Dad snatches the rest of Wellman's mail, pulls the pen out of her hand, turns the chair to the door.

Out.

She's face to face with Mr. Wellman's waistcoat buttons and belt buckle. This the new manager? Mr. Wellman throws his newspaper on the desk, just the way his son Bunk chucks Gerard's books around at school. He looks at his watch. Looks at Dad. You gonna be a bookkeeper like your Dad?

He beams down at her but only his mouth is smiling.

Nope. I'm going to university.

They got degrees in diaper-changing.

I'm going to study Chemistry.

Oh, I see.

He looks at Dad.

Well, I'm afraid there's only room for one of us in here.

Outa here, Dad grumbles.

She heads down the steps to the stack of hats, then looks back to the office-window movie-screen. Dad bends over his books, shifting his gaze to one side, then to the book in front of him, his lips moving as he repeats the figures. Twice as big as her dad, Mr. Wellman hulks over his desk, gazing down, then laughing, pushes Dad's arm, points a stubby finger at his desk. Dad peers over, says something, turns back to his work. Mr. Wellman gets up, hangs his trenchcoat over his chair, nudges Dad again. Dad doesn't smile. Mr. Wellman holds up his hands, then runs them down something mid-air, something wide, then narrow, then wide again — like he's running his hands over that old corset in Mom's trunk — laced up like a shoe, the middle part of an hourglass — like he's running his hands over someone wearing that. Someone like Mom that he's sizing up, running his hands over as though she were a stylish vase he wanted in his store.

Dad nods at Mr. Wellman, presses his lips together, goes back to his figures.

Cora wanders down the aisles toward the sewing section, stopping to rummage crossly through a box of used books. She doesn't want to be a vase for Mr. Wellman, and she doesn't want to smile at him. *Scientific* says a blotched cover, something *Scientific Recreations* — its pages splattered with brown spots and holes. Soak a sugar cube in colloidion solution, she reads, and watch your friends' faces when they can't get it to sink in a cup of tea. Make a bottle cannon by adding tartaric acid to a solution of soda and potash.

The thread counter only has the small spools of Coates mercerized. Mom wants the big ones. She'll have to ask Dad if they've got more in back. He's talking to someone at the front counter — someone in a smart red suit with black collar and cuffs and matching hat — just like the pictures in *Good Housekeeping,* not like the flowered cottons Mom wears — perfect because it's Mme Lumière.

Showing him something — a watercolour she's made of Cold Lake at the edge of town. He's smiling and asking whether she'd like some Fry's Chocolate Creams, on at a very good price this week. Here, try a sample. He holds them out. Smiling like he'd like to give her the whole box. She takes one. He asks her where she learned her painting and she tells him her father was an artist. And yes, he was indeed in the picture galleries. He thinks she'd like some very fine views out at Buffalo Lake, but she rather likes doing farm buildings and elevators. They don't even see her standing here. They're inside a movie screen and she's not in the movie. Mme Lumière likes the Fry's cream, so now he's offering her Charleston Chews. She's not really interested in them — she just popped in because... But he puts his hand in the middle of her back, and steers her toward the shelves of Oh Henry's and Almond Rocas, going on about a new box of Baby Ruths, even though all she wants is the Creams and she just came in because she's made some watercolours into notecards and was wondering if the store...

Cora's stomach goes butterflies like when she says bugger, or takes Bunk's yo-yo, or when she knows she's made a mistake on a Chem test but she can't fix it. He's still looking at Mme Lumière like he's a dog and she's holding up a bone. Cora barges up to the candy shelves and fingers some Baby Ruths. Mme Lumière says how nice to see you, dear. But she's not looking at Cora, she's looking at Dad. She asks Cora if she's found something good.

A book of science experiments. Dad, it's only three cents.

Dya need another book with all from the library. He's still looking at Mme Lumière.

And she's still looking at him, You bet she needs another book;

your daughter's one smart cookie. Top of her class. I hope you're planning to send her to university.

I dunno how — with a family to feed and times like these.

Mr. Wagoner, there are scholarships. You come and see me after school, Cora, and we'll look into it.

Have you got any bigger spools of thread, Cora asks as Mme Lumière leaves the store and crosses Main Street toward the Buffalo Hotel, carrying a box of Fry's Chocolate Creams. Dad doesn't answer, just stares out the window.

Dad.

What?

Thread.

What about it?

———

At the bedroom window, she watches Dad pulling up bean and pea stakes, Elaine behind her, carving away at one of her animals, dropping woodchips she says are only on her side of the quilt.

What're you looking at?

Dad.

What's he doing?

Running back and forth grabbing stakes and piling them.

She feels like punching something. Like running out to Cold Lake as fast as she can. Like jumping up and down on the bed and scattering Elaine and her woodchips to kingdom come. Her father digs and hacks at dead bean roots, raking and smoothing where they were growing, raking out every little bit of the dried stalks. He piles them up, carries them to the compost box, comes back, digs some more, raking like it'll never be neat enough, then dropping the rake and tidying the stakes against the woodshed. It started at the store — this jumpy jiggly feeling. Started with Dad and Mme Lumière.

Mom calls dinner but he says he's not coming in, he's got to finish this before dark. He's started on the tomato stakes. Pulling off green tomatoes and putting them in old peach crates, and piling these on the back stoop. When he finally does come in, he only eats half of what Mom put in the warming oven. Not hungry. I eat too much anyway. He sits in his armchair reading the Bible. Then Gus gets into trouble making too much noise, and Dad makes him get the rope and bend over the bench in the front room, and he gives Gus a hiding.

Lying in bed, she wishes she had her own bed in her own room, like Hilda does, instead of Elaine's whiffling beside her. She fences off Elaine's sleepy arms and legs with a valley of untouched quilt. Hilda's mom and dad sleep in the same bed and so do Netty's. Cora remembers Mom coming out of the bathroom in her nightgown, her hair all down, all wavy and bouncy down her back. Mom standing by the front room heater brushing it, then going into her room. Dad closing the Bible. Staring at the front door. Then following her in there; the door clicking shut behind him. Silence. Then he said her name, Beth. Then her voice said something sharp and questioning like she didn't believe he could be asking her that... Then the door opened, Mom saying I'd like to leave it ajar. Then silence, as he went to his cot in the boys' room.

CHAPTER 5

Let us rise for Number 317 God of Our Fathers. Netty's got a new straw hat. Gold curls always so perfect. Not dull brown. God of our fathers, whose almighty hand, Leads forth in beauty all the starry band. Hilda's in her olive green blazer; chestnut hair or is it auburn? Definitely not brown. Mrs. Maynard's ringed fingers press into the piano keys. The voices drown the piano in a slurry soup LordGodofHosts — polite manners — or wheat host to wheat rust — God all holey like a sponge — Le-e-e-st we forget, Le-e-e-st we for. Get. Find a niche in the voices, don't be show-offy like Mrs. Lawson quavering high above everyone else. Now the first prayer: Almighty and most merciful Father; We have erred and strayed from thy ways...

Aunt Beulah goes to the Toronto symphony and listens to live CNR broadcasts from Simpson's Department Store — Brahms, Schumann, Beethoven — you can get them on the radio out here, can't you? — but Mom can't because we don't have a radio.

Crown him with many crowns, the Lamb upon his throne, Hark! how the heavenly anthem drowns All music but its own. Everyone brushes and plumps sitting down. Knobs of her backbone straighten on ridges of pew. Her legs flatten across the seat.

Pastor Crawford towers over the pulpit. She can hardly see, in the gloom of pulpit shadow, the red asters Mom and Elaine put in a tin jug on the communion table. Jack in the pulpit. Ha — nothing flowery about Pastor Crawford.

Three chairs stand behind him on the platform. Backs all carved into points and bumps — she supposes they're thrones for a white-haired father, a long-haired, bearded son, and a misty holy ghost with drifting muslin eyeholes.

Only hoity toity girls as lives in Toronto go to university, Dad said. Loretta shoulda got married, Dad said, then she wouldn't be so bossy. God forbid you turn out like her or Beulah.

But Aunt Loretta wasn't hoity toity! She was a head nurse. She gave lectures in Edmonton on methods. She prevented infections and saved lives.

She bows her head for the second prayer: O Lord our heavenly Father, high and mighty, King of kings... Voices around her bumble like bees in flower heads. She looks sideways, betting Bunk Wellman's head isn't down. It is but his eyes aren't closed. The room full of whispers and murmurs.

We will rise now for Praise the Lord Who Reigns Above. Mrs. Maynard's muscly arms march up and down the keyboard. The voices sound like Chautauqua violins, high and harsh, low and off-key, blurring and furring the edges of words; only the first and last stand out: We... son; Who... won. Sing... here. Where to sing — what pitch, where to fit — she's too high or too low. Netty fixes her hat and glances over at Bunk.

Our sermon, booms Pastor Crawford at the pulpit, will be on Romans 6: 3-4: Baptism into death — his hair a lion's mane waving out around his head. Hilda says he's fun to talk to when he comes to the farm — he makes you feel all sparkly like sunshine on a lake — he even helps with the dishes. Netty says Hilda has a crush on him. Like Netty has on Bunk, waiting around for him to take her to the Palace and sit in a booth, or take her to a movie. So he can put his hands under her skirt, Hilda says, and inside her sweater.

So many of us as were baptized into Jesus Christ were baptized into his death, Pastor Crawford roars. It's a good thing he's married to Hilda's sister Connie, or Hilda wouldn't give a darn about getting nurse's training. She'd go just like Connie—at home with two tots and expecting another. Cora follows the moulding around the windows, the curved arms of the pews, the carved slats of the Bible racks, to the lace collar and checked wool jacket in the pew in front, and back to Pastor Crawford and the points and bumps of the three thrones.

Before white men, Indians didn't have pulpits. They had manitous and great spirits. They believed in dreams and dances, it said in History. They didn't sit in churches with pointy windows and little diamond panes. They went on fasts like Hiawatha, and wrestled with spirits.

She tells herself to listen to the sermon, instead of thinking about putting a couple of fossils on the communion table. What if she just quit church, went on an Indian fast—in her own teepee at Buffalo Lake—the sun and the moon and the sky her church. Yeah, Dad'd really like that. *Your baptism's two weeks from this Sunday.*

Suppose a man has been condemned to die for a horrible crime. The Pastor glares. Suppose further that he dies, and now by a miracle of God he comes back to life. What a glorious thing to have arisen from the dead! That man will hate forever the thing that made him die. But what is the world he returns to? He wakes to a world of death. He can find no one in the dead around him to converse with. And I say to you, Do not tear up graves to find friends there. Do not open coffins and cry 'come drinking, come out for a game of poker.' No (lion roar), we condemn the dead; we dread the idea of mixing with the dead.

Under the trapdoor on the platform, right next to Pastor Crawford's shiny black shoes, steps go down to the cistern — slosh slewsh, wash the laundry. In baptism, we consent to the watery grave, Pastor Crawford bellows. Last summer he took Netty down there, his trousers and her white communicant dress clinging to their legs, water slapping at their waists. A true believer goes through real death in baptism...Netty closing her eyes, the Pastor leaning her back — water over her face, her cheeks white.

The Pastor stood Netty up again — water sloshed and sucked — flattening her curls into wet lanks, outlining her camisole and garter belt under her soaked dress. Welcome to the membership of Christ, the Pastor beamed at everyone standing around the cistern.

Cora pushes fingers through her skirt tugging at sticking bloomers. Mrs. Maynard, stands up at the piano, pulling her creased dress over her stout middle — a rose pattern with pink felt hat. Pews creak; feet shuffle. Gus quit flicking Dougie like that. Mind your own beeswax. I see the government's going after weed seeds in harvesters again. Sendin round inspectors. Guess so.

Pastor Crawford shoulders his way to the vestibule. Now everyone's fresh laundry blowing on the church lawn. People spewing out of church, all washed and clean. All bright and smart like the gathered shoulders and the little bow on Netty's new V-neck dress with her silk stockings.

I see you've got *it* on. Hilda pokes Netty's ribs.

What?

Your newfound brassiere.

Does it show. Netty throws back her shoulders.

Yeah but you shouldn't wear black under light colours.

Hey Cora, you got one yet?

Netty and Hilda look big-eyed. Like they can see through her blouse to her flatter, lower breasts. Like they can see her garters and bloomers under her school skirt, her legs in lisle stockings. Her private places under her bloomers.

Was it like that — when you got baptized?

Like what?

Like dying and being buried?

It was terribly romantic.

(In school they're studying "Ode to the West Wind" by a Romantic poet.) Why's it romantic?

Huh! I was in the arms of the handsomest man around...leaning back with my eyes closed.

So you've got a crush on him too as well as Bunk!

Hilda and Netty laugh, We've really got to do something about her.

Why's it so important—why do boys make you so...Oh never mind!

She's turning pink.

She's in a snit.

Netty links arms with Hilda, then says loudly behind her hand to Hilda's ear, Has she ever seen hmm hmm at the farm? Because you know what I think. The two of them grinning at her full of mischief. But it doesn't matter. She won't let it matter what they think.

She ambles under the big trees of McNabb Street toward Prairie Avenue and the concrete wall of the town reservoir, Elaine and the boys already racing back to the house where Mom's getting the roast and potatoes ready. Dad walks about a block ahead, in his charcoal suit and grey fedora. A solitary fencepost. Walking away from Pastor Crawford, Mr. Wellman and the Mayor on the church lawn. No, Mr. Wellman and the Mayor didn't think they'd want to do more Bible study this week, Cora heard them say, smirking the way Bunk did at Gerard. And Pastor Crawford was busy with his wife and youngsters—she's expecting you know.

Dad's mouth set in a thin line as he bid the other men goodbye.

They had meetings in the church basement where she'd barged in once, getting her sweater. Pages of numbers in front of them. No sweater in here, Mr. Wellman holding his cigar under the table, the Pastor opening the window. It's behind the piano. She dawdled around the piano bench. Mr. Bond turned the pages of the church account books Dad had prepared. So the answer's no.

Right. No. Next item. Thanks to Mr. Bible Study, she heard them laugh after she closed the door.

She strides after her father, thinking of the Pastor today on the way out of church — I've been meaning to talk to you, his arm around her shoulders. She smelled his shaving soap. He talked low just to her — the hair of his mane touching her ear — You know, Cora, the best way to learn is to teach — we need a tots teacher for Sunday-school; it'd do wonders for your baptism prep. Through her blouse, his fingers tapped and patted and stroked her arm — it made her feel like a piece of bread dough being shaped into a bun. Or a chunk of potato pushed around on a plate. (He did it to Netty and Mrs. Lawson too talking softly to them on their way out of church, like he was telling them some special secret, and they laughed and said something back.) Come and see me in my study, he winked.

Dad's at the concrete wall of the fire reservoir now, he's lifting his hat to someone passing by, someone in a wide straw sunhat holding a small carrying case and a flat thing under their arm. He's stopping to talk. She puts down the case and pulls something out of another bag. It's Mme Lumière in dungarees and a plaid shirt — a bright blue bandana around her neck. She's got her easel and paint box. He's smiling and taking her note card — Very good, you're very talented… They hold the card together — their backs toward her. He reaches his other arm around her shoulders like Pastor Crawford.

Stores in Edmonton and Calgary are taking them. Do you think Wellman and Bond's might?

He leans in closer.

You'll have to show them to the boss. But, say, I've been thinking…

They're facing each other now, a few paces away from Cora's spot in the shadow of the reservoir. He's looking at her like she's dangling a watch and he's hypnotized.

When I set up my accounts, do I put all my expenses in one column or divide them into printing and watercolour supplies?

It'd be best to hire a profession'l. I'm thinking you haven't found a church yet.

I suppose you're right — could you do it, everyone says you're the best in town?

I'm awfly busy — I cd try mebbe. Have you thought of Green Pastures Baptist?

Is that your church?

We have a very fine pastor now, Pastor Crawford. From Boston.

Dad's smiling like the time he let her row the boat out on Buffalo Lake, and he just sat in the sun, casting his line and slowly reeling it in. And she too lay back in the boat, drifting under the blue sky.

What about Sunday then, we could meet in my classroom.

That'd be pretty difficult what with church. We welcome everyone at Green Pastures Baptist by the way.

I could come there instead. I only need about an hour of your time; I can certainly pay you.

No no I don't mind helping a friend. I have a Bible study group meets every Wednesday, p'raps you'd like to join us.

That's very kind of you...

Hi Dad, Mme Lumière.

Oh. Where'd you spring from.

Just on my way home.

Mme Lumière reaches for her bag and paintbox.

Here, let me help you with that. They both pick up the bag.

It's quite alright, she laughs, I can carry my own bag.

He lets it go.

Well I'm off to do the elevators this afternoon. She disappears around the reservoir.

Dad.

What.

He looks at the reservoir like he can see right through it.

Is Mme Lumière a friend?

I dunno. (Still hypnotized, still standing where she left him.)

Yes of course she is. I'm hoping she'll join our church.

He pulls himself into his fencepost and marches off toward home.

Does Mom think she's a friend? I don't think Mom likes her very much.

Her stomach jumps like when Mr. Maynard said things about Indian schools the other men didn't like. Or when Dad told Mom Mr. Wellman was letting Mrs. Lawson go, there wasn't enough business. Or when Hilda's Dad told them he wasn't going to have any wheat this fall.

I don't think Mme Lumière believes in church.

How would you know that?

I think she believes in fossils.

———

Mom sets the roast at Dad's place. At the other end of the table, she drops into her chair and fans herself, her face puffy and shiny with perspiration. Hilda says you go all red like that when your monthlies stop and you go through The Change.

Dad straightens his tie and rests his hands on either side of his plate before the steaming meat. Gus slouches. In front of her plate, Elaine shuffles her tiny wood-carvings of a squirrel, a horse, and a pair of boots.

Hodge are you all right, you look a little...

Fine, I'm fine. Gus sit up straight. Elaine, say grace please.

Bless this food and everyone here amen.

Surely you can do better than that.

Elaine fingers the squirrel.

Dad bows his head. Bless this food O Lord...Gus bow your head, show respect. Bless this food O Lord, and ourselves to Thy loving service; that we may always continue in Thy faith and fear the honor and glory of Thy Name, through Jesus Christ our Lord. Amen.

He jabs a long fork into the beef and curls thin slices away from his knife.

Mom cuts her meat into pieces and adds a tiny blob of gravy. Elbows off the table. She puts a hand on Gus's shoulder. Gus lines up the salt and pepper between him and Dougie.

Cora, are you having any?

He's looking over all their heads like they're not even there.

Aren't you hungry dear. Mom's hand on her arm.

Cora I'm waiting for your plate.

He drops a slice onto it, keeping his eyes on the meat.

Only half a potato, Hodge dear, are you sure you're alright.

Of course I'm sure. Please quit askin.

It's just that you haven't been yourself lately.

Mom's looking at him; but Dad's looking at his potato.

Cora would rather open her Chemistry book to the periodic table with its families of elements each having the same number of electrons in their outer shells. The noblest elements are so stable they don't combine with others and when the others combine it's so they can be as stable as the noble elements. She'd rather play a game with Gus, sitting across from her, building dams and moats for his gravy. Bet you don't know how to float metal on water.

No one can float metal on water.

I can.

How can you? Dougie waves his fork. Can I float my fork?

No but you can float a pin.

Why Cora — why does it float?

Because water molecules grab onto each other and they push away from air molecules.

Jesus floated on water.

He didn't float. He walked.

Did he walk on the backs of molecules? Is that how he did it, Dad?

Mom fans her flushed face, rests her head on a hand.

Jesus has nothing to do with molecules.

Cora says molecules hug each other. Dougie wraps his arms around himself.

Did Jesus hug people?

Dad stacks meat on potato, shoves it in, staring at the pot-bellied stove and the Bible beside his armchair. He loads his fork again.

Dad?

Don't talk nonsense.

There's a picture of him in Sunday school holding children on his lap.

They didn't have cameras, silly.

If Jesus were really tiny he could float on water like a pin.

Don't take His name in vain.

What does vain mean?

Stuck up.

No it means getting nowhere.

Elaine crosses the room to her mother's sewing basket.

Where do you think you're going?

I'm just getting a pin so Cora can show us.

We need some wire too.

Get back here and finish your dinner.

Gus dashes down the hall, slamming the back door, and returns with a piece of copper wire. Cora bends the wire into a little platform for the pin and lowers it onto the water in her glass. See how it's pressing down the skin of the water. Just like a person pressing down a mattress on a bed. But it doesn't break through.

Let's do another one.

It's sticking to the first one.

Let me put one in.

Go get your own wire.

Hey, let Dougie have a turn.

They're making a raft.

How many can you get on there?

Five?

I bet I can do ten.

Maybe we can cover the whole water glass.

Maybe God put pins down on the water so Jesus had a raft.

Elaine floats her carved boots on her glass of water.

God didn't need pins; he made the water hold Jesus up.

Was it frozen?

No, he made Jesus float through the air.

No, it says he *walked* on the water.

Maybe he put logs on the water.

How did he make the molecules?

He didn't make the molecules; he just made animals, plants and people. The molecules were already there.

No, God made everything so he must have made the molecules.

Dad, were the molecules already there, or did God make them? What?

Were the molecules already there?

God has nothing to do with molecules. Elaine, clear the table please. Gus, no dessert till you finish your dinner.

But the Bible says God made everything in six days.

Yeah, he made everything in six days.

Then he must have made molecules.

Maybe God is the molecules, Cora blurts out from some strange place in herself she'd never felt before. It's God that keeps atoms together in the molecules and molecules together in the plants and animals.

I don't want to hear one more word about God and molecules.

What about dinosaurs — did God make them too?

Stop this. Just stop it. Dad pounds the table bouncing the knives and forks.

Hodge are you all right? You look a little pale?

I'm fine. Fine. Just fine. Why do you keep saying that? What happened to dessert?

Cora, the whipping cream's in the cellar.

Cora grasps the withers, breathing in horsy warmth of mane and shoulder, as she hoists herself onto the back of Jock. They trot out the gate, jouncing knock-shake — Hilda on Joe, and Netty on Mrs. Maynard's mare. Let's go past the Nuisance Ground. She skips into a thudding Clydesdale canter — human to animal, animal to animal — holding to the surge and flex of his immense back, wind pulling out her hair behind.

Whoa Jock. He tosses his head, jingling the reins, and rumbles to Joe, then looks around at Cora as if to say what're we doing just standing here, Where's my wagon load. He ripples his neck skin shooing off a fly. She tries to ripple the skin on her arm. It doesn't move.

Seventy-five million years ago, Cora says, we could have been riding barylambdas.

Barrel-whatas?

Like rhinos crossed with bears, they had hairy, clawed feet and long fat tails.

How big?

About the size of a pony.

Where'd you get that idea.

From a library book on animals of the past.

I bet these barrel-doodles'd rather eat us than let us ride them.

No, they ate marsh plants. The whole prairie was a sea. With huge lizards and turtles, the mosasaurs and archelons.

Moso stars — wasn't he in the Bible?

He was under King Arch Along.

Quit it, I'm serious. (She should've kept quiet.)

So actually we'd be under water.

Riding our motor sores.

We'd have long snouts so we could still breathe.

Oh shut up.

How come it's not sea now then.

I'm not telling. (Why had she even mentioned it?)

Oh tell, for Pete's sake, we really want to know.

No you don't.

Sure we do.

No, you just want to talk about clothes and Seward Johnson. (Now she's in a huff. She doesn't even want to look at them.)

Okay let's ride over to the Nuisance Ground. Then you can tell us. (Hilda the peacemaker.)

They find old trunks — like Dad's in the attic — a couch with its stuffing flying out, a black buggy — no wheels, no seats — half a hay rake buried in liquor bottles, a stove missing its front — what a jumble. Like the tangle of skeletons and shells that made fossils at the bottom of the old sea.

Someone moves behind a bathtub, crashing through tin cans.

Who was that?

There's a wardrobe missing a back — maybe she could fix it up — have a proper place for clothes — instead of the apple crates.

Someone's pitched a tent.

Where?

On the far side next to that big rusty thing with cogwheels and levers.

Someone's living here.

There's a lotta men outa work.

There's no door on one side. Where would she put it, anyway? A man carries an old washtub up to the edge of the tip.

Hilda, is that who I think it is. Netty on the mare so small beside Hilda on the great Joe.

The man turns around, waves.

Yep, the one and only Seward.

(He'll come over here and we'll never go for our ride. Maybe she could just leave them and canter out to the coal mine. Just run away.)

He's beaming up at her, calling her Hildy instead of Hilda. Howdy Cora, Howdy Netty. Mrs. Maynard sent him for old washtubs she could use for storing root veg. She's even blushing and laughing. And he's getting down on bended knee with prayer hands. But she's waving him away.

Why're we going to the barn?

Us to know and you to find out, Hilda smiles.

We saw you blushing over Seward.

Why don't you go on Saturday, Cora joins in. For once they're teasing Hilda, not her.

Cuz I don't know if I really like him that much.

You must like him if he makes you blush.

You're blushing now, Hilda gives Netty a shove, Why don't *you* offer to go then.

I just might, he's so... Netty rolls her eyes, I don't know...

That's just it — so I-don't-know.

Hilda swings open the side door to the barn.

What's that stink!

That's what we're coming to see; cover your mouth with a hanky and breathe through that.

They clamber over a pile of straw to the thick boards of a wall. Finger on her lips, Hilda points to some wide cracks and knot-holes. On the other side of the wall, two pigs nose around each other in a large square pen.

The one with black patches is the boar; he's the one that stinks, Hilda whispers.

The boar noses the other pig, then roots and shoves it. On the far side of the pen, Seward also watches the pigs.

The other one's a gilt in heat.

(Cora thinks of sprints, the hundred-yard dash.) What's a gilt?

A virgin female pig.

(Mary in her drapery and halo.)

You know what heat is, Netty whispers.

Not exactly.

That's when she's ready for mating; they get it every three weeks.

They're going to make her watch something horrible, like steers holding their tails out for plops of shit. But if she doesn't watch, they'll laugh all the more and say she's too chicken. They've got their arms latched behind her. You can't go through life not knowing this, Netty pinches her arm.

The boar kisses the gilt's nose, then runs his nose down her flank, then kisses her behind. He nudges her and shoves her, climbs up on her haunches, drops down.

See how rigid she's standing; that means she's ready.

Ready for what. This is sickening.

Just watch, you'll get it.

The boar shoves the gilt, heaving her up in the air.

He'll smash her in two.

No he won't, it's all perfectly natural.

What's that pink thing.

That's what he does his job with.

You mean he...

Yeah, he puts it inside...

The boar gets his front legs astride the gilt.

Attaboy, Seward says, give'r a good one.

She doesn't look like she likes it.

She likes it alright; look at her eyes.

The boar thrusts and puffs and grunts; the gilt stands locked up, jolting with each thrust, eyes half closed.

She's made in exactly the right shape for him.

Go boy, Seward says, keep it up.

The boar's legs hold the sides of the gilt, his thrusts are faster, harder. The gilt grunts and squeals.

What's *he* doing here?

Seward...he has to...to make sure they mate...

Why...

Because, silly, if they don't mate there won't be any piglets.

You mean...

Yup, that's the way it works...

Humans too...

Yup...humans too.

The animals shudder in a final spasm, stay locked together for several minutes.

Good boy, stay up there, Seward mutters.

The longer he stays up there, the better.

Like more pollen for a flower, Netty adds.

The boar slides off the gilt's back, his thing hanging slack below his belly. He wanders into a corner of the pen and flops down.

That is a happy pig.

The gilt wanders round the pen, then rubs against the water trough.

How long before she has piglets?

Sixteen weeks.

And then she has the boar again?

A little while after—yeah.

And then she has more piglets.

Yeah.

You make it sound so mechanical. (Netty rolls her eyes.) It's love. It's what makes the world go round.

The word wanders back and forth in Cora's head. Jesus loves me. This I know. For the Bible tells me so. Shepherds turning flowers into caps and skirts for shepherdesses. A boy on an urn who can never kiss the girl he's chasing. Love altering not. In Heavenly Love Abiding. Answer 48: to love the Lord our God— the sum of the ten commandments.

Do pigs love?

Who cares about pigs, I'm going, Netty bounces out the barn door, Are you helping me clean after school tomorrow?

Oh sure, I guess so.

Hilda's arm grasps Cora's waist as though she wants Cora to be all cuddly and kitteny. She wants to toss back the arm like she does if Elaine strays across the centre line of the bed, but she doesn't toss it back, because then she wouldn't be a friend. She lets the arm pull her into the house and upstairs to Mrs. Maynard's vanity to try out the curling iron.

I want to try it out on yours, Hilda sits her down in front of the mirror, Mine's too short.

Why would I curl it?

So Gerard'll notice you.

What for?! So he'll wanta do that?!

Hey, don't be mad at me — Netty's done it.

Is she going to have a baby?

No.

How do you know?

They had a sheath.

So his...?

Yeah his stuff doesn't...

Stuff...

It squirts when they...

Oh...Was it Bunk?

Yeah.

Where?

One of the rooms at the hotel.

And that's all they want?

They?

Boys...men.

No — of course not...there's a lot more to it.

What? What's it got to do with fossils or going to university?

They want to take care of you and protect you.

From what?

From...I dunno, from not so nice men, I guess.

Mme Lumière doesn't bother with that.

She will...one day...All the men look at her.

No she won't — she's like my Aunt Loretta. She's never going to bother with babies and sewing.

The right man changes everything, you'll see.

I'd have to be different — I'd have to be not myself.

I mean look at Mom and Dad! They adore each other.

Mrs. Maynard's nightie lies tossed with Mr. Maynard's night-shirt over the bedstead, his drawers and suspenders hang on the wing chair.

Do they...

More than likely, Hilda brushes out Cora's hair. They sleep together every night.

My Mom and Dad don't.

Don't what.

Sleep in the same bed.

Oh.

Dad sleeps in the boys' room on a cot.

Why?

I dunno...

Hilda's hands run through Cora's hair, piling it up on her head, parting it, combing it off to one side, then combing it a different way — like Mom's hands used to — Cora wishing Mom's hands would go on for hours combing and parting and braiding and fixing. Like waves of Buffalo Lake washing over her, bobbing her body in little sticks of driftwood along the shore.

If I cut my hair like a boy's...

Whatever for? You've got beautiful hair.

CHAPTER 6

Dad's not going for a walk today, he's got *things to attend to*. He's told them to go off by themselves. They stand on the back porch. Gus wants to go to the coal mine and shoot gophers. Elaine says she's not going anywhere if they're shooting animals. Dougie climbs on the side fence and teeters along the top rail, stepping between wild cucumber vines. You go where you want, I'm staying here, Cora says. No one moves. I'm staying too, Dougie says, jumping down from the fence. No you're not. You're all going for a walk. *By yourself*. Cora shoos them away from her.

Hey where's Dad going?

He walks down Taylor Street toward Prairie Avenue, in his shirtsleeves. Dad you forgot your hat, Dougie yells, but he doesn't stop, doesn't even turn his head.

She takes a shortcut to the lane behind the houses, dashes past garden huts and coal sheds. He's still on Prairie Avenue — the walking fencepost — turning onto Main Street. What's he going up there for? He can't be going to the store. It's Sunday. She rounds the corner onto Main, hurries past the Palace Pharmacy and the Stettler Theatre poster for *Devil to Pay* with Ronald

Colman—two women tussling over a man in a pencil moustache, one pulling his tie, while he gazes at the other.

Well well, hello Miss Wagoner—Cora isn't it?

Mr. Rupert. Yes. I'm Cora.

Standing there in front of her, he seems to puff out his suit jacket, with its crisp silk handkerchief, till he's as wide as the sidewalk. His pale blue eyes peer into her from under a light grey fedora. He doesn't go to Green Pastures Baptist. He goes to the Anglican church where the reverend wears long black robes and burns incense during the service.

Where are you off to in such a hurry?

Just out for a walk. (She keeps her eye on Dad crossing Main toward McNabb.)

How's your father?

Well. (A fat gold chain runs out of the Judge's waistcoat to some other part of his clothes.) Thank you.

He didn't look that well a moment ago. Went right by me, on the Lord's day, without so much as a hello.

Oh. I guess... he didn't see you.

Pretty hard not to see someone when you're walking on the same sidewalk.

Oh. Yes, I guess it is.

I've seen you around Cold Lake, haven't I? (The Judge had fined a man $30 for walking off with a box of potatoes at the back of Wellman and Bond's store.)

I go there sometimes.

I advise you to stay away from there.

Why?

It's no place for a young lady, with all these drifters and dead-beats around.

Yes, I guess maybe it isn't.

When she gets to McNabb she sees Dad heading toward the reservoir and the elevators. Hands in his pockets looking at the ground. So he's going for a walk anyway, without them. Just doesn't want to see how many different birds they can spot, doesn't want to talk to them. He walks around the elevators and onto the tracks, putting something in his mouth, then cupping his hands around it. Smoke rises — he's smoking a cigarette — on Sunday! Walking down the tracks toward Cold Lake, staring at the ties under his feet. He scares up a killdeer; then leans on a fence, ignoring the bird swooping around him. It might as well not be there. Even he might as well not be there, might as well be a fencepost gazing at the tiny body of water. His hands dangle over the top rail. He takes a long puff, then dangles his hand again. Finally he throws down the cigarette and grinds it into the ground with his foot before turning back toward the elevators and up McNabb toward the church.

The pews are empty. Maybe he's gone to the basement. Pastor Crawford preached today about a man who picked up sticks on a Sunday, deliberately defying the Lord's order *thou shalt do no manner of work;* his sin brought shame on the whole congregation and he was stoned to death. She takes off her shoes and steals along past the pews, heel into a floorboard — cat walk — Indian walk — rolling smoothly to sole and toe, close to the wall away from the basement door. Answer 91: *Every sin deserves God's wrath in this life, and in that to come.* Heel to toe. Sole to board. Past the lectern for scripture readers. *Repent unto life to escape God's curse.* Heel, sole, toe. To the communion table with its tin jug emptied of her mother's flowers. The pulpit looms over her. What if she stepped onto the platform? What if she conducted her own prayer to spirits of Lake and Killdeer? Answer 101: *Profess repentance to our Lord and obedience to no other.*

She seizes the jug and turns it upside down, jumping like a spooked horse as it clunks the table. Lurching up behind the pulpit, she puffs up her hair like Pastor Crawford's mane and surveys her congregation of square empty pews. *Here is the church, here is the steeple. Open the doors and here's all the people.* Rows of fingers. Church inside out. She holds her arms straight out from her sides, palms up to the sky. How to call to a spirit or a dream — nothing comes to her — nothing at all — just emptiness, blank space — the meaninglessness of holding her arms out like this.

Light footsteps clip into the vestibule. Cora dashes past the throne-chairs and into the shadows behind the piano. There's no exit from the platform except down the basement steps or into the church office which looks locked. Heavier, scuffing footsteps sound from the basement.

Oh, Mr. Wagoner — there you are.

Dad stands at the top of the basement steps.

I thought I might find you here. Mme Lumière's green jacket and matching cloche hat appear in the vestibule, the V of her lapels showing a silk blouse printed in black and white plumes, matching her black handbag and pumps. Under one arm a new green ledger like the ones Dad keeps for Wellman and Bond's store.

I don't think...

Look what I've brought... She holds out the ledger.

Mrs....

Call me Aimée...

What are you doing here?

I've sold quite a number to stores in Edmonton and Calgary...

Mrs....

Aimée.

We can't... Dad crosses his arms and pulls himself up, swelling his chest and shoulders and planting his feet in the aisle in front of her the way he does when he's talking to the men on the church board. The way she's looking at him — it's like French class, when she's waiting for the correct form of a verb.

This one's perfect for a card. (She holds out one of her watercolours.) The dock at Cold Lake balances so well with the cottonwoods.

Don't you know where we are? He turns on his heel and stares out one of the peaked windows along the side wall.

You were going to give me some pointers. She follows him to

the window, holding a bundle of newly printed greeting cards. I wanted you to have these.

He turns toward her, his shirtsleeves crushed where he'd grasped them, and takes the bundle of cards. She sits down in a pew and pulls scraps of paper from her handbag. These are my notes of sales and expenses.

Dad slumps into the pew and picks up a piece of paper, then another one. You've got to divide these into Accounts Receivable and Accounts Paid.

And then I write it down?

His fingers brush her fingers as he takes the papers.

He leans toward her and rustles through other papers on the seat of the pew, mumbling something about expenses and fixed and variable costs, reciting a list of accounts she should set up for equipment, office supplies, inventory, rent, travel — like he's rhyming off dates in history.

She watches him from under her cloche hat, her lips a bright red Cupid's bow. Then her gaze shifts around the room. That jug's upside down.

What?

That jug on the table under the pulpit — it's upside down.

Oh.

It looks like it'll tip over.

He mutters something Cora can't hear. Then says he'll show her how to set up the ledger. Write everything down in its proper account: office supplies, raw materials, mailing charges… Their heads are almost touching over the book. Debit side… No, a sale's on the credit side. Debit Accounts Receivable.

And then when I get the money?

Debit Cash.

I thought debit meant you took away something.

Sometimes it's an increase and sometimes a decrease.

She sits sideways, her arm resting on the back of the pew, her other hand waving vaguely toward the three throne chairs at the back of the platform. Painting's so much simpler — I just let my hand feel where to paint.

Dad's turned sideways to face her. He's in his fishing boat basking in the sun, her sunshine falling all over him.

I uh...

She turns back to him.

Your hat...

What about my hat?

It's...it suits you.

Oh...yes...Very kind of you to...

She smiles at him with her bright red lips, looks at the ceiling, then back at him.

It's like the boar and the gilt when he put his nose on her nose and ran it down her flank, and he nudged her all over. Dad and Mme Lumière, their arms touching, their heads together. She's like the gilt, waiting for him. Even Mme Lumière, in her perfect suit and hat that made him look at her...

Why Hodge, I didn't think to see you here. Pastor Crawford blocks the vestibule doorway. Don't believe I've had the pleasure. He sticks out a hand, beaming at Mme Lumière. Dad stands up, squeezes out from between the Pastor and Mme Lumière. She shakes his hand. Aimée Lumière.

Hope I'm not interrupting anything.

Mr. Wagoner's giving me some advice on accounting.

Hodge come into the office when you're done there.

Pastor Crawford disappears behind the frosted window of the office door.

Mme Lumière gathers up her ledger and note pages, spilling scraps on the floor.

Dad bends to pick them up.

It's alright...I can.

He hands them to her.

Oh...thanks.

She taps the edges of the pages on the seat of the pew.

Did you give any thought to...

She taps and tidies the papers, even though they're already straight.

To...?

The Bible study...

She glances up, then shoves the papers into the ledger.

I don't think...

She looks at him, then down again, then moves out of the pew.

Take your time on it, Dad says, his hand on her back, ushering her toward the vestibule.

Thanks for your help.

They face each other in the doorway.

I'll haveta finish this next...

But she's gone down the steps.

CHAPTER 7

Dad's at work, Mom's at the church doing women's auxiliary, the others out hurling wild cucumbers.

She opens Dad's bureau, unfolds a pair of long underwear, holds it against her waist, puts it back next to the box where he stores church collection money — God's money — understand! Don't ever touch that or I'll cane ya so ya don't know what for. She touches the box — ha! — then a tie, some drawers, and some socks. She takes these and some other clothes back to her room. Takes off her blouse and skirt, then her bloomers. Legs and bum bare. Showing herself. The part no one sees. The part even she doesn't see. The part babies come from. A hole mixed up with pee and blood. There must be more than one hole. She reaches for the mirror, then puts it back. She's going to be Gabriel Dumont. She's going to ride with Louis Riel. Even if she just has a hole.

Her hand reaches for the mirror again and stops it in front of the big dimple in the middle of her stomach — its long lip like the lid of an eye. She opens the eye — inside all puckered like the blossom end of an apple. Why did people have these? She moves the mirror to the large brown patch on her shoulder — her other way to be, that doesn't care about holes. Outside church and school and town, like Gabriel Dumont and his rebels. But the hole is there, saying you only have a hole, like the gilt for the boar—how can you be a Gabriel Dumont? Her hand moves on and places the mirror between her legs. A tangle of hair shows and the round hills of her bum-cheeks curving into a crack. Dimly under the hair, two lips of flesh and between them a mound. Not a hole. A mound. She pushes the hair apart till she sees the darker red of the hole. Her icy fingers graze the mound, and it calls back to her icy fingers. Why does the mound call like that? Why is it so tender?

She puts the mirror back on the crate and pulls on her father's drawers. The buttoned flap hangs down between her legs. She pulls the strings at the sides drawing the cloth around her waist and the flap over her mound. He has a thing, like the boar. He can pull it right through this flap. She tries on his black wool trousers with their row of buttons hidden in a fold. Her mound calls to the fingers doing up the buttons. She puts on a white shirt. Sneaks back into his bureau for some cufflinks. The smell of him in the waistcoat. Like old shoes. She slips crisp shirted arms through the armholes of the waistcoat.

Now she will wrap the wide end of the tie around the narrow end, draw the wide under and over the loop around her neck, and push it down the centre of the knot. Now she will find her trajectory—that other way of being. She strides around the front room, her hands in her pockets, the tie-knot firmly tightened, tie tucked inside her waistcoat. She can be principal of the school, head of the church board, manager of a grain elevator. She can be Louis Riel's adjutant general. Trap General Crozier in a valley and beat back his troops. Command 200 at Batoche. Halt General Middleton and the Canadians.

What are you doing? Elaine stands in the kitchen door, holding a skipping rope.

I'm going to be Gabriel Dumont.

In Dad's clothes!?

It's for a pageant in the fair.

You look stupid.

Not as stupid as you in your frilled skirt and baggy stockings.

You look like that clown at the Chautauqua.

You look like a brainless toadstool.

Oh shut up — no one's going to be fooled.

Cora studies herself in her mother's dresser mirror. (If she tied back her hair... But it sticks out in a fluffy knob.)

Who's Gabriel Dumont?

If you don't know I'm not telling.

I bet he didn't wear a tie.

Oh bugger off.

Cora clumps back to their room and slumps on the bed, then slowly slides off Dad's clothes. Elaine's right, the brat. Dad's old dungarees and gardening hat make a better pageant costume. Her skirt and bloomers and blouse lie crumpled on the floor, old skin shed by a snake. She tries dungarees and an old red sweater, snugs in his belt, rolls up the pant legs. Then wanders back into the boys' room with its bats and baseball gloves, its plaid shirts, toy train engine and tin soldiers — Dad's rifle polished on its rack. His gun — only hers when he says so. Now she will say so. She breaks it — no shells inside. She snaps it back and sights the sewing machine.

But she must go further. She stuffs her hair up into the hat. Long wavy strands hang down around her bathroom-mirror face. Why should she wear a hat? Inside the cabinet, Dad's barber scissors and clippers lie on the shelf — Dad's to snip. He put bowls or pots on their heads, cut around them, ran the clippers up to the edges. Now she'll cut *her* way. She forks her fingers into fields of hair and slashes it off at the back of her head. Then pulls out hair on one side and hacks it off above her ear. Prongs her fingers through the other side and cuts an inch from the scalp. Long dark swaths of hair fall around her. She mows Dad's clippers from her neck to above her ears till it's short on the sides but long on top like Bunk's. Her neck and head feel cool and free.

What on earth have you done to your hair?

Mom's staring at her from the kitchen.

I want a more boyish look.

Your father'll be furious, and if he catches you in those dungarees he won't be pleased either.

It's for my school pageant, remember? I'm Gabriel Dumont.

You didn't have to cut your hair!

Mom, can you trim it around the back? I couldn't really see.

She drops a sack of sugar on the table, Why are you in such a rush?

What rush?! It's a school project.

She pokes at Cora's hair, pushing it this way and that, You want your own way.

It'll grow back.

But there's things you don't understand. She pulls the hair down as long as it'll go, suggesting Cora could wear a kerchief till it's long again. Mrs. McKickly and Hilda's grandmother wore kerchiefs, with tent-like coats and baggy stockings. They carried their shopping bags into Wellman and Bond's and stood in the aisles. Looking. Never knowing which thing they wanted, Dad fumed.

Cora sits on the toilet while she combs and snips. She asks Mom what she doesn't understand, anyway, but Mom just tells her not to be in such a rush to get things her own way. Your father and the Pastor want the best for you. (Mom's fingers running through her hair like gentle waves at Buffalo Lake.) You can do things your way when you're on your own, and you'll be glad of what they taught you.

She makes Cora turn around face to face, Darling I want you to be the best you can, you've got to believe that (she clasps Cora's arms), but there's things you need to learn before you go your own way.

Mom, how come you and Dad don't sleep in the same bed, like Mr. And Mrs. Maynard?

Suddenly she has to get dinner ready, finish Cora's hair later, your father'll be home any minute. She's back to the kitchen, pouring the sugar into its canister, clunking the lid on.

Mom, don't you love him?

She's at the sink now, running the peeler over a potato so the bits fly up the side of the porcelain.

Mom?

The skinned potato plops into a pot, If you must know, it was doctor's orders, after Dougie was born.

Why?

Dad barges in wanting to know if this is how we're bringin up our daughters now, cuttin their hair like boys' and giving them dungarees to wear?

His black fedora and black overcoat fill the room.

It wasn't *my* idea.

You! (he points at Cora) get out of those dungarees and back into proper clothes.

It's a costume for school.

You're not wearing that to school or anywhere else.

He turns his back on them, and plunks his hat on its peg and his coat on its hook.

Hodge, for Pete's sake give her some elbow room.

What's that sposed to mean?

It's just a school play; they always wear costumes.

She kin stay out of it. School's for yr subjects, not plays.

So is church for meeting Mme. Lumière?

Stomach lurch. As soon as she says it, Cora knows she shouldn't have — that it'll change everything because now they know she knows what she shouldn't, and she can never be the same to them after that. But she must go on, butterfly stomach — she must find her own way.

I don't know what yr talkin about.

Helping her do her account books last Sunday — are you in love with her?

Mom drops the potato peeler, and just leaves it on the floor. She wanders toward the kitchen table.

Hodge?

See what you've done, ya stupid girl, you've hurt yr mother no end!

Hodge...you met her in the church?

After all she does for you—makes yr clothes, cooks yr meals—does yr washin—and this is how you thank her.

He gets his belt off, pushing her down on a chair and grabbing her hand, and she holds it out to get it over with, but Mom's saying no—she's grabbing the belt—she wants to know what's going on, what happened in the church. Nothin's goin on. Then what's she talking about? I dunno, you better ask her. He throws the belt down and walks out the back door.

She tries not to tell Mom anything. Just says he was there in the pews showing Mme Lumière how to do accounts, and the Pastor came in. But Mom wants to know what she meant about being in love. Cora says she doesn't really know what it means, it's just a phrase Netty and Hilda say when they think you like a boy. Then Elaine and the boys come in and start laughing at her hair and dungarees. It's not funny; it's just a haircut. They look at Mom's face and stop. She changes back into her skirt and blouse, and tells Mom she'll get supper if she wants to lie down for a bit, and Mom goes into her room and doesn't come out when supper's ready. It's all her fault really—she shouldn't have said what she said but she can't go back now. Elaine and the boys want to know how come it's just them eating dinner, and Cora says, don't worry, Mom's not feeling well. Dad's gone out. When's he coming home? I don't know.

He comes in after the house is dark and she's lying in bed on her side of the quilt valley. She hears him walking in sock feet across the kitchen, stopping outside his door. Sees a crack of light go on around the edge of her own slightly open door. Light from Mom's room—bright, then dim again as a door swings over it.

Hears him say Beth, I'm sorry. The blurred muffle of her answer. His lower tones, her higher ones, his lower answer, hers — soft, then hard, more determined, and definite. Then quite clearly, I've seen the Pastor, I've been at the church praying. Mom's murmur as though she's lost or tired. Then his voice, I've been askin for His forgiveness. Her voice rises like she's asking him a question, then his mutters like he's repeating something over and over — trustin Him to show me the way. They mumble and mutter for a long time after that, but she can't understand any of it.

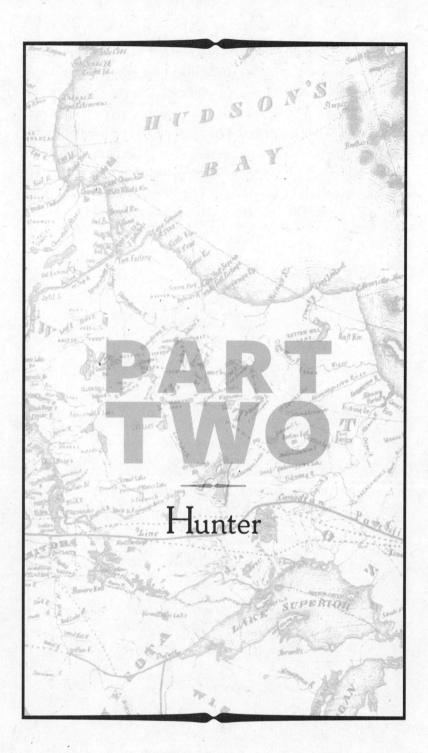

PART TWO

Hunter

CHAPTER 8

Hunter grips the cow's halter and pulls her along the road, trying to stay ahead of the dust from his father's footsteps. His stomach growls, maybe they'll stop at Auntie May's on the way to the government man — Auntie May always has cookies. Now his arm aches again. He runs around to the other side of the cow and holds on with that arm. Dust clings to the long soft hair inside her ears, dust all over her black and white face and her sides and rump with its sticking out bones. Because everywhere is turning to dust now, land drying up, even his mother's and Auntie Marge's garden that he watered with can after can from the pump has smaller carrots this year and stubby ears of corn, tops of beets all yellow and holey. He touches the cow's flank with a willow branch to keep up with his father — Hunter can tell she doesn't want to walk along with them, milk bag bashing side to side. Empty now for a long time. Why couldn't they have milk again? His father squirting into a foamy bucket, squirting to Hunter's tongue and the dogs' tongues, warm sweet milk, then next day thick cream for berries.

I don't think Nikâwiy wants to sell the cow.

His father pulls out his honey-smelling tobacco from the pocket of his leather vest — She's just worried it'll cost too much.

It costs money to sell something?

You have to have permission to sell, sometimes you have to pay to get permission.

Maybe she could have a calf and we could have milk again.

Maybe, but I'd have to feed her through the winter.

Will we get another cow?

Maybe, after the winter.

Maybe, but it doesn't sound like his father's planning to. They've had the cow as long as he can remember. It doesn't feel right to sell her; it's like when Tom and Fish-eyes went away to school; like someone punched a hole in the side of his house and just left it there all winter.

They stop and talk to Father Clarence, walking to his house near the church at the far end of the village.

Hey Daniel, how's your Auntie Marge?

Okay I guess, legs are shaky but she's good help for Mary.

I want to thank you for all the work you and your brother did building my coal shed.

Oh, that's alright Father Clarence.

Mass will be a little cozier and less smoky.

So many fathers — Dad — Father Clarence — Our Father who art in heaven up above the stars in the night sky — Jesus wasn't a father — he was a son — did he have a grandfather, aunts, uncles, and cousins? Before Tom and Fish-eyes went away, Father Clarence marked out a diamond in the field behind the church and taught them how to play baseball after Sunday school, he even batted the ball himself and ran around the bases.

Say, Daniel, could you use extra blankets for the winter?

That's kind of you, but...

I've got some I don't need — come round tomorrow and pick them up.

The government man's house has a porch all around it and lots of rooms inside with couches and chairs and smooth walls, not just logs. Stairs go up to the bedrooms. Mr. McDonald, the government man, has a table in a room off to the side of the house where his father and Uncle Lenny and Uncle Arthur and Uncle Jack go to see him, but right now he's not in that room. Uncle Jack says there's a window between that room and the other part of the house where Mr. McDonald can look and see if any of the men are there to see him. He must not be looking right now.

Hunter ties the cow to a hitching rail beside Uncle Arthur's horse and its cart of firewood. If only he had an apple or a carrot. He pulls his fingers through the horse's mane and rubs the long brown neck. Bin here quite awhile, Uncle Arthur's saying to his father, He's here, but Mrs. McDonald says he's busy. Joe's here too with fox pelts. Gotta get'm into town by the end of the day, doesn't know if he'll make it.

Who's the firewood for?

CNR.

All you get's twenty-five cents a load.

Lotsa loads; it adds up. After awhile you get the rest from Ottawa.

Hunter wonders why an Indian called Ottawa would get Uncle Arthur's money. He wanders over to Mr. McDonald's barn with its shiny red car and farm wagon, and climbs into the hay loft where he can see out the gate of the Reserve to môniyâw land — used to be our land, Grampa said — and back across the grassland toward home. Somewhere out there his father's steers are sticking their noses into the dusty grass, searching for food. Maybe he can see them if he looks hard enough. He counts the boxcars on a faraway train, tiny as a snake crawling at his feet. In the old days, Grampa said, our people could ride for free on trains. The Queen promised this when she made the treaty so we could go and see her if anyone was giving us trouble. She knew our people would be treated poorly. She made the treaty so she could own Canada and she promised us nets and bullets. The king, her grandson, still owns it, too, but now we have to pay to go on the train and we don't always get what she promised.

Come see what I found, Shorty bounds into the loft with Friendly panting right behind him, hanging out his dripping tongue. Behind the storehouse, they climb on a sawhorse to peer in a high window at sacks of flour and sugar; slabs of bacon dangle from the beams.

If we work for Mr. McDonald he might give us some.

How d'you know?

He gave bacon to Nohkomnam when she cleaned his house.

What could we do?

Chop wood, weed his garden.

How do we get him to let us?

Go ask him.

Hunter follows Shorty back to Mr. McDonald's porch where Uncle Joe is sitting on the steps, scraping mud off his shoe with a stick. Uncle Arthur chews grass, leaning against a post with his eyes closed. Faint noises bump and thump from the main house, then go quiet. The door to the room with the table is open. No one's inside.

Hunter picks a grass stalk. It tastes dusty like he put his tongue on the road. He spits it out. His father pushes honey-smelling tobacco into the bowl of his pipe, poking it down with the end of a match. Then clips the match with his thumbnail till it bursts into flame and he sucks the pipe into its sweet puffs of smoke. When you're old enough to buy your own, his father says, not now. Shorty makes Friendly roll on his back with his paws in the air. Let's make'm do tricks, jump for sticks. But Shorty rolls on his back beside Friendly and shuts his eyes.

Hey Nîstâw, Uncle Joe pulls out his cards, let's play Heads Up. Uncle Arthur opens one eye, shuts it. Joe deals him two cards, deals himself two cards on the porch floor. Don't I get to cut?

Sure. Joe picks up the cards, shuffles them. So cut then. Arthur slides down to the floor. Dad doesn't like cards, says they make you do stupid things. So areya in? Ya I'm in. Whaddaya bettin? Arthur drops a penny. Joe adds a penny, then deals three more cards face up. That's called the Flop, since you're watchin, Joe nods at Hunter. I'll raise ya. Two pennies drop. Then two more. Dad gets up off the porch, puts his pipe away, walks over to the cow. Guess I'm outa pennies. You can owe me, Arthur says. Joe drops some pebbles.

Hunter sits on the hitching rail next to his father. Dad's got his knife out cutting away at a chip of firewood that looks like a thumb. He smells of smoke and horse. What is it?

I dunno, what do you think it is. He holds it up.

When Dad gave him his own knife, Mom made a sheath for it out of deer hide. She put beads on it too. It's his favourite thing, next to riding Kîyasiw.

Looks like a thumb.

I think it looks like a horse head.

Where's his eyes and nose?

I'll show you — here's his mouth, here's his chest, here's his mane flowing out in the wind as he runs.

Like Kîyasiw.

Yeah, like Kîyasiw.

Nohtâwiy.

What Natonam?

We're not going to sell Kîyasiw are we?

I hope not.

The sun is already falling out of the sky by the time Uncle Joe gets a piece of paper so he can sell his pelts and Uncle Arthur can drive his load of wood to the CNR. Why does Uncle Arthur shake Mr. McDonald's hand so much, smiling and saying thank you over and over like he can't say it enough times?

Are you sure you wanta sell that cow, you know it's gonna cost you. Mr. McDonald crosses his arms and looks out the door like he'd rather be out there than talking to Dad sitting across from him, placing his big black hat carefully on his knee.

Not enough hay to feed my steers, with the drought.

Mr. McDonald moves some papers around on his desk, looks at Dad, says nothing.

I need to sell the cow to buy hay for the winter.

Well, you know the rules.

When times are hard, you sometimes change the rules.

It costs $18 for a permit to sell a cow.

To buy a cow only costs $10. I could give you two, three dollars, that's all.

The government didn't give you a cow so you could sell it.

Then I'll have to sell a steer.

How many steers've you got?

Five head.

No permits for steers in the fall.

Now is summer.

It's the end of summer. No permits for steers till spring.

My steers'll starve.

Go find work, earn the money to buy hay.

You know there's no work now; no wheat harvest — no jobs stooking.

Go on the road crew.

Mr. McDonald closes up some books on his table. Dad says nothing, just looks at the floorboards.

Your boy ready for school?

If there's a teacher here, my boy'll go to school.

Indian children go to boarding school now.

My boy knows how to read; he doesn't need boarding school.

He needs to learn farming methods; learn to make a living for himself.

His father stands up, puts his hat on.

He can learn that here.

Going out the door Dad's shoulders bend over like when his

sister was buried, wrapped in cloth. The priest said she should have a coffin but she didn't want one. Dad didn't talk to anyone much then. He probably doesn't want to talk now.

Make sure he's back here in two weeks and ready to go with the other children, Mr. McDonald calls out. The law says all Indian children from six to fifteen *must* be in school, and your boy's ten.

— ◆ —

Hunter's mother gives him fried bannock, and says I thought so when Dad shakes his head. What's the use of a cow with no milk, Auntie Marge, pulling yarn from an old sweater, tsks and winds the wool into a ball, might as well sell it. Bannock, soft on the inside, crunchy on the outside, good with Auntie's jam. Auntie Marge who is even Dad's Auntie told him she had a little cabin, before Dad was born, where she used to go fishing by herself and clean the fish and smoke them over a fire. Then a bear smelled the fish and came sniffing around her boat and her drying racks. Her little dog was scared of the bear but she threw a stick at it and it went away. At night she took the fish and her dog into her cabin. The next day the bear came back and she had to take everything inside again. The bear sat in front of her drying racks washing its face with its paw, rubbing behind its ears and scratching under its armpits just like a person.

Grampa's scraping bits of fur and rust off traps for Uncle Jack. No time, now, for pakesîwin, or stories about hunting bears. Go get me a pail of water with some hot in it from the stove.

You can tell where a bear is sleeping in the winter from the mist leaking out the top of his den, Grampa said. You open the top of his den and wait till he sticks his head up, then you shoot him. No, I can't show you Grampa said. That was in the old days up north, no bears live around here.

Dad takes the axe and saw off the porch, bangs the door shut. Now take this brush and scrub, Grampa tells him when he brings the pail, I'll tell you one story about coyotes. They're pretty smart, people say they're hard to catch, but I used to trap lots of them. I would find coyote tracks where they follow each other from place to place and I'd set my trap there, then cover it with snow. Coyotes are curious, always sticking their nose into things. I would ride my horse up and down on either side of the trap making lots of tracks, just like the wild horses. Coyotes wanted to know about these tracks, they came sniffing around them and then they got caught. I used to get pretty good money for those pelts — five, six dollars. Hey, don't be too much like a coyote, Nôsisim.

When they finish the traps, Grampa's eyes close and his head falls to his chest just sitting in his chair. Hunter follows Dad into the bush behind the cabin, watches him notch out an undercut on the trunk of an old aspen, then whack in on the other side, his axe spraying chips like snow over the ground till only a thin band of wood keeps the trunk together and Dad pushes the tree down. Dad hands Hunter the axe, You chop the branches.

Not just one way, Dad always told him, hit it from one side, then the other side making a little V shape. Then cut in from the other side of the branch too. Hold the axe at the end of the handle. But it's not so heavy, Hunter thinks, if you slide your hands toward the blade.

Am I going to school with Tom and Eagle? Shorty's going.

Dad says nothing, just keeps ramming the buck saw back and forth across the trunk of the old half-dead aspen, pushing the end down so it doesn't pinch the blade.

You got those branches off?

Hunter whacks into one. Uncle Lenny let Tom and Fish-eyes go to the faraway school, but Dad says no. The tree bounces, leaving only a small cut from his axe. He whacks harder till the branch is off, then lays it across one of Dad's logs and chops it into firewood lengths.

Mom and Dad are walking to town today, not back till after dark. Hunter's supposed to be chopping logs, but instead he sorts through the woodshed for something to make a bird-trap like Grannie told him about. He tries propping a piece of firewood on a sliver of kindling. No. Silly. Need a flat board. Not clunky axed stuff. He roams around outside the cabin, finds some grey boards growing into the grass. Too long. Looks under the house between the floor and the ground. Ends of fire-logs, broken cup and plate, rowboat oars, muddy glass jars, tin of green paint, top all rusty. A slivery plank about three feet long. What to prop it on. He needs string too.

In the main room of the cabin Rose-Berry's cutting up yellow newspaper at the table, beside her a calendar picture of a bridge — its top swoops down, then up the way swallows fly.

Auntie Marge, sewing a patch on some pants — there might be some baling twine by the water barrel. He kicks around the tank on the porch, cracked boots, clothes-pins, the well bucket. Yanks out a hunk of twine untwisting itself into separate threads. Like it's made of long brown hair or dried grass.

Rose-Berry's pencil would be just right to prop up his board. No, you can't borrow it. A fork maybe from the jar on the window sill. No forks outside, why don't you get on with chopping wood?

Behind the woodshed, he breaks off some willow bush, then lops it down to a short stick on the chopping block. Ties the baling string to the stick.

He takes the trail over hummocky prairie down to the creek that eats the ground under the grass. Props one end of the board on the stick, runs the baling twine back to a bush. Then pulls a match from his pocket. Stuffs it in the corner of his mouth like Uncle Arthur. When will the blackbirds come, like Grannie said. He pulls back behind the bush, then crawls into the hummocky grass, finds a dead beetle, some dried weed stalks, a clump of last-year's seed-heads, and sprinkles the bait in his trap. Noises in the night had woken him — Mom and Dad talking — you know what can happen if you don't have a permit. Thumps like Dad punched something. Shh, Mom saying, Complain, we get nothing.

Hunter curls his fingers around a match and tries to light it with his thumbnail the way Dad does it but he chips all the white part off without making it spark.

Apistikakes lands on the branches over his head. Scolding him ka ka ka — silly boy, you think any bird's going to be stupid enough to fly into your trap, not when I'm around telling everyone.

Back at the woodshed, he brings the axe down on the end of a log. Hits a knot. The blade stuck. Axe and wood now a giant hammer to pound down till the split breaks and just the stick of the cross-branch holds the pieces together. After awhile Mom and Dad's voices were quiet in the dark — gone back to sleep — then they started up again, through the wall like a thunderstorm at the edge of the sky — turning a stone in the bottom of Hunter's stomach — Dad's voice rumbling, Mom a high sharp bird, promise me you will not sell that cow without a permit — then his words punching holes — we need hay. No. Shh, you'll wake the kids. Rose-Berry and Auntie Marge dark hills on their side of the room. He held his hands over his ears, made their words back into thunder and birds — back to the edge of sky.

Hunter splits the round into two then the two into four. Stack. One round done. How many to go? He sits down on the block. Rose-Berry's inside washing dishes.

Something comes to him he saw once in town — kids bouncing up and down on either end — he tips over the chop-block, uncovering a mess of sow bugs. That long wood grown over in the grass — he drags a piece back to the chop-block, places it across the round. Yells till Rose-Berry comes to the door.

Up light as a cloud he flies, then plops when she kicks off. They put their heads in the middle, feet hanging off the ends — watch the jumping sky and bushes. Then feet in the middle, heads at the ends — push off with hands — upsidedown cabin — rightsideup woodshed, upsidedown well, rightsideup outhouse.

They stand in the middle where the plank crosses the round, then inch out to the ends, keeping the board level. Then, not too fast, he drops, she flies, tilts, waving her arms around, laughing, catches her balance. Steps out on her end. Whoop up, crazy stomach. Feet almost off the board. Land. Hit the ground. Rose-Berry mid-air, landing hard, bouncing him up. He landing harder. Rose-Berry bouncing higher. Till she jumps off and he lands, thunk, dead. Chunk of stone.

Let's build our own house, we won't hear them if they talk the bad talk at night. They pull the rest of the boards out of the grass. Lean them together in a teepee. Cover them with an old piece of canvas, leaving a smoke hole at the top. He gets rocks from the creek, makes a fire circle. Auntie Marge lets them take out blankets for beds, lets them eat stew beside their campfire and toast scraps of bannock. Grampa even says they can sleep on his bearskin.

After dark, they make candles out of slivers of burning wood. The candles flame, turn to glowing embers, then snuff into black smoking stubs. Wave it through the air — light it up again. Like a firefly. They make torches of burning sticks and race around the field near the house throwing sparks from the torches. They're fireflies and the whole black sky above's full of starry fireflies.

———

Mom pushes him out the door saying, Go see Kokôm today, go with Rose-Berry. He doesn't want to walk that long way. She gives them bannock, not to eat till they get there.

They follow the trail through willow bush, scaring a rabbit out of its tangled holes. Some men are coming to take away kids, Rose-Berry says. Take them to the faraway school. Why don't we go to school? Kids that go there never come back. What happens to them? They disappear.

Eagle and Tom and Fish-eyes will never come back?

Not for a long time, maybe never.

He thought of Shorty — Uncle Arthur was letting him go. Maybe Hunter would never see him again.

Onocayikowiw circling overhead. Why don't we have our school with Miss McFarlane?

Dad says the government has no money for that school; now they make all the kids go to the far-away one. Long legs of a frog jump into bulrushes along the creek. Grannie says they stretched when the mudhen dropped him in a tree and he hung there reaching for water.

He picks a rush and bops Rose-Berry on the head with its velvet tail.

Did the Wihtikiw eat them, he asked her.

Who?

The kids that never come back.

Maybe, I don't know.

Maybe — like Nokomnan says — they needed stronger dreams.

Maybe.

How do you get strong dreams?

You have to dream a lot — not just dreams at night. Like Nimosôminan says — you have to go away by yourself, not eat anything for five days, just make it hard for yourself, like standing up all day, then the dreams come. Are you going to do that, Nîtisân, Are you going to go out in a little teepee by yourself? She bonks him with a bulrush. He whirls around and bonks her twice as hard. She breaks the end off and rubs bulrush fluff in his hair, but he gets her arms behind her back, both of them laughing so hard they can't stop. She elbows him off.

At the longest part of the trail through open prairie, his legs tell him stop, sit down on a rock. Rose-Berry brushes out fluff from his hair. Gives him a comb. Hey, look nice for Nohkomnan. He asks Rose-Berry what about the children out past Bear Lake, they came back from that school.

Now there's something wrong with them. Something eating them inside. They cough all the time, trying to cough it out.

She runs around his rock, crossing her eyes, sticking out her tongue, arms out like giant hawk wings. Better watch out, Wihti-kiw will get you.

———◆———

Sun low in the sky, he asks Dad let's go fishing, now when the bugs are out and they'll be jumping but Dad doesn't want to. Covered in dust, like someone poured sand all over him, he sits at the table on the chair with no back, facing Mom. Black smeared on him too. Smells funny, like gasoline. Dad digs in his pocket. Puts a silver coin on the table. A quarter—that's all they gave you for a whole day. Dad says nothing. They leave the quarter sitting there between them. Don't look at him standing there.

Môniyâw get twice as much, Uncle Jack squirts oil into a trap.

In his chair, Grampa sits with his eyes closed, too tired to play the hand game. Even Mihkosiw, flopped under the stove, just taps the end of his tail, doesn't lift his head.

Have some hot water from the stove for a wash Nitikwatim—Auntie Marge pours tea for Dad.

I'll go with you tomorrow, Dan, Uncle Jack says, that way the quarters'll pile up faster, eh?

Hunter takes the fishing rod down to the creek. Rose-Berry digs up a beetle and a worm. He pushes the hook through their bodies, drops it in the water. Grannie said in the old days men built fences in the creek pushing the fish into a long narrow place where the men would scoop them out in nets made of thin willow branches. Lotsa fish. Lots for everyone.

How could we build a fence across the creek, he asks his sister. I dunno.

She says she knows how Dad gets covered with sand. I'll show you tomorrow but it's farther than Nohkomnan's house.

———◆———

Rose-Berry takes him through the willow bush, past the bulrushes, along the tired-legs trail, past Grannie's house, through a patch of aspen trees, and a patch of misâskwatômin. Remember, we picked berries here. They pull a few dried sweet ones from the branches.

She stops him at the edge of the Saskatoon bushes. You see that dust, that's where he is. A clump of men raking, shoveling, and pushing wheelbarrows on a long strip of dug-up ground where the wind blows swirls of dust. Both ways, the strip goes, out to the edge of the sky. A machine spewing black smoke rolls along on chains of metal squares dragging a mat of wheels through the dirt and gravel behind it. Another machine pointing a finger in the air hoists a bucket of black dripping muck onto the dug-up strip. Hunter holds his nose. Worse than the shit-house.

A man yells. Dad and Uncle Jack and Eagle's dad bend over the black muck spreading it with rakes. Other men stand around or sit under little roofs over their machines. No no no, the man yells again. This way. Yelling man grabs the rake out of Dad's hands. Swoops it this way and that over the dirt. Thrusts it back at him. Crosses his arms. Eagle's dad, Uncle Jack and Dad push and pull at the muck. Dad wiping his face with his sleeve, his face all black.

Hunter steps out of the Saskatoon bushes. No you don't, Rose-Berry pulls him back. You go out there and those men'll grab you, take you away.

We have to get Dad away from there.

You can't.

Why not.

Because Mr. McDonald says he has to go there and build a road.

Tell Dad, let's go fishing. Build a fence to catch lots of fish like Nohkomnan says.

What's that. I don't remember anything about fishing with a fence.

The men make nets out of skinny willow sticks, they scoop them up. Lots of fish for everybody.

I dunno.

All the way back, they talk about how to stop Dad.

———————

He's snoring, Rose-Berry whispers in the dark. Hunter takes a silvery fish off his hook, the fish is snoring, these fish are so lazy he catches them easily, puts them in his bucket, but the fish walk on their tails snoring back into the river. He's snoring, Rose-Berry whispers. I'm fishing, he says. Gotta get Dad's clothes, Rose-Berry whispers.

He stumbles up to the door of their room, Rose-Berry behind him. They crawl over to the chair under the window, slide the dusty gasoline-smelly pants and shirt off the chair, Rose-Berry takes the rest of his clothes off the hook, they back out of the room. He grabs Dad's boots and jacket off the porch. Then out into the night sky of firefly stars.

Someone's grabbing him through his blanket. Sun patch of morning on the wall. Where's my clothes you little rascal. Dad's arm around him lugging him past Mom at the stove, past the water barrel, the jumble of boots, out to the well pump. Gimme my clothes or it's a cold shower. Dad in just his undershorts. Promise you won't go back to that stinky black dirt. Where's my clothes. Promise. Gimme my clothes first. He wriggles free and runs back into the house under the warmth of his blanket.

Dad's heavy footsteps right behind him clump into the room. He tears off the blanket. Rose-Berry yanks it away and slings it over his head. They tangle it round his arms. Dad the mostos roars, lowers his blanket-snarled head and charges. They roll away, grab more blankets and heap them on his butting head. He snatches Rose-Berry, then Hunter, trapping them in a corner. His big arms squeeze around them.

Hey Danny let's go. Uncle Jack and Eagle's dad poke their heads into the room. Got no clothes, Dad says. Thieves took'm.

Guess you'll have to go like that.

Guess so.

Gonna get tar and sand all over your tootsies.

He walks out of the house in his bare feet and undershorts with Uncle Jack and Uncle Norm.

———•———

Past the church and graveyard, in the empty hut that used to be Miss McFarlane's school, Rose-Berry is the teacher. She climbs on the window ledge and finds a tiny piece of chalk in her stash at the top of the frame. Stett-ler, she writes on the board. Makes him sound it out. In-de-pend-ent. News.

Wind blows into the room turning the pages of her news-papers — no more glass in the windows.

What's independent?

On your own.

How can news be on its own?

It's just the name of it, like you're called Hunter.

What's Stettler?

A town.

Why's the news like that — by itself?

It's better news when it's like that.

Why?

Because dependent news is bad.

My turn. He skips pages with nothing but columns of tiny words till he comes to one showing a plate of muffins next to the word Magic. Magic Baking Powder, she reads, Miss McFarlane's Recipe for Graham Gems.

Is our teacher Miss McFarlane in the newspaper now.

No, silly. Just the same name, I guess.

A man's face on the page stares at him through black spectacles as though he's done something wrong. Like the man's saying, You're lying, I'm not very pleased with you. Next to him a little man, smaller than staring-man's head stands up straight, long row of buttons on his front, all tidy like a good boy, beside a stack of words tall as he is. Soft wool under-wear, he reads, closed cr-ot-ch sty-le with firm-ly sewn seams, buttons and button holes.

What's crotch?

Part between your legs.

Boys are different.

Yeah.

Girls make babies between their legs.

So.

So show me how you do it.

It grows inside you and then it comes out.

Where?

Through a hole.

You have a hole there.

Yeah.

Always something brushing against his legs, rubbing against his pants, against his hand, against his bed tick. Something he carried along, like a set of coloured stones that Uncle Lenny gave him. Something sticking out that he could hold. Something making showers of pee on the leaves. Something to write his name in the snow. Something that felt good sometimes when he touched secretly in bed.

So it's nothing. (He points.) Like a woodpecker hole or a rabbit burrow.

No silly.

Just air blowing through. Like an empty pot.

No. It's closed. It's touching itself.

Show me.

There's nothing to see.

Then she agrees, if he shows his. She pulls up her skirt and drops her drawers. Light fuzz of dark hair. Two little folds of skin between her legs.

How do you pee?

He drops his pants.

Is your stick always getting in the way, she laughs, Does it freeze like an icicle? How can you sit?

Does the hole go all the way to her stomach? Do babies fall on the floor? No of course not, it's just like when Uncle Lenny's dog had puppies. They come out slowly, all wrinkled and slimy. Does it hurt?

There's more to it than that, you know.

What.

Boys have to do their part.

Like this. He seized her braids and put his lips on hers. She stuck her tongue out and pushed him off.

CHAPTER 9

Noises at night — Dad's rumbling thunderstorm — Mom's higher birdcalls. Hunter peers through the slightly open door. She sits at the table, her hair not braided, falling in waves over her face. You promised.

We have to get hay; we've got mouths to feed.

Arthur did that — he went to jail.

Look, I said I'm sorry.

Who did you sell her to?

A farmer, other side of Ponoka.

What if he goes to McDonald?

Joe sold some firewood to him, he never complained.

What am I going to do with you in jail?

I won't be going — anyway at least we'll have hay for the steers and steers for us to eat.

Hunter crawls back under his blanket. Tomorrow he'll catch a fish for Mom. He'll watch not to get the line tangled, like Dad says. He'll go to Bear Lake where the heron stands and catch fish and bring them to Mom for supper.

Go now — the both a you go — out in the willow bush, out past the lake — don't even go to Kokôm's house.

Why?

Government men are coming.

Go now. Don't come back till dark.

Government men again, looking for more kids. Now that Eagle and Tom and Ernie and Lizzie and even Shorty are gone to school — no more kids except babies. In the willow bush, he gathers leaves to make cigarettes like Grannie did. How'll you dry them? She's reading her newspaper. Crown's Corn Syrup tin bigger than three people next to it. A man with his eyes closed poking his nose into the hair of a woman, and a woman with her strap falling off her shoulder looking cross. He picks curled-up leaves from the ground, crushes them in his fingers. Begs some of her newspaper to roll up the leaves. You watch out or I'll do what that man did to Nohkomnan. What? Make you cigarettes out of cow pats. She tears off two small squares of newspaper.

They puff at the cigarettes. Paper burning too quick into large black flakes around the damp willow leaves. He holds his smoke between thumb and fingers cupped in his hand like Uncle Jack and Uncle Norm. Sticks his other thumb into a pocket. Brings the cigarette to his lips, breathes in. Coughs. Dizzy and strange. The cigarette burns to a crooked twist of charred paper.

We should have a pipe like the old men at the Sun Dance.

How're we going to get that?

He hacks off a branch with his knife, and saws away at it until he gets a short length. He scrapes the bark off, marking the fatter end for the bowl. How're you going to make the hole go through, Rose-Berry asks as he scoops at the bowl with the point of the blade.

I dunno. He chucks the thing away. Grabs another stick and slices at the end until it's sharp and pointed and sticks in the ground.

He pulls out the sling Grampa made for him by cutting a thong from a beef hide, then cutting it in half, and knotting each half to two holes in a square of hide. Practice, Grampa said, you can bring down a deer with one of these. On Rose-Berry's page the good-boy buttons-up-the-front man stands beside a boot that comes up to his waist.

Get some stones.

No, you get some stones.

Down at the river edge under a high bank, he fills his pockets. If only Eagle and Shorty were here they'd whack mudballs. Or pick off gophers with Eagle's dad's rifle.

Half way across the tired-legs prairie, they lie in the grass staring into blue and counting clouds racing on the wind. That one's going to get to the big one before that one. No, not the moose-horns one, the rabbit one. Mountains of mud balls float past. Then pipes, smoking like trains. Dad the mostos charges across the sky. Hunter climbs on Dad's back but it's bumpy and lumpy, it's melting under him — only grass and dirt where he's sleeping. Mouth dry. Flies buzzing on his face in the sun.

At Bear Lake they hurl stones around their heads letting them fly at a birch tree. Rose-Berry doesn't feel like hunting for more stones in the dried mud. They push into the prickles of their favourite sihta, the only one for miles around, and clamber up branches, worn with footsteps. She breaks off some pitch — Nohkomnan says you can chew this. Tastes sharp. Not as bad as chokecherries. Sticky rocks on his tongue. He spits it out. You're s'posed to make it like Wrigley's.

Who wants Wrigley's?

At the top they hook arms around the softer bark and pick out tiny houses of Uncle Lenny, Uncle Arthur and their house, then Father Clarence's house, the church and beyond that the empty school hut. Dust rises on the road from Mr. McDonald's house — a red dot on a horse. Farther away down another long road are more houses where Grannie lives with Auntie Ethel, Uncle Arthur, Shorty and baby Mary and Auntie Ethel's cousin Alex and his son, cousin Ernie who's been at the far-away school for a long time.

Who're all the red men.

Police, I guess.

Another red dot canters down to Uncle Arthur's place. Another one out to the priest's house. Tiny red men with big hats — they crisscross the prairie between the houses. They ride up to their house, where Mom's hanging clothes to dry.

———◆———

After dark he and Rose-Berry find their way to the little square of light in their house.

They took your Dad away, Mom tells them.

Who took him?

Police.

Why?

Because of the cow.

That farmer went to Mr. McDonald, Auntie Marge talks to her knitting, Why did he buy her then?

I told him not to sell without a permit.

Why does he have to have a permit? Hunter sits on a chair backwards, legs on either side of the seat like Dad does. Mom's eyes poke into him almost like she's mad he even said it.

Môniyâw get better prices for their cows (Uncle Jack scrapes at fat and blood of a fox pelt) when we can't sell ours.

That hay he got — the steers don't like it, Grampa pushes a cloth through the barrel of Dad's shotgun.

What the hell are they gonna eat, Uncle drops his scraping knife.

What jail? Hunter asks his mother as she clatters a pan on the stove.

In Edmonton.

How long for?

I don't know; I'll have to find out if he can get help.

Mom sits at the table with a pile of baling twine — untangling knots — laying strands to one side. He's not sure she'd like it if he put his arm around her like Dad does.

He rubs sleep from his eyes, opens the oven. No bannock. Stove's cold.

Get dressed and wake up your sister.

Where's Nitosis?

Walking to Mr. McDonald.

Hunter wonders if she can go that far on her shaky legs.

Why?

See if he'll give her food rations for old people.

Rose-Berry pushes him away, pulls the blanket over her head.

I'm stealing your newspapers, gonna burn them, he says.

Your knife's going straight into the lake if I bother to dig it up.

He looks where he usually hides it. It's gone.

Where is it?

She stays wrapped in her blanket quiet as a hill. He dresses, wanders back to his mother in the main room.

I need water and firewood.

Where's Nimosôm?

Trying to find out why the steers aren't eating the hay.

I'm hungry.

I know. Maybe Uncle Jack will shoot a duck today.

He pumps water into the bucket, lugs it sloshing to the porch, tips it into the water tank.

Do I have to fill it?

Five buckets is okay.

The bucket pulls his arm apart at the elbow. Bangs against his leg, leaving wet patches on his pants.

What're you doing?

She knots one end of the baling twine so that it makes a small loop and threads the other end through the loop. I have no flour today, she tells him. You and Rose-Berry go to Uncle Lenny's, Auntie May'll give you some bannock.

Uncle Arthur and Uncle Joe crowd around Uncle Lenny's table. Smell of meat stew from Auntie May's stove. Hunter's stomach growls.

McDonald says go work on the road.

You going to the road work?

I'll get by, trapping, cutting firewood.

Uncle Arthur rolls a cigarette. Uncle Joe tips his chair back, leans on the wall. No one says anything. Then they talk about Daniel, Hunter's father.

A guest of His Majesty.

How long d'ya reckon he'll be in there?

Three months maybe.

Food's not bad in jail—beef, coffee, bacon.

Indoor plumbing too.

Even give ya tobacco.

Auntie May fills a jar with some hot stew. Puts it in a flour sack to carry. You take this to your mom, she tells him and Rose-Berry. Bannock crunching in his mouth.

Mom's laid out many pieces of twine on the table, with one end made into a loop and the other threaded through it. Hold them carefully so they don't tangle.

She leads him and Rose-Berry into the willow bush. Tie the snare to a low branch over their trail, she tells them. Tie it very tight. Use little sticks to keep the loop apart. When they run through it, the sticks'll fall away and the noose'll tighten.

Why don't we just shoot them.

I don't have time to sit around all day waiting for rabbits to come by.

Rose-Berry and I'll shoot them.

Kids don't play with guns, anyway maybe we don't have that many bullets.

We should shoot one of the steers for food.

We will when it gets colder.

He searches out rabbit paths in the old dried grass and little gaps between the willows. The unwinding baling string doesn't want to tie onto branches. Rose-Berry's got way more done than he does.

———

With small knives, Mom and Auntie Marge cut stitches in the seam of a flour sack, yanking out bits of thread and leaving holes along the cloth edges. Mom snips the sack into short fat strips.

Dad in jail. Not like kick the can. Fish-eyes tagging him. Gotcha. You're in jail, you stay here. At the can. No cheating. Only way you get outta jail is if Tom or Eagle kicks the can. Then you can run. You're free. But I'll catch ya anyway, so I wouldn't bother. Dad's jail not like that. Dad's jail — bars in a stone wall — like that book when they still went to Miss McFarlane's school. The Dungeon. Dad's jail a pile of straw. A bucket and rats. The man in the dungeon was a prince pretending to be a poor man. He knew the answer to the king's questions, and the king let him out of the dungeon, and gave him his daughter to marry, and he became a prince again.

Eagle's dad went to jail once. Nothing wrong with it — Dad owed some money, Eagle said. Why'd he owe money? Sold some wood without getting permission from Mr. McDonald. Mr. McDonald said he had to pay it back but he didn't have it any more. Didn't have the wood either. Eagle hurled his sling around, let a stone go. Couldn't pay. The stone hit, bull's eye.

Father Clarence says you can get hung if you go to jail, Fish-eyes made his sling into a noose and looped it around Hunter's neck. They tie your hands behind your back. Open a trapdoor and you gag. Your face turns purple, your head swells up and bursts. They cut you down. Guts squish out through your neck hole. Turkey vultures come round for dinner. Peck peck peck.

Mmmmmmm. Yum. Dead Indian. No they don't. Sure, they cut you down, you fall like a sack a wheat — dead! No guts spilling out. Sure do, your neck all busted — big sticky mess. Peck peck peck. Mmmmmm. Indian brains. Gobble up your stomach. Eagle poked Hunter in the gut. Vultures peck off your willy. Scoop out your eyeballs.

You don't go to school your Mom and Dad'll probly go to jail — you'll probly go too. How come you aren't gonna go to school like us? The Wihtikiw's at that school, Dad says. No such thing as Wihtikiw. Like Father Clarence says, Only savages believe that. You gonna wear feathers on your head and shoot arrows. Savages burn in hell, Father Clarence says. After the vultures've chomped on your dick, you wake up down there. They tie you to a stake and bury you in red hot coals. Your dick burns off and it comes back and it burns off. And you never die. Red hot coals on your tongue. Red hot coals in your eyes. Red hot coals on your balls. They cut you open, put red hot coals in your stomach. You never die.

Only way you don't burn is if you pray to God, like Father Clarence says, Please forgive me. I am a sinner. Eagle whirled a rock in his sling over his head, then whapped it hard on the ground. You tell Father Clarence your sins. Eagle swung up his sling and beat the dirt till the leather snapped. Fish-eyes got down on his knees and put his hands together. Bless me Father for I have sinned. Say ten Glory Be's.

Glory bees. Like the ones buzzing in goldenrod.

Fish-eyes scrunched his eyes. Glory be to the Father. Louder. Glory be...

Stop. Hunter yanked at Eagle. This's stupid. Let's play Four Winds. Forget it. Stupid Indian game. Don't wanta be no savage.

Hunter wants to ask Mom whether they can visit Dad and whether the Wihtikiw could be in Dad's jail but she looks like she doesn't want to talk.

In the morning Rose-Berry sits at the table sewing Mom's strips of flour-sack into tubes — in front of her, a catalogue page cut in the shape of a little man. She doesn't want to go to their favourite look-out tree. Doesn't want to read newspaper in the old school house. You get water and wood. Help Mom, with Dad away. No time for games. Mom's checking the snares.

What're you making?

Dolls. Mom wants to sew them and sell them. So we can buy flour and bacon.

Her eyes not laughing. Eyes like muddy water. She hunches over, pinches the cloth together and pricks a tiny stitch with her needle. Lots of stitches just to make one doll he thinks.

He runs along the trail to the willow bush. Finds Mom tying a loop of baling twine to a branch, propping it open with sticks. Go check that patch. She pushes further into the branches. Wâpos is tricky Grannie said. He steals nuts. Then when people catch him, he says don't throw me into that willow bush, whatever you do don't throw me in there, I am so afraid of it. That is just where we will throw you, they say, throwing him in the middle of all the sticks and branches. Ha ha. Wâpos laughs. Thank you very much.

He finds a rabbit with its foot caught in the snare, the other three scrabbling at sticks and dirt, bending the snare branch flat to the ground. He puts his hands on the brown fur, the pounding heart, the snorting breaths. The animal kicks. Its hind legs claw his knees. He holds it down. Mom takes its head in one hand shoulders in the other, twists hard. Fur goes limp. No more kicks. No more heartbeat. Take it back to the house. Take the big knife, use the wood chopping block, cut its head off. Tie it up by its back legs in the woodshed.

From the hanging fur, blood drips on bark and wood chips. Wâpos crying big rabbit tears, Wîsahkecâhk my shoulders are so narrow. Foolish Wâpos, Grannie said, you thought you were so important with your two girlfriends. Each one squeezing into you trying to get your attention. Then they both left you — couldn't care less. Foolish Wâpos, your shoulders will always be narrow.

Mom slits open little brother Wâpos, spilling innards into a bucket. Go bury these in leaves way out back with the head. No, wait. She cuts off the paws and the tail. Lucky rabbit foot. Only the left one. Can I have the fur? Knife goes under the skin. Her hand pulls it back from the meat. She slices under the handless Wâpos arms, red underside of fur, skin clinging to shiny muscle.

When you hunt a bear and you kill one, Grampa said, it's not because you are so smart; it's because the bear gives itself to you. The bear is part of the bear spirit — it gives you part of itself so you can live. You must thank the bear spirit and ask it to come back.

He carries the head by the ears into the aspens and pincherries behind the shed, where he digs a small grave. Next to the innards, he lays the head and feet, even the lucky one, covers them with dirt and leaves and marks the grave with a rock. Wâpos, I will remember you. Have lots of girlfriends, Wâpos, and come back to us, like Nimosôm said.

All afternoon he thinks about Wâpos in Mom's pot. If he eats the pieces, will they turn into whole rabbits, jump around in the bushes inside him. He chops wood, stacks it on the porch. Is it ready yet? No. He brings in bucket after bucket filling the water tank to the top. Is it ready? It doesn't cook any faster cuz you're hungry. I'm going down to the river. Stay out of sight okay.

After sundown Mom opens the front of the stove beside the table with its six plates. Hot-coal-light of the stove-grate shines on Mom's and Uncle Jack's faces as he scoops innards out of some ducks he shot, and Mom yanks off handfuls of feathers. They talk about Uncle Norman's cow getting hit by a train.

McDonald's gonna butcher it for rations.

What's he paying Norman for the meat?

Dunno. Has to wait for Ottawa to set the price.

That could be months, Auntie Marge says to her knitting, Anyway who's he going to give them to — I'm seventy-eight years old and he tells me, no your nephew will look after you. My nephew's in jail, thanks to you, I said. Even Father Clarence thinks that's not right.

In the lamplight beside his bed, Grampa cleans shells with a nail and pokes in powder, shot and wad. Maybe later they'll play the hand game — which one's got the shell, which one the rabbit bone, Grampa holding his hands behind his back, singing away you'll never guess — is it this one, holding up a fist, or this one, ha, you'll never guess. But now Hunter is too hungry. Rose-Berry not looking at him, just looking down down down at her plate. Wâpos runs in his mouth. Arms and legs without paws. Ribs without head, swimming out of Mom's stewpot on the stove. Hopping down inside him, into the rabbit holes inside him.

He lines up flour-sack doll arms on the table. Faded strawberries and polka-dot and blue-and-yellow check stuffed with dried grass. Legless armless bodies saying Mills Ltd. He joins legs to legs, legs to arms. A row of heads with pale flower-covered eyes like Auntie's wallpaper. Hair of red and blue stripes. Mouths and teeth of black-and-white plaid. He joins four legs to a head. Mother of Wîsahkecâhk. Her head cut off by her husband because she liked a snake man. Please Mom, never hold any snakes. He rolls the head across the table. Wait for me, my children. They run away. Wait for me, you're making me so sad leaving me behind. As far as they run, she's always behind them. Wîsahkecâhk and his little brother make forests, mountains, fires — no matter what, she's calling wait for me. Until she falls into a huge river and Wîsahkecâhk turns her into namewak and she swims away.

———◆———

Mom, Uncle Jack and Grampa stand by the stove when he gets up. No one saying anything, like they were all talking about something they didn't want him to hear.

Where's Auntie Marge?

Outside digging up potatoes and carrots.

That hay's bad, Grampa crosses his arms, that person sold Nikosis bad hay. It's mouldy.

Maybe we can trade for something with Bob Tail Farm.

Shoot one of the steers, dry the meat.

That's a big job for Auntie.

No bannock today, Mom tells him. You go to Auntie May's. I'll bring in wood and water, help Auntie Marge dig up carrots. No you get Rose-Berry, go to Auntie May's, she has breakfast for you. When you get back I have something to tell you. Are you going to sew your dolls? That's for me to know; go get Rose-Berry. What did you eat? Get Rose-Berry, go to Auntie May's.

Why, he asks Rose-Berry, on the path to Auntie May's.

Mom's going away.

Where?

To see Dad.

Why can't we stay with Nimosôm, Auntie Marge and Uncle Jack.

Because.

Because what.

She's going to stay in Edmonton, try to help Dad get out.

So.

Hey you two. Auntie May's on hands and knees rubbing a small lino island on the floorboards near her stove. He swoops into the rocking chair, tucks his feet on a rung and pumps it letting the room swing back and forth. Rose-Berry snuggles into the striped blanket on Auntie May's couch. Auntie wrings out her cloth, Guess I won't see you for a while. Arm around him bringing him to the table. Plate of stove-warm bannock and lard. Where're you going? Oh... your mom'll tell you. She digs in her cupboard and brings out a small jar of jam she's been saving specially for them. Then hauls out a suitcase from behind the couch. This was Lizzie's. Faint-patterned flour-sack. Maybe fit you, Rose-Berry.

After they've eaten, they stand on the front steps saying good-bye, Auntie's big arm presses him into her soft roundness—Rose-Berry's eyes like a scared cat. You take care of each other now. She stands on the steps waving till they're almost back at their house.

Sit down I want to tell you something. Mom's voice is low and mad and sad. She takes his hand and Rose-Berry's and they sit on Grampa's bed looking back at the dishes and dishpan on the table under the window. She tells them Father Clarence thinks it's not fair that Dad is in jail. Father Clarence thinks she should go to Edmonton to see if she can help Dad. She pulls in Hunter and Rose-Berry close and warm surrounding him with her smell of sweetgrass and wood smoke.

Always we've kept you away from the faraway school. It's better for you here. But now your dad needs help, I must go to Edmonton and you must go to that school.

Why don't we go with you to Edmonton?

No place for kids there and anyway if they saw you they would take you away to one of those schools. At least this way you'll be with your cousins.

We kin stay here with Auntie Marge and Uncle Jack and Nimosôm.

Father Clarence says it's better if you go to school now with the other kids, the school has more food and clothes for you than here.

We kin go to Auntie May's or Auntie Ethel's.

Mom's arm pulls him in tight and close, Rose-Berry, too, Mom's sides shaking, keeping tears to herself, and it makes him mad that someone made her feel this way—mad so he could take a gun and shoot that person. After a while she tells them, You need to learn things you can't learn here. So you don't have to be poor like people here. The school will teach you how to make money for yourself. Have a better life.

But...

You go visit Kokôm, say goodbye, she tells them, so you are ready tomorrow.

But she holds onto them for a long time on Grampa's bed, not letting them go to Grannie's, just listening to the fire crack in the stove, and he wants to be the best he can for her, just forget about that stone turning in his stomach.

Grannie's like a small bird beside him, hooked wing-bones pulling him, one side, Rose-Berry the other, to sit on her bench, lean against the logs of her hut, look at the woodchips around Uncle Arthur's chop block, the axe biting into the top of it. Baby Mary cries in the main house, Auntie Ethel shushes her, sings a little song to her.

Tell us a story. No not today. Just one. Thought you came to say goodbye. Grannie's eyes behind her glasses big as an owl's. Just one story. You'll be gone a long time. Pulleeease. Okay then, I'll tell you a little one.

Wîsahkecâhk was hungry, you know, he saw a lot of ducks and geese out on the lake but he couldn't catch them. Instead he made a big bundle of sticks and carried it along on his back. Pretty soon the birds wanted to know what that bundle was for. Special dance, Wîsahkecâhk told them, but I don't have anyone to dance for. The birds said, we'll come to your dance. First I have to build a lodge, he said. He put down his bundle, and made a lodge out of the sticks. That doorway to your lodge is very small, said the birds. You must have just such a tiny door in the lodge of my special dance he told them. Now all of you must gather wood for a fire in the lodge. The ducks and geese made a big stack in the middle of it. Wîsahkecâhk gathered all the birds inside. Now my friends he told them, I can't sing unless you shut your eyes. When you hear me sing you shut your eyes and dance. He began to sing, and the birds shut their eyes and danced around the fire. Wîsahkecâhk sang a little louder, and at the same time laughed to himself. He snatched a goose and wrung its neck, then another one and another, all the time singing loudly. He put his catch in the fire to roast. Just one bird opened his eyes. That was the hell-diver. My friends we've been tricked again he shouted, run away if you can.

———•———

In the morning, Mom sits him in a chair, parts his hair and combs it back and smooth down to his shoulders. Gotta look good today.

Fast as little bird chippings, Auntie Marge's knitting needles click from her chair.

What food do they have in Edmonton?

I'll find something. Mom's hands press hard into his shoulders holding him against her stomach. I'll be alright.

When do we get out of that school?

Chipping chipping chipping knitting needles, Auntie Marge frowning.

It might be a while. You go and learn how to get a job so you can live better. Have better food, better clothes. Better place for your children.

But she's not really saying this. It's something Father Clarence told her, and she doesn't really believe it. Uncle Jack goes out, then comes back a minute later with some harness and stands by the stove, Guess I might as well clean this. He stands there a while then gets out a rag.

I don't want better things; I want to live here with you and Rose-Berry and Dad and Auntie and Uncle and Nimosôm.

Mom's hands press harder into his shoulders.

When'll we be home again? When when when?

Maybe Christmas, maybe summer. You do what they say at that school, then they might let you come home sooner.

When'll we see Dad?

When'll we see you and Auntie and Uncle and Nimosôm and Nohkôm?

She doesn't answer.

Hey, Natonam, Uncle looks up from his harness, I thought you were going to be the man of the house. But with you gone, I guess I'll have to be.

Mom makes him put on his good shirt that used to be Eagle's that she patched. Just do your best and don't think about running away from that school. I will not be here. Your father will not be here. Stay with your cousins Tom and Fish-eyes and Ernie and the other boys from here. If you come here the school men will take you away again, and it will be worse for you when you go back.

She doesn't look at them. She looks at the dress she's tying into a bundle for Rose-Berry, and the catalogue pages she's laying inside his shoes to cover up holes. She hands him a paper bag with Dad's old shoes inside. Soon you'll be big enough. He adds his knife with its leather cover that Dad made. She braids Rose-Berry's hair tight and neat, ties it with red wool. White rabbits with long ears and fluffy tails jump all over Rose-Berry's dress that was Lizzie's. White rabbits hopping on pink flowers.

Don't complain when you're there, or you will not be liked. Make sure you get along well with everyone. Do what your teachers say, don't be looking crossly at them. In front of them keep your eyes down and your hands still.

Follow the right thing to do by seeing what others do, Grampa coughs a little, just like when we play the hand game, don't talk. Your dad will be proud of you.

Knocking sounds on the door. Two men in black suits with lots of buttons down the front. We're here for the children. She holds him out in front of her, brushes his hair back behind his ears. I have something for you. The men say, Hurry up, we haven't got all day.

Uncle and Grampa stand up, and face the men in black suits, making them stop talking, making them look away while Mom takes some things from her pocket and fits them into their hands —a flour-sack owl for Rose-Berry and a horse for him. Its mane and tail of rabbit fur. She pulls him and Rose-Berry close so they all press into each other. Auntie Marge too, arms all around them.

Then the men go on either side and take them to a black automobile. They point to the back seat. Sit here. The men slam the door. Long as he can see out the back window, Hunter watches Mom and Auntie and Uncle and Grampa standing on the step of the cabin, just standing there, like they are frozen.

CHAPTER 10

One black-suited man takes him, the other takes Rose-
Berry to another door in the building that towers over them like
all the town buildings piled into one. Down a long room past a
statue of the Virgin Mary, past many doors, into a room with a
big table piled with blue shirts and pants, socks, undershorts, even
coats, hats, mitts, shoes and boots.

Father Haffman, we have a new boy.

So I see, Father Lafarge. The man beside the table smiles but
his eyes are empty. Hunter looks down, like mom told him, while
Father Haffman gives Father Lafarge a pile of blue clothes.

What's your name, the Father wants to know.

Hunter.

Christian boys must have proper Christian names. In this
school your Christian name will be Vincent.

Hunter keeps his eyes on the floorboards.

Answer me!

The woodgrain is like water. If he could just sink into it.

Look at me!

He glances up. Pale eyes fixed on him.

What is your name?

Vincent.

Boys in this school have numbers.

Hunter stares down at the floorboards.

Your number is 37. Look at me!

Pale eyes, then down again.

Vincent what is your number?

Thirty-seven.

Remember it. Go with Father Lafarge.

So many buttons on the men's cassocks, he will just count the buttons, maybe there are thirty-seven, he will count—this is what you do in school. But Father Lafarge is behind him pushing him into a room with shiny white and black walls, holes in the floor. Pipes and cross-shaped things stick out of the wall. Sit. Father Lafarge pushes him down on a wooden stool and goes to another room. Hunter keeps his eyes on the buttons as Father Lafarge comes back holding long-pointed scissors, then almost tips off the stool when the Father grabs his hair from behind. Snip, snip, the Father keeping himself arm's length away—snip, snip—his black hair scatters over the white floor. Father Lafarge brushes his cassock, buttons bulging almost pop, white face bending down turns red. Tsk. Tsk. On another stool a little metal plow with long handles and fine teeth.

Father Lafarge picks up the plow. Hunter swerves. Hold still. A hand grabs his shoulder and crunches him down on the stool. The plow snap-snicks over his head. Shock of cold on his scalp. Then clouds of hairs in his eyes, nose, mouth. Father Lafarge brushes his black cassock and tsks. Hunter touches his head. Just prickle. Nothing over him. No roof to be safe from sharp things falling—scissors, plows, rocks. No roof to keep him warm. Hands down, Father Lafarge growls. Metal to scalp—click click click. He shivers, like punches of ice inside.

The Father hands him a broom and a shovel with a short handle. He sweeps his roof into the shovel. Over there. Next room. With the squirrel tail, he lifts the lid. Drops his roof into the flames. Some of it spills on the stove top. The Father scowls. Tsks. Wrong again. Count the buttons. No roof to protect him. Vincent. 37. Vincent. 37. Remember.

Father Lafarge smears lamp oil on his head. Smells like Dad after he shoveled black stuff on the road. Hunter swipes his hand across it. Coughs at the fumes. His hand stinks. His head stinks. Clothes off, Vincent. In there. Into the shiny black-and-white room. Father Lafarge picks up Hunter's paper bag, holds it out, end of his arm. Drops it on the white floor.

Throw your clothes there. He points at the paper bag, Dad's shoes inside, his knife inside. Hunter pulls his shirt slowly over his head wiping away lamp oil. Then shoes off. Pants. Socks. Underwear. Father Lafarge turns the crosses. Water spews out of the wall. Under there. The man pulls him back, rubs soap on him, soap like it's made of rose thorns. Scratch scratch scratch.

He runs around behind the Father, then back under the water and scrubs at the lamp oil. The Father grabs him. Hunter slips in a puddle. Splashes soapy water over the Father's black skirts. Then stomps his foot in the puddle, stone turning in stomach — mad like the time he punched Tom for throwing mud on Rose-Berry. Little bastard. The Father cuts the water, brushes at his skirts. Flings a towel at Hunter. Into the puddle. Dry yourself. He makes him wear a blue shirt and blue pants. Shoes bent and scuffed from someone else's feet.

Burn that. He points to the clothes and bag, hands him the broom and shovel. His head—prickly nothing—stinks of lamp oil.

Hunter snatches the toy horse from the pile of clothes, and stuffs it in his pocket. He pulls the knife from the bag. Father Lafarge grabs it, Boys don't have knives here. He slips it into his buttoned skirts. Dad's knife. Dad-made knife. Speak English, Vincent. Hunter seizes the skirts and Dad-made thonged leather sheath. Cloth tears. The Father kicks, and shoves his lamp-oil head. He butts at the man, ripping his skirt. Gets his hand on the knife. The Father pulls something black from his skirt and whaps it across Hunter's back. Black leather thing slaps his ribs, his bum, his legs — his arms holding knife, till he lets it go.

Put that in the fire. The father points.

Flames lick up his old pants and shirt, the bag with Dad's shoes.

Carry those. The Father points at the pile of blue clothes, marches him upstairs, then up more stairs to a room full of beds. So many beds he can't count them all, almost can't see where the long rows end, each bed with a fence at the top and bottom.

———◆———

In the morning a Father clangs a bell up and down the rows of beds. Get moving NOW. Line up. Blue shirts and pants, blue boys. Newboy, stink-head. They leave a space around him. I said Line. Up. The Father shakes him, tells him to wake up! Hunter keeps his eyes down, his hands at his sides. What's your number Vincent? He doesn't remember. Stupid Vincent — what did Father Haffman tell you? Hunter looks at his shoes. Look at me, what's your number? It's on the back of his shirt but he can't see the back now. It's thirty what? Other boys look at him. Someone whispers. Thirty-seven Hunter says to the floor. Louder. Thirty-seven. Now, march.

Two rows of blue pants, blue shirts, brown feet clunk down the stairs. Quiet! Stay in line. Past doors to other rooms of blue boys lining up. Clunk-shuffle to the green room. Green benches, green tables. Tin bowl, tin spoon. Hunter, Hunter, it's me. Where? Blue shirts, clipped prickly heads all the same. It's me — Tom. Blue shirts, brown hands grabbing at the pile of white slices till they disappear. Passing bowls of grey mush. Other side of the room, rows of blue girls in blue and white dresses, same chopped off hair. Is that one Rose-Berry? That one? That one? Someone grabs his bowl. You don't want it I'll eat it. It's me — Tom. All up and down the table. It's me — Tom. Which one, which one? Heads

down to tin bowls. Hands rubbing white slices round and round
till bowls are shiny again.

———•———

A bell clangs till he can't hear his thoughts. Brown shoes of blue
pants and blue shirts clunk-shuffle to a grey room with brown
desks — huge cross with Jesus nailed to it hanging over the desks
like it might fall on the boys' heads if they did anything wrong.
Someone hands him a little book. Chopped-off hair — someone
he used to know. It's Tom but they call him Thomas here. Piece
of paper, pencil. He opens the book to Jesus — head under gold
circle surrounded by yellow-haired children, pink and blue.

Vincent, say the daily offering.

Hunter keeps his eyes on the gold circle around the head of
Jesus.

Stand up!

He scrapes his chair back, keeping his eyes down.

Turn to page 13.

The book's back is broken. The pages stick and clump.

Read the offering!

O Sacred Heart of Jesus!

Louder.

O Sacred Heart of Jesus!

I implore

(The words boom. Eyes of the other boys stare.)

That I may ever love Thee

More and more.

Close the book.

He puts the broken thing back together.

Say it properly. It's not a nursery rhyme!

O Sacred Heart of Jesus!

I implore

Implore implore — nothing comes next.

Write it out till you can say it without looking. Be ready in ten minutes.

Paul, say your Act of Faith.

O my God! I firmly believe all the sacred truths which Thy Catholic Church believes and teaches; because Thou has revealed them, who canst neither deceive nor be deceived.

Hunter drifts to the grey sky through the small high windows. Wonders, is there grass here to run through, is there wet sweet smell of willows, is there a river that eats away the ground? He drifts back to Tom across the aisle—something shiny in his hand.

Vincent! (A cane hits his back.)

O Sacred Heart of Jesus! I implore, that I may ever love Thee more and more.

Thomas, say the Creed.

Tom turns pages in his broken book.

Close the book!

I believe in one God, the Father Almighty, Maker of heaven and earth, and of all things visible and invisible. And in one Lord Jesus Christ, the only begotten Son of God, born of the Fathe…born of the Father…of…of God, of very God…

Wrong.

The Father bangs the cane on his desk.

All of you copy out the Creed till you can say it without looking!

The Father piles himself like black sacks of flour into the chair behind his desk. Keeping his head down, rubbing the dull pencil over his paper, Hunter touches the tiny pointed ears and mane of rabbit fur on the toy horse in his pocket. Eagle's somewhere in these rows of boys but they call him John here, they call Shorty Edmund and Ernie George. What do they call Rose-Berry? *Begotten not made,* he writes, *being of one substance* [what is substance?] *with the Father…* Keeping his head down he glances at the Father sitting under the huge cross and looking out the window. A marble rolls into Hunter's foot. He picks it up. The boy behind thumps his back, holds out his hand. Hunter hears the marble roll along the floor to another boy. Father Lafarge — some boys call him Lardface — knocks over his chair, puffing, and stomps down between the desks. Only half done?! Write faster! He twists Hunter's ear, then hips and behind of the Father jiggle up the row, bend to pick up the chair. He flops down, mops his head, stares out the window. The marble rolls down the next row. Next one to do that's getting the cane. Across the room, a tall boy, muscles like a man, makes his thumb and forefinger into a ring, runs his other forefinger in, out, in, out. Corner of his eye, Father Lafarge catches it. What'd you just do? Muscles hunches over his book. You, Paul, I'm talking to you. The Father, hands on desk — frog hands, arms fat as legs drag belly up. Nothin, Father. You did something with your hands. Got an itch, Father. The marble rolls down the far side of the room. Tom puts his hand over his mouth. The Father turns. Belly slides off desk. Chair tips. He grabs it, puffing. *And I believe in the Holy Ghost, the Lord and Life-giver,* Hunter copies. Then he tries to remember the first part but only gets as far as *came down from heaven and was… was.* He looks at the next word *incarnate.* It sounds like a train. The marble rolls down on Muscles' side. Tom drops his hand, head down to paper, tongue in the side of his mouth, printing pencil words. The Father grabs him by the ear. Pulls him to the front, pulls a pointed hat down over his eyes, makes him stand there facing the class. Wasn't him Father. It was number 19 sir. The marble rolls down another row. It was 23 Father. Another marble. Number 5 did it, Father Lafarge, sir. Thirty-one, sir. No one mentions Eagle's number or Tom's.

Quiet! Recite the Prayer for Confession!

Now sir? Everyone?

Yes. Everyone! Now!

Have mercy on me, O Lord. I am a sinner. I have disobeyed Thee. I am not worthy to speak to Thee… Hunter follows along, mouthing the words with the other boys.

You shalt not, you shalt not, shalt not, not, not. Fly buzzes against the window. Father White runs his fingers up and down his row of buttons. Buttonfingers, some boys call him. Watch out for Buttonfingers at night. Shalt not take the name of the Lord. One two three four five six seven eight nine ten. Name name name name name. Vain vain vain vain vain. Then another You you you, shalt shalt shalt, not not not. The the the the the. Of of of of of. In in in in in. The door opens to the swish swish of big black sleeves and long black dress, so many skirts she has no feet, white skirt around her neck, too.—huge cross dangling on top of it. She stops in front of Father White. Hands hidden in her skirts—hidden in pockets—she could pull out scissors, knitting needles, a scrub-brush to hit you with. The Father leans back in his chair, folds arms on his buttoned stomach. He finishes here first. Father White, it's getting late. She puts her hand on her hip, swaying the string of beads with its cross hanging from her belt. He slides his fingers along his buttons. Shrugs.

Vincent hand me your paper.

Hunter follows the curtains of black flumping cloth, the black cloth instead of hair growing from her puffy, jiggly face. Big white wings growing out of her head. Down the hall, where a blue-suited boy pushes a broom, wide as a fishing rod is long, back and forth, pushing dust fluffs. Come with me, Martin. She makes him push the dust fluffs into a corner. Follow me. To the green room with the green benches and empty green tables. Four girls sit on a bench. All covered in blue and white squares. Their dresses all the same —so many little squares he can't look at them, their hair all the same chopped off at their ears. Brown eyes above four white collars. Eight white cuffs.

He and Martin and two other boys stand in front of the girls. One comes toward him. Makes him sit beside her on the bench.

Another girl rushes up to Martin. Nîtisân.

Nîtisân.

Brother. Sister. Is the girl next to him...?

The nun flaps out on her black skirts. Silver cross flip flop, dangles on her fat white front. No Indian words. You speak English. Hands back in her pockets—ready on a ruler or maybe a needle like she poked into Shorty's tongue for speaking Indian words.

Rose-Berry puts her finger over her lips.

What do they call you, Hunter asks.

Margaret.

He touches the place where her braids used to be. Fingers her blue and white squares that make his eyes crazy. She smoothes a rip in his shirt sleeve.

Namoya. Môniyâhkâso.

What did I just say Martin?

Not to speak Indian, Miss Winston.

What did she just do?

I'm sorry Ma'am.

No visit with your sister.

She didn't mean it ma'am.

Back to your sweeping, Martin. The nun shoos the boy and his sister out opposite doors of the room.

Rose-Berry puts her fingers through her fingers, pressing her hands into the white and blue squares in her lap. Fingers pressing knuckles till the cords in her arms stand out. Hunter makes his hands circle around a big space. She looks at him, eyes frown, What's that?

He walks two fingers of his right hand and two fingers of his left hand down one of his blue legs. Close-together finger people. She frowns. Shrugs her shoulders. Grabs blue and white squared cloth of her skirt and sews it with a pretend needle. Over and over her hand goes poking the blue and white squares, stitching pretend thread. He makes his pretend needle sew his pants to her dress.

The nun flumps her black skirts across the room. Vincent, Margaret. You talk out loud. No whispering. Talk English.

Rose-Berry's right hand wrestles the left hand. Twisting knuckles, fingers fighting fingers, in blue and white squares.

When will Mom come, another blue boy asks his sister.

Never. She will never come.

Then why don't we go find her.

Rose-Berry looks out the window. Her foot pushes her knee up and down shaking her skirt.

Hunter puts his hand on the fighting hands. Still hands. Quiet hands. Count the floorboards one two three four. Rose-Berry's hand wraps around his.

No touching. (Eyes under her white hood, like a hawk ready to pounce).

Sorry, Miss Winston.

Sit further apart. She makes him move down the bench. Rose-Berry pinches her hands between her knees.

In the hall, a father clangs a bell. Miss Winston plumps her skirts and claps. Visiting time is over. Go to your line-up.

He stays on the bench. Rose-Berry sits very straight. Off go the other blue and white girls. Blue boys swirl past them, lining up for afternoon chores.

Miss Winston flaps between them. Flip flop silver cross. She pushes them off the bench.

Visiting time is OVER. White-winged jiggly face so close her spit hits his lips.

———————

Hunter rams a spade in dust-cloud dirt. Dangles himself dead-weed over the handle, hands heavy, eyes in sun-glare see every-thing white. Tom in his row flops over his spade. Shorty tries to get his legs dangling too. He topples over. Hunter pries at a potato plant. Pitches back on his bum. Flops down on the dirt and stares up into the blue. Buttonfingers's coming. Buttonfingers. A father waves a pitchfork at some boys working down the row. Hunter rolls back onto his knees and heaves at the plant with his spade till it comes free. He digs around in the dirt with his hands for potatoes, and carries them over to the wheelbarrow. Father White stabs his pitchfork into the ground. Hunter shoves a spade at the next plant. Use your foot, Vincent. Black arms grab his leg, put Hunter's left foot on the spade. Push down. The Father stands over him while Hunter pushes and rocks the spade-handle, prying up the plant, then digs up dust clouds with his hands, burrowing for potatoes.

What's this? Father White waves a half a potato at him.

Hunter stands up. I'm sorry sir.

What did I say? The Father grabs the pitchfork.

Don't cut into them, sir.

Lazy boy. Watch where you dig.

The Father marches down the row, poking Tom with the fork handle, Too slow. Work faster Thomas.

———

Christmas comes. Hunter does not go home. He copies words from the wall of a classroom. Holy holy holy. Lord God Almighty. The eyes of the nun standing at the front stab into him from the shadows under her white-edged hood. What do you want Vincent? Nothing ma'am. Then get on with your work. He prints the letters of each word between lines of his notebook. *I am the Lord thy God; you shall have no other god before me.* Maybe if he does it very neatly, maybe this time he'll get a letter. Like Tom did — a piece of paper folded into another special piece of paper — from Tom's mother, Auntie May — Auntie Lena and Uncle Norm have a new baby, a little sister Theresa for Eagle — on All Saints' Day, Father Clarence got everyone together for a hockey game and Uncle Lenny scored three goals.

Outside the window nothing but gray sky. He counts the squares of sky in the window panes. Finished yet Vincent? No ma'am. Then stop looking out the window.

Can I see it, Hunter asked Tom in the dorm?

She didn't give it to me.

Yes she did, what'd you do with it.

She made me give it back

Did it say anything about Mom? Is my Dad out of jail?

No. I don't know.

About Nimosôm.

No.

Once Dad got a letter and it was about his brother in Edmonton. He left it on the table. Went out and saddled up Kîyasiw. He will not live long the letter said.

Did it say anyone was dying?

No.

Hunter walks to the front of the rows of desks.

What do you want, Vincent?

Please ma'am, do you have a letter for me?

I told you last Sunday — no letters till you've been here for twelve months.

Even though I don't get letters, please can I write to my mom?

No letters home, till you get one.

———◆———

Hunter heaves wooden handles and pushes a barrow lump bump dustcloud slow along a row rattling its shovels and forks. He gets stuck on a hummock, so rests awhile. Father Oxford — the one some boys call Warty — waves his stick — Not there. Over there, over there. Hunter yanks the handles, dust-cloud lump bump drag-arm. All morning digging: kick shovel in, break up the dirt, move along the row, kick shovel in, break up the dirt, move along. Breathing dust, eating dust, eyes full of dust. Afternoon: cut seed potatoes. Clean the dirt off with this scrub brush, the Father says, CUT TWO EYES TO A PIECE! OR THREE! Put them in the barrow. Do you know what eyes are? Yes Father.

He scrubs at the dirt, but it clings in dried clumps. Dust-cloud.

Cough-spit, scrub brush. With the trimming knife, he hacks open a potato, peels it, chops slices into his mouth, then into his pocket. Father Oxford moves down the row, poking Tom — dig faster, I want these potatoes planted this afternoon. Tom digs hard, clouds of dust around the Father. He moves off. Tom slows down. Hunter cuts a piece with two eyes, scratches in nose and mouth, and chucks the face in the barrow. A potato hits him in the head. Eagle winks. Shorty: Father Oxford, sir, Eagle's cut his hand. Let's see. Back to work then, Edmund.

Eagle holds up a red grubby smear. Better go see the sister. Edmund where are you going with that barrow. Over here. Not over there. The barrow tips. For pity sake. Father Oxford clumps down the field after Shorty waving his stick — Get them all back in the barrow immediately.

Eagle nods his head. Hunter follows, knife in pocket, into a thicket of aspens, keeping foot silent not to crack branches and sticks. Eagle points. Slide past that trunk. He crouches, watches Eagle, rock still. Hunter silent as a tree-shadow sliding. Then a slow womp-womp of grouse wings. Eagle points to a stump, its tree fallen, mossed, clawed with bushes. Eagle's hands tell him, Slide along the ground along the tree, Eagle one side, Hunter the other. Eagle makes his hands into clawing fingers, crouches, hand-calls to Hunter, Come here. Womp-womp-womp whirr of grouse-wing. Up to branches overhead. Eagle — palms up — wait. Sun winks through crisscrossing new-budded branches. A woodpecker flashes red, then rat-a-tat chipping. Old leaves stir under the fallen tree. Eagle's hand calls, come. Bushes scratch over his eyes, nose, cheeks. Eagle's hands reach to the shadowy hollow under the fallen tree, to bird scratch, bird-head peck peck, neck stretching — bird-eye. Eagle darts in, snatches. Grey-brown feathers flap, Eagle grabbing leg, feathers snowfall — Go. Go. Hunter's fingers close on scrabbling foot, head, wing, drag it out through scratching bushes. Eagle tucks the bird under his arm, and twists hard till the head dangles.

Another rustle under the log. Hunter grabs. Wings flail, foot claws the air, as he clutches at fanned quills. The bird claws him — his fingers empty but for tufts of feathers. Eagle shrugs, Next time. Hunter stabs the trimming knife into a black-kneed aspen. Gimme that. Find firewood. Hunter gathers bark peelings, twigs, sticks. Heaps them around a charred cooking pot hidden in some stones. Eagle slips his knife under the feathers, pulling the skin away. Slices open the belly, spilling bird guts. Chucks bird in the pot, claps on the sooty handle-less lid. They build the fire around and over the pot. Go. Go. Hunter slips back to the potato field.

———◆———

Water in washbasin. Soap slip. Out the hand-mouth — weasel out of Wihtikiw. Hurry up wouldja. Soap float. White weasel-coat splatted with Wihtikiw guts. Hands scrub brown hands, brown cheeks of brown face. Never-white cheeks. Wîsahkecâhk made weasel's fur white. Float a soap boat. Weasel killed the Wihtikiw but his tail will always have a little black tip. Here try this, Father O'Reilly handed him a floor-scrubbing brush, Maybe that'll get the brown off.

No stove in the dorm. Hunter shivers, changing into thin pajamas, hanging blue shirt and pants on the fence at the end of his bed. Pocket of hunted bird-meat in the pants. Next bed Cousin Ernie coughs and coughs, pulls a sheet over his head. No Wihtikiw silly, Shorty says. Then why is Cousin Ernie? He's always like that. Other-side bed, Mouse wipes tears, hides his face in his knees.

Eagle farts setting off snickers and snorts and more farts. Muscles and Bone push into Hunter, Muscles holding out his hand. Gimme a piece. What? I know you got something. Muscles grabs Hunter's pants. It's for my cousin. Muscles snatches Hunter's horse. Gimme a piece or you can kiss this goodbye. It's for my cousin, he's sick. Muscles stomps on the horse. Hunter yanks the pants, tearing the pocket.

Give his pants back, Eagle shoves between Hunter and Muscles.

Whaddaya you care?

I said give them back.

What is he, your little baby?

Bone swings at Eagle. Eagle brushes him off and punches Muscles in the stomach. Bone leaps on Eagle and Fish-eyes on Bone, mashing Hunter's pants and the toy horse into the floor. Buttonfingers's coming. Buttonfingers. Ernie coughs, sinks into the bunk, his sheets and blankets seem empty—no one there. Father White shishes his cassock along the rows of beds with their white metal fences. What's going on here? The father's strap slices Hunter's shoulders. Vincent get your clothes off the floor. Everyone kneel for prayers. Hunter puts his hands together, elbows on cold bars of bed-rail, closes his eyes, teeth clacking in the cold. Thomas, say the prayer. Me Father. YES YOU.

Lord, I have passed another day

And—cough cough—Thee for Thy care.

Forgive my faults in work or play

And listen—cough cough cough—prayer.

Thy favour gives me daily bread

And friends, who all my wants supply:

And—cough cough cough cough—my head,

Preserved and guarded by Thine eye.

Amen.

Bedfence at his head, bedfence at his feet. Bed to bed to bed each one almost touching the next—long road of beds: Ernie's bed next to Shorty's bed next to Fish-eyes' bed next to number 13's bed next to Muscles' bed. Other side past Mouse to Tom to Eagle to Bone to Martin to numbers and more numbers. Switch snaps to dark, his eyes dancing bed fences, then he opens his eyes to window-shadow dog-bark. The father's footsteps. Click, the door shuts.

Will it open again—click—in black night? Will the black cassock come back, pad pad along bed after bed, father-hands slipping under covers, boy stumbling after him to the rooms where the fathers live? This time coming for him?

Dog-bark to night-sky. Dog barks to faraway dog-bark. Mouse snuffles. Bone mutters, Shuddup Mouse don't be sucha crybaby.

Shuddup Bone, let'm cry if he feels like it.

Mouse misses his mommy.

Shuddup Fish-eyes, Muscles growls.

Bone's pajama shadow, dark-headed, leaps past bedfences to Mouse's snuffling. Shuddup Mouse or I'll stuff yr head in a pillow. Leave'm alone. Heads, arms tangle outlined in night window. Hunter follows Shorty, grabs Bone's kicking foot. Leave'm alone, Bonehead. Fight fight. Arms grab him from behind. Blankets twist sheets, he gets a fist, then a knee in his stomach. He kicks, butts. Elbows knees heads thump to floor. Bed scrapes screech metal to metal. Piss off bastard. Stupid crybaby. Buttonfingers Buttonfingers. Clumps sound in the hallway, footsteps. Footscamper. Snap. Switch. What's going on in here? Nothing Father, having a pee. What's that bed doing there? Tripped, Father. No more noise. Switch snap. Hunter's eyes dance streaks of light.

Mouse snuffles. Shuddup crybaby. Hunter reaches under his pillow for the toy horse. Reaches over to Mouse's bed. Hey, Mouse, I got a little friend for you. A small hand takes the horse under the covers.

———

Miss Winston's chalk taps and shhhes over the blackboard. What is the fourth commandment? Who is the most important father? How do you honour Him? Who else must you obey? Hunter copies the questions into his notebook, then drifts back to the path along the river at home, through the willow bush to the bulrushes and his favorite spruce. Grannie—in her little cabin next to Auntie Ethel—can she still tell him about Wîsahkecâhk boasting he could make noise longer than the river. All summer and fall he sat beside it saying blblbl blblblbl but it still kept making its noise. Surely in winter it would stop, but no—all winter Wîsahkecâhk sat beside the river saying blblbl blblblbl. The river kept talking till the spring flood. Wîsahkecâhk sat there saying blblbl blblblbl, water up to his neck. Then he had to walk away. The river had won.

Is Grannie still in her little cabin—how long will she wait to tell him stories again? Is Dad still in jail or does he have to work on the road? Is Mom making dolls?

Miss Winston's chalk slides and squeaks the answers to the questions. God is the most important father. Obey his will. Policemen. Teachers. Priests.

Tom got another letter from Auntie May—on Treaty Day they had dancing and singing in the big tent—Uncle Arthur shot a deer and gave everyone dinner—Auntie Ethel and Uncle Arthur's Baby Mary is coughing and has to go to the doctor—Tom must eat lots and stay warm. Winter is coming.

Maybe today Miss Winston will let Hunter have the letter she showed him last time. Some of the boys are even allowed to write a letter home, but not Tom. He's not allowed even though he's been here for two years. Miss Winston flumps in her black skirts down the rows of desks handing out paper to the boys who will write letters.

If Hunter had a paper he would write to Mom and Dad—Rose-Berry doesn't talk much—Cousin Ernie's glad Hunter has the bed next to him—they don't learn things here like in Miss McFarlane's school—just pick rocks, load wood, Rose-Berry works in the laundry—please can we come home.

Miss Winston's ruler raps his desk. Why haven't you finished yet?

Please Ma'am, could I have my letter today?

How many times! What's the rule about letters?

Not till twelve months, please Ma'am how many months have I been here?

Eleven.

Hunter gets out of the desk and stands facing her huge cross and hawk eyes under her great winged hood.

I need to write a letter to my Dad and my Mom.

No you don't. They can't read anyway.

My Grannie too and my Auntie Marge and Uncle Jack.

They're not your family now; we're your family. No need to write to us.

Her ruler hits his ear. Sit down and copy the answers.

Somehow they can read, he knows they can, they sent him a letter. Maybe Father Clarence wrote it for them; he can read to them too. The letters home go in a canvas sack with the postman's horse and cart every Monday afternoon. Maybe he can give the postman his own letter, not bother with Miss Winston's paper, he can fold his own envelope, Eagle knows what to write on it.

———◆———

Stupid Indian, Father Haffman, drags Eagle to the front of the classroom. Father Haffman doesn't wear a cassock like Father White and Father Oxford. Father Haffman wears sharp folded trousers and shiny shoes. Trousers make his legs look like knives. Muscles calls him Ice-eyes. Useless know-nothing. Why are you so stupid?

Eagle looks nowhere and everywhere. Like he's standing all day by himself, never sitting down, proving he can stand for a whole day, or even five days, like Grampa said you have to so dreams will come. Hunter softly tears two pages out of the back of his notebook, folds one, pockets it, slipping the other into the middle of his notebook.

Eagle says nothing.

I said, Why are you so stupid?

Eagle looks past the father — like he can see right through the walls of the school all the way to where the sun comes from. Answer me. Father Haffman's pointer thumps Eagle's back.

Nimosôm, Hunter writes. Some families come to this school to see their children. I need Nikâwiy to come. I have to talk to her. The Sister says I cannot have my letter. Please can you tell Nikâwiy to come?

He folds the page and pockets it.

Look at me and answer me. Father Haffman pushes Eagle so he almost falls down.

What is the capital of Canada, Hunter copies from the board, Who is the Prime Minister of Canada?

I'll tell you why you're so stupid. The father holds his face an inch in front of Eagle's.

You were born stupid — stupid and useless.

A father in the hall clangs a bell. Line up, the father Ice-eyes commands, Two rows, in the hall. Yesterday they walked back and forth in lines in front of the school while a man pointed a camera. Everyone stepping at the same time, right left, right left, two long lines of boys, two long lines of girls. Then Hunter, Shorty and Bone pulled feathers off chickens. Hunter spread too many feathers around. Stupid Indian, Father Ice-eyes said, Can't do anything right can you?

Eagle, beside Hunter in the line up, still looks like he's standing for five days. I need your help Cousin, Hunter keeps his eyes on the boy in front of him.

Eagle says nothing. They clunk shuffle to the dining room with its green tables and green benches, even its walls gray and green. If only they could have some of that chicken they took the feathers off but it's mushy grey-green soup and a slice of bread. Gimme some of your lard, Shorty nudges him. What lard? Shorty reaches under the table to where Hunter had saved some from breakfast. Shorty waves a finger full. Not all of it!

Suddenly no one's talking. Father Oxford marches Ernie to

the front of the room under the cross with its bleeding hands and sad body of Jesus. Pots of grey-green soup sit on the tables with ladles beside them.

What do you say George?

Ernie coughs.

Speak up George!

I took something, Ernie mumbles.

Louder. Tell everyone in the room.

I took some meat.

Was it your meat?

No.

Who did it belong to?

It belonged to Cook.

Ernie looks far away over everyone's heads, staring out like Eagle did in Father Haffman's classroom, like he could fly through the back wall.

What did you do with it?

I ate it.

Louder.

I ate it.

What do we call someone who takes something that belongs to another?

A thief.

What are you then?

A thief.

Ernie's shirt hangs loose around his arms and chest, his pants seem too big, like he's almost not there inside his clothes. He coughs again.

Besides Cook and your school, who else have you offended?

Our Lord.

What do you say then to our Lord so that He will forgive you?

O my God, I am heartily sorry for my sin; I detest it because it offends Thee, and I firmly purpose by Thy holy grace, never to sin again.

The Father makes Ernie say it louder two more times, until Ernie starts coughing again.

What does God say to thieves?

Thou shalt not steal.

What else?

Give back what you took.

Boys at the tables snicker and laugh.

Quiet!

If you can't give it back what does God tell you to do?

Make amends.

How are you going to do that?

Ernie shrugs his shoulders. Stares beyond the back wall.

I'll tell you how, the Father says, Go without what you took. Make an example for others in this school who may be thinking of doing what you did.

Father Oxford makes Ernie hold out his hands. He brings the strap down lots of times, hard like he's axing a tree. Then he makes Ernie stand there saying his rosary while everyone eats. Everyone except Ernie. You can have mine Hunter says, giving Shorty his slice of bread.

———

In the dark dorm, Muscles and Bone have shut up. No one's farting. No one's whispering. Hunter counts the stars inside the shadowy window panes. Beside him Ernie breathes like a saw on wood, then for a long time he doesn't. Hunter reaches out and touches his cousin's bed covers. Faint up and down.

A long time has passed since Eagle glued his envelope together and wrote on it: Mr. and Mrs. Daniel George, Grampa George, Uncle Jack and Auntie Marge, Maskipeton, Alberta. A long time since he ran over to the postman — Hey Mister. What son? Can you take my letter? Well, it doesn't even have a stamp on it! Please sir. You can't send a letter unless it's got a stamp on it, son. Then he got Tom to rip off the stamp from his next letter and Eagle glued it on and he went to the postman again with his white-footed horse that looked like Kîyasiw. Please sir, it's to my Mom, my sister is dying. This wasn't true, but if he said it, the man might take the letter. Oh, the postman said, Alright give it me. Will you take it to her today? Oh no, it'll take a week I reckon. Thank you sir. Thank you. Thank you. He ran back to the field and picked up another stone from the turned sods, carried it to the wheelbarrow, clumped across the dusty clods for another.

What were you doing away from your job? Father Oxford whacked him.

Patting the horse, sir.

Whack. No you weren't, you were talking to the postman.

Father Oxford—Bone called him Warty because of his nose—stomped over to the postman. The postman got down off his wagon. Took off his cap, put it back on. Father Warty pointed back to Hunter in the field. Hunter looked sideways as he bent, picked up another rock. Father Warty waved his hands back and forth, like no, never! in front of the postman. He looked in the cart. Hunter picked up another rock, carried it to the wheelbarrow.

A long time has passed since then. They must have got his letter by now. No one has come. Maybe Dad is still in jail. Maybe Mom is still in Edmonton and Grampa can't find her. Ernie saws again. The father didn't even notice that Ernie wasn't kneeling on his bed for prayers.

———

Grey light fills the grey window bars, the grey wall, the grey torn-paper ceiling. Grey light on the grey blanket-hills between fences. Grey ceiling-mark makes itself into head and legs, tail and mane. Hunter rides the grey mark before bell clang. Something's missing. Mouse sleeps beside him, toy horse in his hand on the pillow. Mouse turns, arm over eyes, pulling soft sleepy breaths. Hunter rides the grey mark across the ceiling down the wall, jumps the window, runs to the next, flies out in the grey light. Something's missing. A father came in the night, black shadow, hands fingering stomach of buttons.

Something's missing. It's too quiet. Ernie's not sawing. Ernie's better. No more coughing. Hunter rides the ceiling-mark over the window, how long till the clanging and washing and morning church. Heaven and hell. And burn in hell. Ernie's eyelids are grey, his blanket is low and flat like nothing's there. Hunter places a hand on Ernie's chest. Nothing. Nothing. Nistes, Nistes wake up. He shakes Ernie's shoulder. Wake up, wake up. Ernie's head flops and rolls on the pillow — dead like the rabbit when Mom twisted its neck.

Father Father — Hunter runs out to the hall, past grey doors to other boys, past the room of toilets and sinks, out where he's not supposed to be past the couch where the night Father lies but he's not there now. He goes down the stairs, past the Virgin Mary statue, past the door to the green tables and tin plates — past the outside door — he could run out there now, run forever away from this place but he carries on to the rooms where the fathers live — the rooms where boys never go except the ones that get chocolate at night. Father, Father.

What are you doing here, get back to bed, Father O'Reilly comes toward him tying his cassock. What's going on — Father Oxford sticks his head out another door.

Ernie's dead Father. Hunter turns and runs back upstairs.

Bone, Eagle, Shorty, Mouse, Fish-eyes stand around Ernie's bed. No one moves. Even Muscles says nothing, as Father O'Reilly picks up Ernie, and carries him down the hall toward the sick room. Everyone stands there looking at Ernie's empty bed. Cousin Ernie — yesterday in front of Hunter in the line-up, then saying Contrition to Father O'Reilly, then eating the extra bread Hunter passed him at dinner. Cousin Ernie remembering Grannie's story about Wîsahkecâhk and the river. What will happen to him now?

Will Uncle Alex come? Will Father Clarence put a white cross over him in the graveyard behind his church? Hunter smoothes Ernie's sheets, they still feel warm, still smell of old flowers like Ernie.

Whatsa matter, he your lover boy—Bone pushes Hunter's face into the bed. Hunter mashes his shoulder into Bone's ribs twisting him down onto his own bed. Bone knees him in the stomach. Hunter's mattress is bloody. It crashes to the floor. Stupid little fuck you broke your bed. Now you'll get it.

Father Oxford clangs the bell. Up now. Make your beds.

Father Oxford.

Get dressed. Chapel's in ten minutes.

Father Oxford. Hunter pulls at his sleeve.

What's your bed doing on the floor. Put it back together.

Father Oxford.

What.

What will they do with Ernie?

The doctor will decide.

Line up. Shortest in front. Quiet. Walk down stairs, past the green room of green tables, out the door, down the steps, across the gravel, over the Chapel doorstep. Line up beside the pews. Stand straight, look straight at number 17 on Tom's shirt. Not to other pews' blue and white dresses — maybe Rose-Berry. Clack. Right knee to floor. Stay. Clack. Rise. Clack. Other knee to floor. Stay.

CHAPTER 11

Go out of here, Hunter thinks. Wait till Father O'Reilly passes, flashing his torch over sleeping and not sleeping boys, then slip down the dark hall, down the stairs, past the grey-green room with benches and tables. Out to the night. Walk, maybe one day maybe two days, to the train tracks. Find his way back to Grampa and Grannie, Auntie Marge and Uncle Jack. Mom and Dad too if they're not in Edmonton.

Now in Ernie's bed, on Ernie's pillow, his own bed broken on the floor between him and Mouse. Where did Ernie go? Black cassocks passed at night, up and down the row of beds. Black skirts spread black wings over a sleeping boy. Next day that boy didn't get up till the Father tipped over the bed. Even if he tipped Ernie's bed, he couldn't get up now. Ernie's inside the Wihtikiw. Turn into weasel, dive down Wihtikiw's mouth and stab his heart, then Ernie would come back.

Lucky it's not winter — they'd put Ernie outside and freeze him, Fish-eyes said. Two months later send him home. Like my cousin out past Bear Lake. School told his dad, come and get your son, he's not well. My uncle got here, found out his boy had been dead two months. My uncle put him on a sled. Three days' walk to get home. A storm came up. Started blizzarding. They found my uncle frozen in the snow. He put his blanket around his boy to keep him warm.

Ernie's in heaven, Mouse, Tom said.

Where's heaven?

In the sky with the angels.

Ernie ain't in no heaven, Eagle said.

Where is he then, in hell, Fish-eyes made his knuckles crack like the snapping of a grouse neck.

Ain't no heaven, no hell—Ernie's in the ground eating dirt.

Where then?

Past the barns in the dug-up piles.

How d'you know?

I saw them put the sack in the ground.

Will they dig him up when his dad comes?

Those dug-up piles, Eagle said, that's no graveyard—they just put the dirt back, forget about it.

Like Ernie was never here, no place to go back, say hello to Ernie in the ground. Go out of here—go home, tell Uncle Alex where his son is so he can take him home too. The door opens, torchlight flashes through Hunter's eyelids. He tries not to scrunch them, tries to keep them from wiggling all over his eyeballs. At the end of the room, the Father stands with the torch off. He strikes a match, lights a cigarette. Tobacco smoke wafts through the air, itching Hunter's throat. Black cassock up and down the bed road at night. Where did you go? Nowhere. What did he do? Nothing. Did you get chocolate? So—what if I did? A mattress button digs into his shoulder. At last the Father stubs out his cigarette, flicks on the torch and goes back down the rows of beds, closing the door behind him.

Hunter dresses in his blue shirt and blue pants. He grabs his shoes, a big potato sack and the knife lifted from harvest trimming. He piles his own blankets under the covers on Ernie's bed then slides down the row of moonlit boys. The night couch is empty; the Father has gone back to his friends downstairs. Hunter creeps down the first flight. Then footsteps — the Father coming back up. The last runaway Father Haffman beat with a piece of wood till he bled through his shirt, in front of everyone at the lunch tables. Then they chained him to his bed. Hunter darts into the lavatory, and stands on a toilet. Footsteps pass by, then return. Hunter hoists himself on the tops of the stall walls, lies across them and flattens himself against the main wall. The Father marches in, flashing his torch and batting back stall doors one after another. He opens Hunter's stall, then passes on to the next, turns around at the end, slamming the door behind him.

Hunter eases himself down, one foot on a toilet-paper holder, another on a water pipe. The paper holder gives way and he falls with a thud. He waits in faint moonlight, counting to a hundred in the pissy poopy smell, then climbs back on the toilet ready to spring at the slightest sound. Brave like Uncle Lenny said — old times, men did brave things. Our grandfather sent away his wife and children — that's me and Uncle Norman — and stayed alone in his teepee to lure the Blackfoot up real close, Blackfoot even shot him — right through the arm — then he fired shots and all his brothers ambushed the Blackfoot.

No one to ambush if he gets caught here.

He slides out of the stall, puts his ear to the lavatory door. Nothing. He pulls the door. It doesn't move. Somehow the Father locked it. He climbs on a sink and up on a window ledge, slides open the window; an old crooked-limbed tree right underneath waits to snarl him in its spiky branches. The Father's footsteps again in the hall. Off the ledge. There's only one way out.

I know you're in here you little bastard. Snap of the lock. Flapping of cassock — the Father kicks into the room, banging the door back; his black skirts swish past. Before the Father turns around, Hunter slips from behind the door and into the hall. He sneaks down the stairs in bare feet, his shoes in the sack over his shoulder. Men talk and laugh in the green room with green tables. Past the green room is the door out of the school.

Fathers swing open the door and clatter into the hall — Father Oxford with his crosses, Father Haffman carrying a Bible — smiling and talking. Hunter ducks behind the wooden skirts of the Virgin Mary. Smell of roast chicken — green-room door swings shut. Father White aims an imaginary croquet mallet hitting a ball to Father Haffman, Father Lafarge carries a plate of butter tarts and a bubbly brown glass toward the Fathers' rooms. A big hollow place in Hunter's ribs growls furiously. Quiet. Quiet. Push in stomach. Father O'Reilly is pounding down the stairs. Run. Now.

In the moonlight, the dogs rush on him barking and snarling. That's how they caught the last runaway — with the dogs, which they lock up during the day and only let out at night. He pulls a grouse carcass from his sack and hurls it as far away as possible, then runs in the opposite direction, past the kitchen coal chute, past the parade ground, past the black automobiles, past tractors and wagons, past the harvesting shed, the rock-picking field, the cow barn, past the dug-up piles of dirt where Ernie is. Till he's running through trees and the school lights disappear behind him.

He stops to put his shoes on. Listening for dogs. Thinking of Rose-Berry asleep in a row of girls — girls like Mouse and Muscles, girls like Ernie, Rose-Berry not knowing he's gone now. But he will tell Mom and she'll come and get Rose-Berry away from here.

He wanders on through moonlight-white trunks — his stomach sloshing empty.

CHAPTER 12

Leaves, branches — not grey torn-paper ceiling. No blanket, just moss and the potato sack that's almost as big as he is. Dogs. Where are the dogs? No dogs. Everything's still, except something scratching, and a thump. He sits up scattering leaves. Something spotted flies up. He stumbles to his feet. Something blacknosed, black-eyed — nubs of antler. Flick flick, white tail — bounds and jumps — leaving empty tree-trunks, far as he can see. Space all around him — no clang of bells, no line-up, no bed fences no walls even — no Father-yelling.

He stumbles into a tiny trickle almost buried in leaves. Scoops water and drinks. Splashes his face. Where's the sun? Where's he going to go? He stands up — stomach hole sloshing — finds himself falling sideways — eyes full of fireflies. He rolls over in the leaves. Legs feel empty — no bones in them. On the ground, he curls up — shivering, scrunching into himself for heat. Eyes closed. If he could pull the ground over him like a cover, he'd be warmer. Dig under the ground. He reaches one arm blindly around him, pulls at a handful of leaves. But if the dogs come. But his legs don't move. But if he stays here, he'll die like Ernie back at school. And

Dad will. And Rose-Berry and Mom and Grampa and Grannie.
He rolls over into something solid. Holds onto the tree. Pulls
himself up. Still his legs won't move. He slides down the tree, sits
at the base of it—knees into his chin, backbone into hard bumps
and ridges of tree-bark. If Eagle and Tom were here. He picks up
some leaves with a stick. Chucks the stick into the woods. Whomp
whomp whomp. Not far from where the stick landed.

If Eagle and Tom were here, they'd.

And he will now... if he can move from this tree. He thinks
of Grannie, how hard it is for her to move now, and one of her
stories comes into his head, about Wîsahkecâhk when he had
nothing and he went to a Frenchman who was buying furs, but
Wîsahkecâhk had no furs. He said to the Frenchman, give me
some blankets and a gun and I'll get lots of furs and pay you
back. The Frenchman gave him the blankets and the gun but
Wîsahkecâhk just gave them to his wife. His wife thought he
was stupid. He had no furs but he went back to the Frenchman
and said give me some poison. He told the Frenchman it was to
kill the wolves with. The Frenchman gave him the poison. Then
Wîsahkecâhk got some melted fat from his wife. He mixed in
the poison and hardened it into little cakes. When he saw a
wolf, he called him over. Why do you want to kill me, the wolf
asked. Wîsahkecâhk said all he wanted was the wolf to call the
other wolves and foxes so Wîsahkecâhk could preach to them.
Lots of wolves and foxes sat in a circle around Wîsahkecâhk.
He told them if they believed in religion they would live forever. Do you believe, he said. As each one said yes, Wîsahkecâhk
put a little fat-cake between his teeth. Soon they were all dead.

Hunter stands up next to the tree. You might hear some talk
Grannie said, don't always believe everything you hear. But there's
no one talking here. Except scritching and scratching in the falling yellow leaves.

Shoes off, he slowly circles the spot in the fallen leaves — the
soles of his feet mould themselves over sticks, not to snap. Eyes

scour browns, grays, yellows of leaves for the browns and grays of feathers. A magpie shrieks its warning. He stands still as the aspen trunks. Magpie go away. Grouse turns its eye this way that way. Waits. Grouse pecks leaves, twigs, rustling ground. Get behind it, get a tree between, bird foot up — bird eye here there. Still as a tree trunk. Bird head bird peck. Now. Grab. Birdneck. Feathery rasping bird claws. Shove it kicking and flapping into the ground. Twist it. Hard. Harder. Hard into leaf mess. Snap and limp. Now the knife from his sack. He hacks at the bird's neck.

———————

He breaks off some rosehips and munches them with raw pieces of bird. Berry picking — Mom and Grannie — what do they call this? Red thing. Staring at him. Cree word locked up somewhere. Rose fruit. Rose-berry. Okiniy. Good for you, Grannie said. Sour but good. Rose-Berry. Where is she? Far away across the gravel marching ground of the big white school he saw her two days ago, blue squared dress, chopped off hair. In a line-up of blue squared dresses. Staring at the ground. A nun flapped back and forth in front of them, waving her arms at a girl with a sheet over her head.

He puts the rest of the bird in the sack. Go now, he tells himself, go before the dogs come, find shoes, find the sun, go away from the sun. That way's where home is. His hand reaches for red clusters close to the ground — wîsakimin — handfuls — mouthfuls — another clump — over there even more. Go now. Walk away from here. Maybe find a train he can sneak onto.

He finds his shoes, cleans the knife in the trickle of water. Wanders through tree trunks.

———————

Dust in his mouth. Dust in his hair, his eyes. Far as he can see road. Dust. Tree clumps. Road ahead cut through fields of stubs of yellow grass. Road to the sky. Sun high overhead. Drying the grass stubs. Drying the leaves off trees. Drying up all the trickles and ponds he could drink.

Something squeaks and snorts behind him. A man and horses pulling something. Hide. Where? Mowed fields stretch away all around. Run then. A man with horses can't follow.

His legs won't run. He lets the farmer pull along side him. Horses blow through their noses and clump up dust clouds.

Aint you sposed to be in school?

Say nothing. Keep walking.

Hey kid, ya deaf?

Red-faced man. Blue overalls. Torn leg Mom called a three-corner tear.

So ye kin hear then.

Tired old man. He'd never catch him if he decided to run. Stop then; let him go by.

Whoa, boys. Whoa.

The empty wagon holds three sacks of grain. It's pulling a two-wheeled thing with a seat and long arm of teeth raised up like half an open jaw.

What's the matter, aint ya never seen a mower before?

He remembers something like it at the school, cutting hay. All day they pitched it onto wagons. All day. Itching. Sun crazy. All day Father yelling, Lazy boys.

Where ya goin?

Train.

Long ways to the train from here.

How far?

Hop on I'll take ya part way.

A blue jug sits behind the man's seat.

Go on climb up.

Foot in a wheel-spoke, he heaves himself into the wagon.

Giddup, boys.

Hunter flops down on a grain sack. Must ask the man for water.

He slides down to wood slats in the jigging joggling wagon. Ask the man. He must sit up, not rest his head on the fat grain-sack pillow. Head up. Must ask him. Ask the man. For the blue jug. He's pouring water but his cup keeps missing it. Ask the red-faced man. To pour. He's suddenly awake again in the fields of yellow stubs. The blue jug sits under the wooden slat holding the man's bum. Ask. The man's arm reaches out big iron teeth. Now the jug's on the mower seat behind them. The man's arm reaches to the mower. Now Mr. Red-face is on the mower seat. The blue jug's in the wagon. No one is driving...

———

He jolts awake, head up off the sack. The wagon's stopped, wheels still, horses flicking tails. His mouth is a dust-hole. A mouth of grain-sack. His tongue's a wooden board. Dried as the fields of yellow stubs. Dry as grasshoppers.

I should really take ya to the school but that'd be three hours outa my way. Or I could call the police that's another two hours to the nearest telephone. Still have to get this thing over to Asker's.

Sir.

Oh it's sir is it.

You got any water?

Sure. 'S'in the jug. Hop out and open the gate.

He grabs the jug. Warm wet on his wooden tongue.

Oh, okay. I got all day.

It tastes of the rusty jug. Drink anyway. Drink more. More.

Eh! Time ta hop out. Ya keep going that way, tracks're about another coupla miles.

———

He walks toward the sun falling out of the sky — maybe he's half-way to the tracks from where the farmer let him off, maybe even closer, walking, walking endlessly, farther than he's ever walked. A hundred times farther than the tired-legs walk to Grannie's house. Around him giant shadows of bushes and fence posts stretch out across yellow grass stubs. Thistle-shadows tall as houses.

He finds misâskwatômin — dried on bushes — better than fresh ones. Not many though. Birds got them. Cool in the shadow of the berry patch, he picks off wrinkled berries here and there. He mustn't stop. Must keep going to the tracks before dark. Stomach hole under his ribs growls.

He drags the rest of the bird out, covered with sack grit. Wiping the knife on his pants, he hacks off pieces of bird, then chucks away bones. Raw meat slides around in his mouth like wiggling worms. Chew and chew. Swallow anyway. Better with berries. Chew the wiggly-worm meat. Find more berries over there.

He winds into the bushes on the paths of animals, away from the section road, filling his mouth with wrinkled berries and raw grouse. Another clump. Then another.

A muddy plaid shirt lies across the trail. Muddy pants too. Not just thrown away — a body inside them. In the crook of its arm is a corked bottle. He pushes into the berry bushes, away from its white, grizzled face. The body snores. A dead body. Snoring. Grunting. He gathers his sack and runs through the bushes back to the road. Don't look back. Don't see it.

The sky's on fire. The sun's orange ball is sinking into dark tree-clumps, dark edge of land, dark road. Over his head, dark clouds push like lids over the last of sun's eye, sealing up its fiery light. He must run toward the eye. Run away from night.

The snoring dead thing calls out.

Don't look back. He runs on, hands over his ears, sack flapping on his back.

Behind him on the road, a dark shape weaves back and forth. Talking. Muttering. Calling.

He runs till he gasps for breath. Runs till he can't run. Stops dizzy. Walks backwards.

It still follows. Still talks and chatters.
Cloud lids close the sun's eye—at the edge of sky a slit of pink.
He walks and walks, keeping the shadow behind him.

———

Come with me, Ernie at school says. I'm friends with him. Black
cassocks crowd around. Just down here. Over these mounds.

No Ernie.

My eyes are fine; he's my friend.

Your eyes are gone, Ernie. Only holes.

Hunter wakes to hissing and rumbling, soot smell, oily smell.
Rocks grind into his face. The ground shakes. Something huge,
clacking and spitting roars toward him. He stumbles to his feet.
Leaps back into the bushes. He jumps again as the train lets out
two long hoots.

You sure run fast.

The plaid-shirt dead thing with its white grizzled face laughs
at him.

Want some bread.

Plaid shirt pulls out a crust from his pocket.

What's your name then.

Hunter. (He takes the bread.)

Mine's Louis.

He chews bread in his parched mouth.

Which way you goin?

Maskipeton.

Never heard of it, where's that?

That way.

This train ain't goin that way—it's goin south.

How can I find one going that way?

Git on one goin south, till ya hit the CPR going west.

Hunter follows Louis to the curve where the train has to slow.

CHAPTER 13

On the jiggling floor of a boxcar, Hunter crouches with his sack. A mower and baler parked in a field, some men leaning on rakes, a team and wagon roll past in the open doorway. Looks like we got company, Louis mutters. Sun through cracks in the walls flashes on two men in a dark corner.

Name's Louis. The man holds out his hand to a man in a jacket covered with black and white diamonds.

Teddy, the man says, this here's Quentin. (Patched elbows on his long brown coat.)

Who's your little friend?

All's he's told me is his name's Hunter and he's goin west.

Quentin here's a teacher—where'd you say?

Was a teacher—Lord Strathcona Elementary School, Edmonton.

What was your former life?

Salesman. Britannia Shoes. You?

Milk delivery, Louis says, Union Milk till it was bought up by United Dairies and they let a bunch of us go.

Truck or horse.

Horse. Five A M six days a week. Get me an ice block for the cart, pick up the empties. Deliver the fulls. Milk. Cream. Butter. Eggs. Whatever the missus wanted. Nine years I worked for that company. Never missed a day. Then bingo, it's gone.

Hey kiddo, where're ya from?

Tell them and they make you go back to the school, Hunter thinks. Tell them nowhere.

In the door, a pond shrinking back from white crusted ground, then the black-knobbed trunks of aspen trees.

Haveta be from somewhere. Where's yr dad?

He went to jail.

How long for?

I don't know.

Why's he in jail?

He sold our cow.

That doesn't seem right, why would he go to jail for selling a cow? Mr. Quentin crinkles his eyes like Uncle Jack. Mr. Teddy's black and white diamonds make his eyes crazy.

Was it his cow?

Yeah.

He wishes he'd met Mr. Quentin in the berry bushes instead of Mr. Louis. He asks Mr. Quentin how Dad could get out of jail.

Well he'd have to go before a judge, I guess.

Worse yet—he'd haveta have a lawyer. Diamonds-man rolls a few threads of tobacco in a paper. Cost so much he'd have to go back to jail cuz he couldn't pay.

A field of rusty automobiles without wheels slides past the open door.

What's that—a judge?

He's a man that decides what's fair.

Do you think that man Mr. Judge will go to my Dad's jail?

Hah, that'd be the day. Diamonds-man holds a match to his cigarette. Mr. Judge sits in his courtroom. *You* haveta go to *him*.

The boxcar door holds a yard of steers; then a white church with a blue steeple.

Will they open the jail so my Dad can go?

That's why ya have to have a lawyer. Lawyer gets you outta jail.

Lawyer — what's that?

He's a man that talks to the judge.

Which is why ya have to have lots of money.

Would a quarter be enough?

Hah. More like hundreds of quarters.

My Dad could just talk to the judge himself, like he does to Mr. McDonald.

Only lawyers kin talk to judges — legal talk.

Yeah like lickadated damages and punital damages.

Hey, don't you just have the fancy words?

Milk cart ran over a housewife's foot, I had to go to court'n testify.

Don't confuse the lad. It works like this see — Crinkle-eyes looks at him — There's a thing called the law, and that's the rules of a country. Judges and lawyers apply the rules of the country to everyone else.

Hey what about police — they sure as hell apply the law to you'n me.

Wheat stooks roll past; then some men feeding bales into a machine blowing out a huge stack of straw.

It's complicated, see. There's a lot of rules. That's why you need someone who knows all the rules to talk to the judge.

Yeah there's the rules, then there's the rules about how you can use the rules and what kindsa papers ya haveta have and when ya haveta have'em by. Claims and counterclaims and affadavies and exhibitions.

What if you don't have enough money?

Sometimes the judge'll get you one.

Do you think my Mom could get money?

I don't know son, what does she do?

A crew of men with shovels slides by — men raking black smelly stuff on a road like Dad did.

Eh boys, that's what we could be doin. Road work, fifty cents a day.

My Mom makes bannock. She sews dolls and catches rabbits.

Maybe if she caught a lot of rabbits, she could sell them.

Where is she?

Edmonton.

Dunno how many rabbits she's going to catch in Edmonton.

Depends on how you define rabbits.

The men all laugh.

He pretends to smile. But he doesn't feel like laughing at Mom catching rabbits.

———◆———

It was easy to jump off the train and follow the men onto another one. This'll get us to Alix, Mr. Louis said, You get off there, catch one going north to Ponoka. The clack-clack, clack-clack of wheels underneath makes Hunter sleepy like on the farmer's wagon.

Mr. Louis rolls up his blanket, props his head on it against the wall, and stretches out his legs across the floor. A mass of grey curly hair grows out the top of his shirt. Like a raccoon was living under there. Dad just has skin under his shirt.

Mr. Teddy holds a little mirror in front of his face, combing his hair to the back of his head. It sticks together in thin strings, his scalp showing underneath. Beard stringy too, showing his chin. Can't see chin through Mr. Quentin's beard, or head skin under his hair. His collar's buttoned up, his jacket buttoned over his shirt. Probably no raccoon under there.

Splashes of light flash on/off into the boxcar. Branches and leaves rush by.

Dad doesn't have a beard. Dad has thick dark hair like a horse's mane down to his shoulders. Dad the mostos. Dad. Dad. Dad.

Kin I borrow that.

Mr. Louis holds the mirror up to his face.

Oh boy, gotta do something about this.

He pulls out a small metal box. His beard's like a stubble field. He screws a metal rod into a curved metal roof like a two-sided rake. Then rakes it over the stubble.

Not tryin to shave without soap are ya?

Sometimes Dad pulled hairs out with pinchers.

You'll get razor burn.

Mr. Louis makes the stubble shorter on one side, then rests the rake on his stomach and smoothes the stubble over the rolls of his chin. He starts again on the other side. Ah, the hell with it. The thing's too dull. He unscrews it, puts it back in its box.

Mr. Quentin crosses his arms on top of his knees. His thumb and finger smooth out the corners of his moustache, he stares out the boxcar door. The thumb and finger start together again under his nose and slide out toward his cheeks, out to the points of the moustache. So much moustache, Hunter can't even see the top half of his mouth.

—◆—

The train jolts then slows. Louis slides the door shut.

Git back in the corner. He pulls Hunter to his feet and pushes him into the corner on the door side. The others head back into the shadows of the other corners.

This Alix?

Only gone about twenty miles from the junction — must be Stettler.

Shhhhh!

The train stops.

Mebbe just gettin water.

Shhhhh!

Hissing sounds up the tracks. Warmth of the sun creeps through the wood sides of the car. Men's voices outside are getting closer. No way up inside their box. The door on the other side's bolted with a metal lock.

A dog barks and whines, a voice saying I want all the cars checked. Hunter tightens his grip around his potato sack with its apples, carrots and harvesting knife. The car door slides back, he makes himself flat as the wall. This one's clear. The dog barks, gets its paws up on the doorsill. When I say checked, I mean get into the car and look! Okay, sir. Will do.

Scratching sounds, of nails on wood. Attaboy. The checker heaves the dog into the car. It bounds up to diamonds-man. Shshh, shshsh good boy. Diamonds pats him. The dog wags its tail then bounds off to Louis barking, and growling. Louis kicks him back. The checker bangs his ladder against the car, pulls himself through the door. Stands for a moment. Hey mister you couldn't give a fella a break eh, I gotta buck here for ya.

Okay everyone out, all a ya. You wanta ride the train, you buy a ticket.

Hunter jumps first, whirls back, clambers over the coupling between the cars and runs around the end of a row of grain elevators.

Hey get back here, you.

He weaves between buildings, steering clear of a team and loaded wagon, then crouches in a corner among tall, brown-headed weeds. Someone's talking to horses on the other side of the wall, Whoa, Back, Back, Whoa. An engine fires up, clattering and squeaking something round and round.

———— ◆ ————

Hunter dodges between some grain-hoppers close to the elevator. Hey, Bunk, lookee here! A white boy blocks his exit. Wheeler, over here, we found the Indian runaway. Two more white boys head toward him from the other end.

Watcha got in yr sack, squaw-boy?

Got some scalps in there?

A ladder runs up the side of each grain hopper — then what?

Hunter crawls between the big steel wheels and over the steel rail onto grease-stained ties and crumbled rock under the hoppers. He starts out the other side. A white boy snatches his leg and pulls. Grabbing the metal bars and bolts under the car, Hunter kicks him off. Boys surround him, both sides of the hopper.

Gotcha, squaw-boy.

Gonna take you to the police.

Send ya back to Indian School.

The white boys snatch at him. Hunter kicks their faces. A freight train on the main track grinds past shaking the ground and spewing steam.

Get under there Bunk, push him out — we'll pull 'm.

No way — I ain't goin under no train.

Get outa there ya little feather-head. Bunk kicks under the rail car. Hunter jams his foot on the white boy's boot, pinning it against a train wheel. Bunk falls backward.

Hey get away from those hoppers. What are you doing anyway?!

We found the runaway, Mr. Maynard.

What runaway?

Indian kid off the CPR.

He jumped out of a boxcar, we followed him.

We're gonna take him in to the police like the poster says.

That'd be a change, usually the police are taking you somewhere.

The poster says all Indian kids are s'posed to be in Indian school.

You boys clear out of here and let me handle this. Clear out now, unless you want me to mention to the Police your night chucking Mrs. McKickly's laundry from the top of the water tower.

The white boys let go of his leg and crunch away along the tracks, leaving just the boots and pantlegs of the man standing there.

Son, I'm not going to turn you in to anyone. You come on out from under there when you're ready. Don't wait too long, though — these cars are loading tomorrow.

———◆———

In the darkness he smells oil and soot. Something hard and metal fences him in on a bed of stones and planks. Where's his sack? He rolls over hitting something big and cold — solid blackness poking into his shoulder. Hooks and bars, something coiled. He bangs his elbow and crawls toward a dimly lighter grey patch. His knee hits steel, and something claws his head as he stumbles up — dizzy — spinning stars in his eyes like fireflies, then down to hands and knees. Above him open night sky, moon and stars, nothing heavy and pressing down. He tries to stop his teeth from clacking his jaws as he walks on numb feet to the dark block of a building.

Dry weed heads and thistle pricks snatch at his hands till he reaches the sun-warm wall, and hits something cold, knobbly — a water tap. He turns until it streams out — warm. He cups his hands and drinks. More and more. Cold water now. Cold teeth clacking, cold running like a snake through his chest. He shuts it off and hugs the sun-warm wall to the corner of the building, then follows along to another corner and some steps, where he sits, hunched into a doorway, eating an apple.

On the other side of a field a streetlamp gleams and tiny squares of window-light. Far away a dog barks. A moving speck of light draws a line through the black flatness. Mr. Louis, Mr. Teddy, Mr. Quentin — they're out there maybe somewhere under this moon. Mom, Auntie Marge, Grampa — maybe they see it too.

Grannie said Wîsahkecâhk held on to the legs of a crane, he made the legs stretch longer and longer as they flew. A long way to the moon. Flying and flying. Wîsahkecâhk holding on to the crane all that way. Almost broke his arms. He got to the moon, and painted a red dot on Crane's forehead as a way of thanking her, before she flew back to earth. Wîsahkecâhk liked it on the moon. He settled in and lived there. But the moon kept getting smaller. His seat on the moon got sharper. Finally he was only holding on to the points of the moon. Then it disappeared and he fell back to earth. Sideways and backwards and every which way, Grannie said. He told Earth to make a soft spot for him to land and Earth did that. Wîsahkecâhk fell head first into a mudhole.

Hunter hunches closer to the warmth of the door and the building. Then falls backwards into nothingness, clattering the door into a wall. He's out of the wind, snug inside walls. He closes the door, finds a chair and a table, then the shadow of a round-bellied stove. The room smells of new-cut wood. A patch of silvery moon splashes across one wall. He runs his hands over rounds of flower-petals pressed into metal squares in the wall. A broom stands in the corner. He looks around for a place to hide and sleep. Not enough room under the metal box on legs with its long cord. Nor behind a wooden box with wheels on the sides. He turns the handle on the big wheel, rasping and rattling bits around inside.

Walking into darkness away from the window, he brushes a hanging chain, steps around it, and pitches down into blackness. He clutches at the floor boards, but loses his grip, and slides into a dust-choking hill of loose dry sand. No, not sand. It's thousands of tiny pebbles. He scoops a handful. Tastes a grain, then takes a whole mouthful — teeth grinding the grains into flour, the flour into food. He digs a nest in the grain and sits, eating another mouthful and another and filling his pockets. Wiggling down into the grain till he rests his head on a grainy pillow. His eyes close. Mustn't sleep. The screech of a passing train jolts him awake, and he lurches up. Must get out of here. His feet shift and slide on the loose hill, like trudging through snow. He stumbles into something metal and scoop shaped, a tower of little scoops. Then a ladder back up to the floor.

Along the planks and posts and back past the hanging chain, he finds a narrow passage. The glimmer of moonlight from the window disappears. His head hits something sharp above him, a curved edge with points sticking off it. He wipes a wet trickle off his forehead with his sleeve, then steps into another nook where it's completely black — walls close in around him — a closet — a place to hide. A loop of rope brushes his face. He sweeps it out of the way. Something in the wall jolts and clanks. The floor of his closet rumbles upward, buckling his knees. He crouches, hugging the little patch of floor. Walls brush past him. Nothing to hold onto. Then, with a whack and a thud, his closet floor stops.

———◆———

Hunter wakes to bright light and the smell of cut wood. Boards push into his face. A fly flit-buzzes bumping a window. Past the edge of a crate, grey branches grow like an upsidedown tree into the floor. His nose itches. Don't sneeze, he tells himself. His eyes shoot tears and his nose still itches. The upsidedown tree has six branches. Not branches — pipes with bandages, sometimes a crack coming through even the bandage — the pipes branch out of a corner and spread down into the floor. Maybe under the floor are more branches, maybe leaves. When he gets home, he'll go to Grannie first, in case police are around his house. He has to get back on the train and find another one at somewhere called Alix. His head aches. He closes his eyes.

Killdeers throwing their eyeballs up in trees, then shaking trees till their eyeballs fell back in their heads. Laughed when they did it. Hee hee hee, hmm ha ha, Grannie laughed and chuckled and giggled. Don't laugh so much, tell us the story. The story is laughing. Why're you doing that, Wîsahkecâhk asked the kill-deers. Cuz we have headaches, it makes us feel better. Wîsah-kecâhk wanted to do that trick too. Too hard said the killdeers. I have headaches, Wîsahkecâhk said, show me that trick. No, it's way too hard, anyway you can only do it four times a year. At last Wîsahkecâhk talked them into giving him the trick. He threw his eyeballs up in a cottonwood tree and laughed as they fell back in his head. He laughed and laughed. Pretty soon he did it four times. I still have a headache, he said. He threw up his eyes. They didn't go back in his head. They fell down and scattered on the ground. Wîsahkecâhk felt around on the ground with his hands. He stumbled from tree to tree, bumping into them but he couldn't find his eyes. How will he find his eyes? Grannie asked.

He jolts up to a clattering pup pup pup, squeak and clank rustling and rattling in the ceiling and walls through the upside-down tree branches. Clouds of dust puff out the cracks in the pipes. Something rushing down inside them must be grain but how does it come all the way up here? He's inside a machine grinding grain. He must go down the ladder into the floor — get away from this clacking place.

A man's head blocks the hole when he looks down, his hand on the ladder. Hunter leaps back behind a crate. Boots clump across the floor. A blue handkerchief with white polka dots sticks out of the man's pocket under the X of overall straps. The man bangs something, stopping the grain rushing through the pipes. Something scrapes. Get over there ya bugger. Pushing and shoving, the man bumps and knocks at the grey pipes, then thumps something, starting up the squeaking clank and rustling of grains. His hairy hand reaches for the polkadots, then puts them back in his pocket. His boots stand at the edge of the hole where the flying closet crashed up in the dark. Slowly the man's feet, then his legs, then his body, then his head sink into the floor and disappear.

CHAPTER 14

Cora needs a potato and some wire, for her attic laboratory, but Hilda wants to stop at the elevator after school —
just for a minute, I think Dad's lonely there waiting for grain
to come in — there's hardly any these days. Hilda rambles on —
she loves visiting Dad after school, he gets her to run the kicker
and do wild-oat tests. Or turn the Gerber wheel. Hilda the buffalo — calm and strong. Too strong, too calm, Cora thinks crossly,
too confident things will go her way. And they do go her way.
Because Hilda's family is happy, and Cora's isn't. But how can
she think this way about her friend? She looks over at Hilda
in her plaid skirt and blue blazer. Her friend smiles back, and
Cora wants to link arms but something stops her. Instead she
thinks of the galvanized nail and penny for her experiment, and,
most important, a flashlight bulb. A regular bulb's too big. Then
tells Hilda she's going to do an experiment in her attic laboratory; she's going to make her own electricity. But Hilda's Dad
even shows Hilda how to do experiments in *his* laboratory in the
grain elevator. I test the grain for moisture, Hilda says, It's very
scientific.

There she goes again, everything going right. Well, *she* is going to do her own experiment, she's going to turn electrons in a potato into light.

Cora, are you listening?

What?

You add oil to the grain, then heat it inside a metal box. The water drips out at the bottom, and you measure it.

When they open the door, Mr. Maynard's fixing a cleat to the wall to hold the manlift rope, a cat rubbing up against his leg. He tells the cat to quit mooching and go catch its dinner, while he winds the rope around the cleat. Darnedest thing; when I got here today, the manlift was at the top and the rope snagged, I had to climb all the way up the ladder to the top of the leg to get it, I'm sure I didn't leave it like that. Hilda throws her arms around him and kisses his cheek. Hey partner, he squeezes her. The frown clouding his face vanishes into sunshine.

Hilda wants to take Cora on the manlift to the top of the leg, do the moisture test when they get down. Mr. Maynard adjusts the weights, and Hilda pulls her onto the tiny platform — her arms around Cora, Hilda's breasts and stomach pressing into her, Hilda's breath blowing her hair, Hilda laughing, Shall we dance, as she unhooks the rope. Slats brush Cora's arm, rungs of the ladder brush her bum as they slowly float up the shaft.

From the bright, fly-buzzy room at the top, Cora gazes at the water tower hanging big-bellied over the roofs of houses. Rail lines head out of town — where to, where to — till they're swallowed up by fields and sky.

In a corner of the hot little room, Hilda points to the metal flank of the elevator grain-hopper and shows Cora how you can shift its chute to various giant bins.

What was that?

Each one holds 2500 bushels.

What was that scratching, coughing.

Probably a mouse or maybe a packrat.

It was behind the crate. Cora pulls it aside. There's someone here.

An Indian.

Hunter grabs his sack.

What are you doing here?

I'm going now. He steps onto the ladder.

Wait a minute, Hilda seizes his arm, did my Dad find you under a train?

Maybe. I didn't take anything.

Where do you live.

Nowhere.

Aren't you supposed to be in Indian school?

Hunter says nothing, keeps his eye on the ladder.

Are you running away, Cora asks.

I just slept here. Now I'm going.

Wait, you can't get down with the manlift in the way, Cora stop him.

Cora takes his other arm.

He shrugs her off.

We'll go first, then you can come down on the ladder.

Polka-dot man and the two girls face him at the bottom of the ladder, blocking his way to the door—the tall smiley girl with red-brown hair, and the glasses girl, with boy-hair—sadder, thinner. They've got shiny shoes with new laces, and their dresses aren't faded like Mom's and Rose-Berry's.

Behind the man are his tools and a cat sniffing at his lunch-box. The man makes him sit at a small table, opens the lunchbox, and gives him half a sandwich. Before he can chew his first bite, his hand brings the sandwich to his mouth again, and before he knows what kind of sandwich it is it's gone. The man sends one of the girls for water, and gives Hunter a piece of cake.

The three of them stand over him, when he gets up from the chair, telling him their names: Mr. Maynard, Hilda and Cora, and asking for his. But if he tells, they'll... Then the man says they won't turn him in to police or a school. They ask him where he's from. Nowhere, he says. I don't think there's any towns around here called Nowhere, the man says. Where d'ya want to get to?

Maskipeton.

Maskipeton, Mr. Maynard says, that's up near Ponoka, you got folks there?

Hunter nods. I am Hunter.

He lets Hilda wash the cut on his head and put medicine on it from the first aid box. He lets them take him in a car to a farm. He promises the man, he'll stay at the farm till he gets back later.

He keeps watch on the door as he eats meat and gravy and potatoes that Hilda the smiley girl gives him at a long table in the farm kitchen.

Cora the glasses one thinks they should take him to some place called Rupert's.

He barely trusts us, we can't just pass him on to someone else.

He might trust Mrs. Rupert more — she's Cree.

Dad'll help him; I know he will. Dad'll put you on a train, won't he hon?

He keeps his eyes on a slice of beef, cutting it with a silver fork and a silver knife on a china plate.

If he stays here the whole town'll know by tomorrow morning.

If you walk him to Rupert's, the whole town'll know by tonight, and Judge Rupert'll send him straight back to school.

When will Mr. Maynard come back so he can leave this place.

Glasses and Smiley keep standing there. Looking at him.

Leave now. Just walk away. They can't stop him.

Glasses asks him if he'd like to stay on the farm or talk to a Cree lady in town.

Cree lady.

You can't just go walking through town with him.

We could cut through the fields north of town.

That would take forever, and you'd still have to go along the Camrose road.

Maybe Mrs. Rupert can come here. She asks him whether he can stay here with Hilda, while she gets Mrs. Rupert.

He shrugs.

On Hilda's bicycle, Cora passes Judge Rupert's bear pulling against its collar, wrapping its chain around the post. Then notices Gerard coming toward her, leading a chestnut horse with big white feet through the field beside the drive. She wonders if he's drawn any more pictures of her, then feels red creep into her cheeks.

He pulls an apple from his pocket and holds it out for the horse.

What's his name?

Arrow.

He's big.

Yeah.

Clydesdale?

Clydesdale cross.

I need to speak to your Mom.

Why?

It's about a Cree boy—he's lost I think.

She doesn't know anything about that.

Cora reaches across the fence to pat Arrow's neck. And suddenly she's telling him how she really likes how he draws things, and could he give her a few pointers on their next Art assignment.

I don't know, I just do it. Don't know how.

Maybe she shouldn't have said that. She should just go and look for Mrs. Rupert.

I like your hair by the way, he says as she pushes off, it's different.

Oh. Yeah...it is...My Dad hates it.

Mrs. Rupert brings out tea and a plate of cookies and they sit at either end of a couch under the nostrils and horns of a moose head. Cora tells her story, but Mrs. Rupert says nothing at all, just looks out the window for a long time. Cora doesn't know what to say, Hilda would know but Hilda's back at the farm. She wonders again whether Mrs. Rupert's family still has dances and people who have spirit dreams. What was it like to have that kind of dream, and could a girl have them?

Finally Mrs. Rupert says, If I see this boy my husband will find out and send him to the school. Cora says they just want to help him get back to his parents, Mr. Maynard will probably give him a ticket to get to Ponoka.

If he rides the train without Mr. Maynard, they will just call the police. It's the law that they have to go to that school.

He just wants to see his family, see if they're alright—he hasn't seen them in over a year.

Once they go to those schools, they don't go home again until they are fifteen.

But the school is horrible; they hit the kids a lot; he says his sister is very sad there.

Even if he finds his way home, the agent on the reserve will know everything going on and will send him back.

———— ◆ ————

Hunter goes with Hilda up the creaky stairs of the farmhouse and into her bedroom. It's safe to wait here—no one can come in without my permission. He stands at the window, holding his sack with the knife and the apples, and looks over the porch roof down to the yard. A team of big horses pulls a wagon carrying two men with dusty hair and clothes covered with bits of straw.

In the bedroom, there's a table covered with silver and white boxes, combs, a brush. The table wears a pink and white skirt like a girl and grows a mirror out of one side. The bed wears a pink and white skirt too, and so does a chair. On the floor lies a braided rug, like ones Mom and Auntie Marge make out of sacks and worn-out dungarees.

Hilda sits on her bed with her back to him, then says What am I thinking and offers him the girl chair, but he stays by the window.

His eyes keep coming back to the quilt on the bed. Big squares stitched out of smaller squares climb over the bed like stairs when you see them from the side. Then he sees it again — white rabbits with long ears hopping on pink flowers. Like Lizzie's dress that Rose-Berry wore the day the school men took them away. Mom braiding her hair, tying it with red wool, Mom putting catalogue pages in his shoes, the school men saying, Hurry up, we haven't got all day. Now Rose-Berry's back at that school. By herself.

A loud whistle sounds from the yard, then another — like uncle Lenny makes when he wants to bug his aunt. Hey Hilda Baby, who ya got up there? Can we get a date?

Hilda moves Hunter away from the window and slides up the glass. Get lost, Seward.

Who's yr friend?

None of your business.

Is she pretty?

I said, none of your business.

Well, I guess I'll just have to come up there and introduce myself.

Forget it Seward.

Seward leaps out of the wagon and heads up the porch steps.

He's frozen and empty — like when they went in the car with the school men — as though he's falling off a cliff and tumbling through air, and shrinking to a tiny invisible dot. He watches the dot bouncing around the girl's bedroom. The girl saying, she's going out in the hall to stop Seward. He must stay here. Don't worry, she says, you'll be safe. She has to lock the door to keep Seward out. She closes it, and the lock clacks from the outside.

From the edge of the curtain, he checks the yard. The wagon and the men have gone. He slides up the window. Plates clatter and people laugh and talk from the floor below. Roasted meat smells from the kitchen. He puts his shoes into the sack. Other side of the bedroom door, a man's voice says, Give me a kiss and you can have the key back. Hunter steps out on the porch roof and feels his way along it close to the wall. Impossible to hold wall and sack. He ties the sack to his waist, the porch door bangs and boots clump across the floor. He crouches down. Boots clump down the steps and crunch across the gravel in the yard. Another door opens. Shuts. Hunter scuttles round the corner of the farmhouse sticking to the wall.

The sack gets away from him, sliding down the tin roof till it snags on a rose trellis poking up above the gutter. He inches down toward the sack. Peers over the edge at the rose bush and the trellis.

———————

They're gone now — the girl and her father calling, Hunter... Hunter. You're safe here. We can help you Hunter.

No more footsteps, no more rustling bushes, no more flashes of lamplight. His thorn scratches have stopped bleeding. He pushes out from under boards and chicken wire in a dark shed, and makes his way, under a bowl of stars, along the dusty road — faint sun-heat still in the pebbles and stones. He remembers crossing rail tracks on the way to the farmhouse. He will go back to the tracks, maybe find a coal shed, get out of the cold.

At the white X, two dark lines disappear into trees on both sides. Where's the town, the dogs, the police? Go away from there. He steps along the wooden ties, too cold to stop, and trees close around him. Sometimes he doesn't step far enough and stumbles onto the small rocks instead of a tie. A dark shadow slides through branches over his head. An owl he thinks. Hunting mice. He thinks about owl eggs. Not this time of year. He thinks about the apple pie Hilda gave him.

Faint light like a cloud of glowing dust glimmers through the trees. He walks on. The glimmer brightens, lighting up grey and white trunks of aspens and cottonwoods. Black lines of branches and bushes stand between him and the fire. A man moves around it, a huge man-shadow striding through woods behind him. The man-shadow throws a log in the flames, sparks shoot up into the night.

Hunter steps toward the fire, filling his eyes with it. He can't see where to put his feet in the underbrush. Holes swallow his legs. Leaves and twigs whap his face. He gropes his way forward till he's standing at the border of dark encircling the campfire. The men can't see him, but he can see them laughing and talking. One more step and he'll be in the circle of light, where the men's voices waft into branches overhead, swallowed by the night sky. Their faces are red with firelight and dark with unshaven beards. They're passing a bottle. One of them is Mr. Louis and another in a long coat might be Mr. Quentin from the train.

Best one I ever had was in Edmonton.

Down by the river.

Down by the river — sounds like a song.

Oh boy did she have melons — yeah, she was down under the railway bridge.

East side.

Yeah.

All done up in lace — yeah I know the one.

Feel them melons pressing up against ya.

He'll be comin' round the mountain when he comes.

Ah, shaddup.

I got me a little hot cake over in Red Deer.

Little brown house back a the station.

Yeah, little brown hands too — what they kin do.

Hey pass the jug.

Quit hoggin' it.

Ha ha ha, you and me, Little brown jug, don't I love thee.

The backs of the men are dark lumps against firelight — their eyes dark holes in their red faces. Hunter steps forward. A man in earmuffs jumps up and pulls a shotgun on him. Ah, he's just a kid, leave him be.

Earmuffs sits down, rests the gun between his legs.

They let him sit near the fire. Indian, ain't ya. He nods.

Hey, this here's my little friend, Hunter.

Plaid-jacket Louis tips up the bottle, passes it to long-coat but he doesn't take it. His head hangs on his chest. Comes up, eyes shut, then flops down again. It's not Mr. Quentin.

Where'd you disappear to? Louis asks.

He shrugs, tries to stop his jaw rattling.

A man in a crumpled green suit gives him a coat. They argue about whether he can have Wally's coat, whether Wally's coming back. Hunter puts on Wally's coat and pulls in closer to the red-hot logs. Now they're arguing about whether Wally was still kicking after he got knocked down outside the bar, and whether blood coming out his mouth meant he couldn't breathe. The coat smells like throw-up. He was dead, okay, I've seen dead people, their lips are white like Wally's, their face is grey like his. (Dead like Ernie in the mounds behind the barn.) Better watch it. (Man with thin grey hair, ponytail.) He'll come back and haunt ya. Ponytail offers him the bottle. Here, that'll warm ya up. Hunter takes a swig like the men. He coughs at the scorching liquid—hands the bottle to the next man.

Green suit says what's he doing out here, why isn't he in school. One of those special schools for Indians. Teach ya skills so ya can get a job. Yeah, like us. We all got jobs. The men laugh. Mr. Louis laughs so hard he falls backwards off the log onto the ground behind.

Hunter's going to Ponoka, ain'tcha.

He nods his head.

You gotta go to Alix, then north.

There's a big crossroads in toward town.

Thataway. No. Thataway.

You go down this line then take the other back to Alix.

You gonna know where to get off?

I'll show him, Ponytail offers him a wiener and a roasting stick.

Mom told him, you say thank you when people give you things. You're surely welcome, young man. Ponytail's teeth show. He slides the wiener over the point of the stick and holds it in the fire.

Speaking of wieners, Mr. Louis gets up, heads to the bushes. Green suit holds his hand to his ear, Is it raining yet?

Mr. Louis's pee pounds down on leaves and dirt. Hey Louis, how big's your wiener; is it ready for roasting?

See that tarp over there (Ponytail's teeth smile) there's plenty a room for both of us. I've got an extra blanket too.

One log left on the fire hisses and splutters, embers around it beginning to fade. Night chill creeps through the heat. Ponytail gives Hunter another drink. He gets it down without coughing; he doesn't feel so cold now. Give us a swig, Mr. Louis says.

Nah, go find your own. Bum.

Hunter makes a pillow out of his sack and lies on the ground. Here, have some a this. Ponytail throws a blanket over him and gets under it himself. The other men stumble around in the brush, snapping branches and cursing rocks and roots. Tomorrow Ponytail will ride with him on the train to Alix, show him where to catch the train to Ponoka. Maybe he'll even get home tomorrow. He'll cut through the bush behind Mr. McDonald's house and take the path to Grannie's cabin. If there's no police he'll go home to Grampa, Auntie Marge and Uncle Jack and maybe Mom and Dad'll be there too, not still in Edmonton.

A train shakes the ground, screeching — creaking metal on metal, rattling wheels, and hissing as it jolts and grinds through the woods, filling the air with dust and soot. Clack-clack, clack-clack. Now the clack-clacks are further away. Now the ground's not shaking. The train's going far away. Into the night.

What happened to Mr. Teddy and the teacher Mr. Quentin? How come Mr. Louis came here and not them?

He wishes he were lying beside Mr. Quentin and not Ponytail. Ponytail's eyes are empty like nobody's there, yet they stick into you like arrows. Asking him is he cozy—saying, Two of us'll be warmer than one.

Think of Wîsahkecâhk and the bear, he tells himself. Stay awake till Ponytail's asleep. He scrunches down in the throw-up smelling jacket, making himself still so Ponytail will think he's asleep. An owl hoots.

He remembers Grannie telling him usually Wîsahkecâhk was afraid of Bear. Then he made some arrows, some really sharp ones, from chokecherry wood, and he wasn't afraid. He saw Bear eating some Saskatoon berries. How come you have such a big white ass? he yelled at Bear. How dare you insult me like that, Bear said and he chased after him. Wîsahkecâhk wasn't afraid. He shot one of his arrows. But it broke. He shot another one, and it broke too. Then he had to run. He ran to a tree but he couldn't climb it fast enough. Bear chased him round and round the tree till they wore a path in the ground. Wîsahkecâhk got tireder and tireder...

Hunter's eyes spring open. He must've fallen asleep. He reaches for his knife on the floor beside his tick but his arm's weighted down; it won't move. Dad...Dad, he calls. His mouth won't open. There's a hand over it.

He's not at home with Dad and Mom and Rose-Berry. He's on some sticks and moss in a grey tangle of bushes far away from anywhere. The hand over his mouth smells of sweat and grease. He jerks his head away from the hand. An arm shoves him down, grinding his elbow into a rock. He wrenches back, banging his head into Ponytail's chin. The chin rams into Hunter's neck; the man's breath snorts onto his skin. Jamming his other fist between his body and the sticks, Hunter forces himself upwards. Another hand's touching him between his legs. He bites hard into grease-smelling hand. The other hand's pulling at his pants. He digs his teeth into the palm till the flesh snaps and he tastes blood. Look, you little bugger, I'll give you five bucks. Hunter gnashes his teeth into a finger. You little fucker. The man rolls onto him. Hunter jabs his elbows into ribs, and curls his legs in. He slashes his head into a jaw, a nose, a lip. I said I'll give you five bucks. That's a lotta money. You kin buy a train ticket. Hunter kicks back, hitting a knee, a shin. The man's legs lock around him. He elbows a thigh, and wriggles against the legs. He twists and punches till he hits the man's crotch and the man rolls off.

Hunter shoves away and thrashes into the bushes. A deadfall hits his shin. He stomps down on it and lurches into a hole. His foot snags in something soft. Someone grabs him. He trips. Hey what's going on? It's Mr. Louis. That man under the tarp's no good.

Whaddya mean? Louis heaves himself up. Hunter yanks away.

Wait a minute, what's goin on? Louis grabs him, stumbling to his feet. He smells like wood smoke and wieners and potatoes gone bad — Hunter's sack with his knife still back there on the ground. Thought you were gonna ride with him.

He's no good.

Did he do something to you?

Earliest day lights up a birch trunk among shadowy spruce branches and a wreckage of underbrush, lights the stubble on Louis's face, his hand holding Hunter's arm, leaving dark patches, where his eyes are, looking at Hunter. You okay?

Louis grabs his other arm, holds him there, looking into Hunter's face.

Yeah.

That cocksucker. Where the hell is he? Louis ties up his boots, and crashes into the brush, pushing leaves and twigs out of his way. Ponytail's hunched over. What the hell you think you're doing, you fuckin pervert. Mr. Louis brings a branch down on Ponytail's back. Ponytail plows into Mr. Louis's stomach. They fall onto Hunter's sack, roll around on the ground. Ponytail gets his arm around Mr. Louis's head. You fuckin leave me alone and get outta here. Mr. Louis kicks the air and chokes. Then hooks his legs on Ponytail's head and flips him over. Ponytail squeals like a kicked dog. You fuckin stabbed me you asshole.

Someone should cut you into five thousand pieces.

Mr. Louis sits on top of Ponytail face down on the ground. Git his stuff.

Hunter can't move. Like a steer Dad showed him. Stepped in a sinkhole. Put its foot in. Got it stuck, Dad said, then he put his other foot down to push his foot out and that foot stuck too. Pretty soon all four feet pulling and pushing. Steer sinking up to his knees, his flanks, his shoulders, his neck. Finally only his nose stuck out. Snorting and puffing. But the mud pressed his ribs in, squeezed out all his breath.

Don't stand there, git his stuff, then we'll scram.

Hunter forces one foot off the ground, then the other foot. Flies buzzed around the slimy nose and dead eyes of the steer. He points to the sack under Louis's knee. Louis kicks it away. Hunter grabs it and Ponytail's cloth bag with the leather handles. The tip of his knife sticks through the sack. It's bloody.

Hey gimme that.

Hunter untangles it from the sack and a mess of crushed apples.

Git that rope hangin off the tarp.

Louis ties Ponytail's hands behind his back, then presses the knife point into his neck.

Now listen to me you fuckin cocksucker, you make one move to follow us and this knife'll slice you into threshing chaff.

———◆———

Away from the camp, Hunter sits beside Louis on the tracks, the cold steel jolting into him as if he were sitting on river ice. Two rails glimmering with first light stretch away on either side. A shudder runs through his back. His hands in his pockets make fists and punch each other through leather and cloth.

The man scoops his hand around inside Ponytail's bag. His face is red under its chopped off beard. Little red lines crisscross his nose. He pulls out a wallet — takes out a two-dollar bill and a five. Black shoes — creased and scuffed, a tin of polish. My size, close enough. A bottle like the one they were drinking out of around the fire. The man's throat goes down and up, down and up.

Have a nip.

Hunter shakes his head.

G'wan, it'll warm ya up.

He lets it burn over his tongue, down his throat, up his nose. His eyes run. His clenched fist grinds into his stomach. He gulps smarting liquid, and gulps again.

Hold on, you'll make yourself sick.

Mr. Louis snatches the bottle, drinks three swallows.

You get sick?

Whaddya mean?

You drink this—you get sick?

Naw, not really. He pulls a photograph in a wood frame from Ponytail's bag—a man with a high domed forehead, no mouth, just a tangle of moustache and beard, pale eyes with tiny hard dots. Dark folds of skin under his eyes. His brows meet and crease the skin above his nose, like he can't understand what he's looking at. Louis turns it over. Father, 1906.

Well sometimes if I drink too much I feel a little tired.

Why would it make me sick then?

Cuz you're just a kid.

So why do you give it to me?

Cuz then we'll be buddies.

PART THREE

Cora & Hunter

CHAPTER 15

Fine, she'll be nice and go with Nettie and Bunk along Prairie Avenue in the tree-rustling wind. Ignoring Bunk's How do you do Four-eyes — I mean Miss Wagoner. Thinking instead of men pulling on ropes and tents across the avenue in the exhibition grounds. Bunk and all the rest of them'll have to smarten up when they do the school pageant. Or will he? Will he ruin it for all of them? Nettie tells him to keep his hands to himself, they've got company, and to quit being mean because Cora's her friend.

Uh, Miss Wagoner, would you mind trading a few answers on that practice test?

My name is Cora.

Could I really call you Four— I mean Cora?

Why would I give you the answers?

Cuz I'm really a nice guy, and what're you going to do with them anyway?

Don't give him anything Cora, he doesn't deserve it. Netty's arm links through hers, Netty pulling her along the sidewalk.

Do you even know what potassium bifluoride is?

Why Miss Cora, I guess I rightly do.

Thick pithy smell of coal smoke wafts from a raised fire-pit in front of the blacksmith shop. The barn of the shop holds a mower and buggy — but no sign of Percy.

Someone clanks and bangs. A horse snorts from its hitching rail. Gerard's horse — the Clydesdale cross he was leading when she was looking for Mrs. Rupert. Above him, horseshoes — huge to tiny — hang from spikes in the heavy beams. From the shadowy walls of chains, rods, hammers, wedges and rasps, Gerard emerges carrying a hot shoe to the anvil.

Whaddayou want here? Gerard glares at Bunk.

Nice place. Bunk wanders around picking up pliers and wrenches, puffing the bellows at Netty, pulling the lever on a saw.

Where's Percy?

Fixing a tractor.

Gerard lifts and turns Arrow's hoof, measures the shoe, takes it back to the anvil.

Pretty good for an Indian, hey one day maybe you'll graduate to an automobile.

Get out of here. Gerard raises his hot tongs.

Netty drags Bunk past the hitching rail to the far side of the shop, leaving Cora standing near a stack of empty barrels and racks of V-shaped iron bars. She's waiting like the horse. For what — gazing at the steel jaws of a vise anchored on the workbench. She'd like to stick Bunk's pinkie in and turn its two-foot lever — that's what. Turn it till he what — what was the point?

Gerard bangs a stud into the shoe — his mouth set, his mop of black hair tumbling over his brow. His hand grips the mallet, his arm a stout iron L. Cora clenches her fist around an imaginary handle. She's stepped into the forbidden place of men and man-muscle.

He holds the shoe in the water tank till it's cool. Mom says she saw a Cree boy with an older man walkin in a field off the Camrose Road.

On the far wall of the shop, Bunk presses his hands into the wall, trapping Netty between them. All Cora can see is her skirt on either side of his legs. She wonders whether Netty even thinks about her plans for Normal school.

When?

Gerard picks up the horse's hoof, pulls it between his knees, taps nails through the shoe into the hoof.

I dunno. Maybe yesterday. Day before.

A block away, a steady chunk-clunk of boxcars and grain hoppers grinds south on the CNR line.

I was thinking...he says, then stops. He lets Arrow stand on the shoe, picks up the foot, checks the nails.

I was thinking...we could go look for him if you like.

Okay...

Can you ride double?

You mean now?

Sure.

———————

He mounts Arrow, then gives her a hand up behind the saddle. She feels his heat inches away through the plaid of his shirt—his smell of hay and balsa wood—horses, metal, coal-smoke—where to put her hands—so she doesn't cross a line...like Elaine's sleepy arms over the centre of the bed, so she has to push them back.

CHAPTER 16

Shrugging his jacket up around his ears, Hunter follows the boots of Mr. Louis clumping from tie to tie on the track. The sky's eye is pushing back its lids pouring out pink-gold. It's as though they're walking inside a rose petal. Rose-Berry. Rose petal. Rose-Berry. What is happening to her at school? When will he get Mom to go and see? The man's boots drag off a tie, clump onto the next one. He trips, falls forward, hand grinding into the rocks, rights himself, carries on. Hunter stops to grab a piece of binder twine snagged in a wolf willow. He picks off the white berries. Their mushy green centres taste pasty and dull, but he eats them anyway.

The rose petal fades to milk. Then bright yellow bars of first sunlight. Long shadows of chokecherry and Saskatoon cross the tracks. The man has walked on without him, maybe forgotten him. Hunter strides long steps to catch up. He holds out the twine, measuring it against the length of his arm, against the memory of Grampa cutting a thong from a beef hide, then cutting it in half, and knotting each half to two holes in a square of hide. Grampa's hand on his shoulder, showing him — hold the stone in its pouch

—make the thong tight between your hands. Lean back, start the swing going behind you. Keep your eye on the target. When the stone comes around, let go one thong.

The twine's flimsier than the thong. How will he make the pouch? The man stumbles again, Bloody boots—don't fit—shitty place to walk anyway—the hell'm I doin here—damn banks, DAMN THE BANKS—DAMN THE FAT CATS. A dark stain on his red plaid looks like a thundercloud or maybe a dog's head. The bag bangs against his leg as he walks along, like he's forgotten his arm that's carrying it.

Use a shorter thong for hunting. Grampa placed Hunter's hand next to his thigh with the stone dangling in its pouch. Swing around back—let go as it comes forward. Stand like a tree, just your low arm moves. Hunter shot his sling at gophers and birds; he'd never killed anything. He wishes he had a rifle. For sure now he could shoot rabbits and gophers. Maybe even duck.

Rose-Berry, rose petal, Rose-Berry. He pulls some from thick clusters on the rose bushes along the tracks. Ahead, a fence runs through the middle of the bushes. No, not a fence. It's the thin railings of a bed. Rusty coils of bedsprings grow out of the next bush. Then a broken-rung chair missing its back sits on some burnt papers next to a sink with two pipes to the air.

Mr. Louis heads off the tracks and drops onto the chair. He plunks his elbows on his knees and hangs his head down toward the ground.

You okay mister?

The man sighs, his hand shakes. Just give me a minute.

Hunter picks up a broken china jug with a horse and carriage on it like the one Grannie has that she got when she cleaned Mr. McDonald's house. Because it had a chip out of it. And now it has a crack in it but she still uses it every day, washing it and drying it and putting it on her shelf.

He kicks through a pile of rusty tin cans and bottles past some cart wheels. Hey, I remember you from the train—it's Mr. Teddy from the train ride, in his diamonds jacket, kneeling in front of a ripped-stuffing chair, looking at a mirror, his face all covered in soap—Welcome to Nuisancetown. He scrapes his cheek with a thin straight knife. Mr. Quentin, the man he liked best from the train, is poking some potatoes on top of a smoking stove with no front. Put a lid on them, Mr. Teddy says, they'll cook faster. Mr. Quentin reaches for a pile of charred pots and broken plates.

Wihtikiw, Grannie said, that's a wild spirit—so horrible you can't look at it—raggedy clothes, hair all hanging down, full of filth. He used to be a man, but he got hungry and ate a person. He turned into an evil spirit. When he yells, your bones turn to ice. You might try to shoot him but you can't. No bullet or axe goes through his skin.

Only ones with a strong spirit, Grannie said, could beat the Wihtikiw. Strong from dreams. They could yell as loud as the Wihtikiw, maybe even louder. They could fly up in the air and wrestle with the Wihtikiw till it knew it had lost, and it fell to the ground. Then everyone would circle it and beat it to death and burn it.

Then he sees Earmuffs that pulled the gun on him at the campfire pointing his shotgun at the flapping door of a cupboard that's lost its back. Earmuffs whirls around, pointing at a rusty machine with wheels of teeth, and arms sticking out like a big kwâskohcisîs. Ponytail could be here too.

James 4, verse 7, a man with tangled red hair waves an open Bible, flapping its pages. Submit yourself to God. Humble yourself in the sight of the Lord and he shall lift you up. Surrender to God.

What am I sposed to do, Mr. Teddy wipes away his soap, lie down and starve?

Earmuffs points his gun at Bible-man.

Submit yourself, sinner—submit to God as your king.

God ordains all; therefore I'm already submittin.

Far from it, my friend, submission means acting and doing, seeking the will of God, not sitting around a campfire.

Shaddup or I'll blow your head off. Earmuffs trains his gun on Bible-man.

Hey Mack, don't add murder to your problems, Mr. Quentin turns over small, blackened potatoes with a rusty fork. Mr. Teddy ducks behind his torn-up chair.

I didn't mean any harm, Bible-man drops his book on the chair. Then shaddup.

Earmuffs lowers his gun and points it at a sow thistle growing out of a buggy sinking into the ground.

Something clumps and Hunter turns to see Mr. Louis slump off the chair onto the ground. His eyes are closed and his knees are bent as though they're still shaped around the chair.

Hey Mister, you okay?

The man doesn't answer. His arm shakes.

You could get warm by the stove.

The man groans, he can't get up. Hunter touches the grubby plaid of his coat. Mr. Louis doesn't want Hunter to touch him. He's hot, then cold, he says. I'm afraid for you, Hunter says. The man opens his eyes, and smiles, Can't let my buddy down. His breath is sour potatoes.

Mr. Teddy runs from his chair to the cupboard, sneaking up on Earmuffs who is pointing his gun at the rusty machine. He swings the shotgun up and down the tracks, then back at the machine. Mr. Teddy slides behind a bed-end and the claws of a hay rake. I know you're there, Earmuffs whirls and fixes on the bed-end. From the hay-rake, Mr. Teddy dashes through some rusted tins, and grabs at Earmuffs' knees. He sprawls forward, then rolls and kicks Mr. Teddy in the face. He reaches for the gun. No you don't. Bible-man wanders around with his Bible, staying away from the fight. Mr. Teddy's nose is bleeding, he pushes Earmuffs to the ground and Mr. Quentin pins his legs. Earmuffs kicks, I'll shoot your balls off, ya bastards. Mr. Teddy chucks the gun onto the tracks. You're in no fit state to have this, Mack. Earmuffs lands a boot in Mr. Quentin's leg. Mr. Teddy grabs his arms. Hey St. Paul, give us a hand eh?

Bible-man breaks the shotgun. It's empty of shells. He lays it between a wash-boiler and the stove. The other two men pin Earmuffs to the ground, while he spits in their faces. They roll him over with his arms stretched over his head, one man on his back, the other on his legs. I'll shmt yr bwmlls off, he says to the dirt.

You promise you won't bother anyone, we'll let you go.

I'll shmt yr bwmlls off.

Okay I guess we'll stay here for a while.

I'll shmt yr bwmlls off.

Earmuffs kicks his heels up and bucks the men pinning his arms and butt. Bible-man pokes at the potatoes burning on the stove.

What're we sposed to do, take turns holdin'im down.

Let'im go. There's nothin in the gun.

What if he gets sumthin?

We'll take it away from him?

What if he get's another gun or somethin worse?

How's he going to do that — anyway we'll be long gone.

Hunter turns back to the man beside him. His nose is red. He snores in, then lets his breath out in puffs of steam, filling the air with rotten apples.

Mister, I'm going to go find the train.

The man grunts, What?

The train to Ponoka, remember.

Wait. Louis sits up, clamps his hands to his temples. Wait. He pushes his hands into the sides of his head, then closes his hands over his face. Oh boy. His fingers pull at his cheeks, rub his eyes, he blinks quickly.

I can find it. I'll just walk down this track like you said till I get to the crossroad, then go on the other track. Hunter stuffs the binder twine into his sack-blanket and slings it over his shoulder, his knife dragging it down behind him almost to the ground.

Hold on, Buddy, I'll go with you, show you the ropes. You're gonna need help figuring the trains at Alix. It's not that easy.

Hunter walks down the track, burying his hands in his jacket. The man stumbles to his feet and clumps after him on the ties, then puts an arm around his back, like Dad did one time in the big teepee where a lot of people were dancing. Your turn, Dad said, to give to the Bony Spirit. Go to the centre where the other boys are dancing. Tie your cloth under the face of the Bony Spirit. Give away things, Dad told him, then things will come to you. If you keep things to yourself nothing will come to you, you'll shrivel into bones.

The man paces his steps along the outside of the rails to keep even with Hunter's steps on the inside. You're my buddy, gotta look after my buddy. The man leans into him across the rail, then his foot jams between the rail and his other leg. His weight slumps onto Hunter like a sack of flour and they careen off the tracks toward the men at the stove.

A thin layer of warmth comes to Hunter's face and the fronts of his legs. Walk with the Lord, He will dry your tears, Bible-man mutters, Suffer for the Lord, Take up the cross, Let the Lord crown you with His own hand. Hunter's eyes feel heavy, his stomach gnaws. Four small potatoes smoulder in front of him. No one says anything. Earmuffs lies face down on the ground, no longer bucking the men on his back. The butt of his gun touches Hunter's shoe where he stands behind the stove. He sits on an overturned pail almost breaking through the bottom, and places his sack near the shotgun butt. Louis sways toward the stove then jolts back. He lurches out into the nuisance ground and drags back a small trunk, shedding a rat from its missing corner, then collapses onto it next to Hunter.

This here's my buddy.

Hunter hunches over his knees toward the stove. Bible-man can't see his hand on the gun.

You want, a medal for havin an Indian kid as a buddy?

He winkles the gun out from between the stove and washtub

toward his sack, knocking over some deadwood sticks. He puts his hands back in his pockets, sits up.

The men let Earmuffs go. He stomps around opening a suitcase, dumping a pair of trousers, then overturning a bathtub, with its tattered quilt. Where'd you hide it you bastards. He picks up Bible-man's book, and hurls it at the cupboard.

Just in time for breakfast, eh. The other men look at each other, then at the ground, then at the potatoes. You guys a gotta find your own grub, Mr. Teddy says, Don't mind you soakin up some fire, but that grub was hard to come by and not enough for a fly let alone two more a you.

Hunter inches the gun part way into the sack.

No problem — me'n my buddy — we'll be fine.

Gimme my shotgun, Earmuffs stomps over to the stove.

You sit down and show us you're sane enough to have it back.

Mr. Teddy hands out spuds. Even Earmuffs huddles in around the stove to eat. He downs his potato in two bites.

You're the one that cut up Emery, ain'tcha? Earmuffs stands up.

Dunno what you're talking about, Louis mutters.

Yeah you do. Up the rails, last night. Yeah boys, this's the guy that beat up Emery 'n stabbed him so he almost bled to death.

Who's Emery, Mr. Quentin asks.

You stay outa this, you weren't even there.

Cling to the Lord; obey His will.

This Indian kid shows up in the middle a the night, half frozen. We let him sit at our fire. Emery gives him a jacket and some whiskey. This kid woulda died a cold if he hadn't.

Hunter nudges the sack with the gun around behind him, keeps Mr. Louis between him and the other men.

What'd Emery do to him, why don'tcha tell them that? Louis stands up facing Earmuffs.

What'd Emery do — he gave'm a place to sleep under his tarp, gave him blankets. Steada thanking him, the kid kicks'm in the face'n steals his bag.

Is this the whole truth and nothing but? Mr. Quentin throws a broken table-leg into the fire.

Not only that, he gets whiskey-head here to punch'm up, and stab him.

Hunter backs away from the men, holding the sack behind him, sliding his foot onto a tire, then another tire, then onto a chair seat, heading for the rusty machine, and beyond that some aspens and cottonwoods. He shimmies onto some bottomless boots, and steps to the spokes of a wagon wheel. The wheel shifts, cracking and clinking on bottles. Mr. Louis looks over his shoulder.

Hey wait up buddy, I'm comin' with ya.

Hunter turns, wades through rusted-out stove pipes and darts behind the hay-rake.

He's takin off again.

So what — let him go. Quentin holds his hands over the stove.

He's gotta sack. What's he got in there?

Earmuffs runs around the stove pushing past Quentin and Teddy. My shotgun — where is it — that Indian crook or his friend's got it.

Louis grabs the carpet bag, kicks away the trunk, and follows Hunter over the tires and boots.

Where're ya going. That's Emery's bag, gimme that.

He grabs the bag. Gimme back my shotgun, ya bastard.

Earmuffs turns the bag upside down, spilling out the shoes and polish.

Emery's shoes, gimme those.

Hunter backs away, rolls on some bottles.

Get the kid, you idiots, he's behind the hay-rake.

Teddy pulls out his comb and broken piece of mirror. Quentin opens a book and pulls in to the stove. Hunter keeps a couch between him and Earmuffs.

Wait up buddy. Mr. Louis staggers after him. Hunter veers away into a gulch of rusty tins, rolling and pitching till he reaches some tires. In front of him the track clacks and mutters of a coming train. A bottle flies past his head. He zigzags toward the track. The round nose and spewing stack of the train grinds toward him, grunting and puffing through the trash dump. Between him and the track, a fence of bedsprings lurches up. A bottle hits his ear. He swerves. Another bottle hits the bedframe. The train is a couple of boxcars away, clouding the sun with soot and steam. Hunter leaps past the bedsprings and across the tracks.

CHAPTER 17

Cora leans against the anchoring tree of her rowboat, tearing bulrush leaves into bits, and scattering them in the muddy water. The sun slides down over the horizon but the sky flames against its gathering gloom. Sin is a great dark power, Pastor Crawford said, Sin means doom and eternal wrath, blacker and wilder than the fiercest tornado. The sky is the colour of sin and hell, but she isn't going to heaven anyway, since she isn't baptized. What if she got baptized but didn't really believe in it? Wouldn't that be a sin? What if she ran away like the Cree boy? Would she drift through vacant lots? Live like the dole-office men in nuisance grounds or like tangled-hair women in the shacktown lean-tos that had rags for windows and doors. Or could she run away like Dad did? Just her against the world. Her own adventure.

Some leaves fall into her lap. She looks up to a dark shape caught in the branches. Gus maybe — fooling with her. But it's not Gus. The flapping heel of a battered shoe hangs from a branch — a bare ankle, torn dungarees. She walks around the tree till she can see his face. It's the Cree boy they found at the elevator — staring down at her from a crotch about ten feet up.

Go away. He stubs his foot again and again on the trunk of the tree.

She sits back down in the rowboat. What would Hilda do? For sure Dad'd never hide someone from the police. Where're you going to sleep tonight?

Stay here in the woods.

Then what?

Hop a train.

Where?

That way.

She looks up but can't see in the shadows. Some runaways make it home, Mrs. Rupert said, then the agent and the police send them back to the school. Some runaways never are found again — their parents never know what happened to them. Maybe they got mixed up with some tramps on the road, maybe they died in the cold.

Cora thinks of Aunt Beulah's programs for children's food and health, and the new courses of study she started, sponsored by the Red Cross, at the University of Toronto. If Cora could get to university, she could start programs like Aunt did to help kids like Hunter and stop so much sickness in their schools.

———————

In the attic, she moves a dressmaker's skeleton into a corner beside Dad's old trunk marked Change Islands, Newfoundland. She puts some cookies and canned meat for the boy in the trunk, beside an oilskin coat and a framed photograph of Dad and his sister Ida — in high-necked blouse with puffed sleeves — sitting in front of a painted birch tree and painted lake between velvet curtains.

When Cora was ten, Aunt Ida knitted her way from Newfoundland to Stettler.

All us kids knitted. That's what you did in winter when the wind's blowin the sea topsy turvy. It's easy. She held the skein of wool, over two hands, made them wind it into a ball. Showed them how to cast on. Hold the wool over your finger. Hook it round the needle, pull it through. Like this. Purl stitches. Drop stitches. Slip stitches. How to make ribbing.

Boys knitted too?

Sure they did — had to. Was th'only way we'd of had enough woolies.

Dad knitted!

He was the fastest, he could knit a scarf in two hours.

Dad, Aunt Ida says you can knit things?

Ida, don't meddle. Dad sat in his leather chair reading the gold-edged pages of his Bible.

I'm going to try it. Dougie grabbed a needle and wrapped some yarn around it.

Put that knittin needle down and git outside.

You stay here Dougie, I'm gonna tell you a story about your dad, I bet he's never told you.

Ida, mind yr own business. In the dim light from the single bulb, he squinted and scowled at the page, moving his lips with the words.

Yr dad was ten and I was eight when the diphtheria came. Winter of 1890. Big sisters Betsy and Eliza got it, then big brothers George and Lester, and finally yr dad. They all had the same bed, yr dad and his brothers. Mother and Father moved some beds by the fire in the front room. Eliza got the sofa. The rest of us younger ones got the bed in the girls' room. They left yr dad in the other back room. He was white like a wax candle, his face puffed up like a mushroom. His mouth bleeding. Every night I asked God to save him. I promised God I'd knit his socks and scarves. Don't you go near 'm, Mother said. They gave him up for dead. Stayed out of his room. It smelled terrible, like rotten meat. They tried to feed spoonfuls of broth to Lester and George. Black stuff oozed out of Eliza's nose. Big purple spots on her face and hands. I went into the kitchen and got a little cup a broth for yr dad and snuck into his room. Mother caught me and gave me a hiding. Next day Eliza died. They put her in a coffin out on the front porch. The doctor scraped black outa Betsy's mouth but she died too. You could hear George and Lester all over the house, rasping like saws. The doctor gave them needles. I kept thinkin of Eliza and Betsy freezing inside their wooden boxes on the porch. Were they still inside there, or had they gone to heaven? George died, then Lester died. Four coffins on the front porch. Only yr dad was left. I didn't want him to go to heaven. I wanted him to stay right here and be my best friend. And God answered my prayers.

Didn't he, Hodge, she looked over at her brother.

Guess so, he mumbled, not looking up.

Aunt Ida?

What dear?

Didn't you pray for Lester and George and Eliza and Betsy?

Course I did, oh yes, I prayed for them too.

Beside her pile of books, Cora lays out horse blankets for the boy. One day she'll work in a laboratory like Madame Curie and find out how to cure diseases like diphtheria.

On her plank table, she cuts a raw potato in half, pushes a penny into one half and a galvanized nail into the other, connects the penny and the nail with wire, and then wraps the wires around the stem of a flashlight bulb. She pulls the cord to the overhead light — leaving a tiny glow from her experiment.

———————

Mom, sewing sewing sewing a patch on Dougie's trousers, folds the edges under as she hems. A stitch in time saves…Each of her stitches worth nine…the patch worth five hundred then. Till the patch wears out. Clothes patched and repatched till they're so tattered you can see through them, their weave loosened to frayed threads and wispy fibres, rags finally shredded, sent to the compost heap, rotted away to molecules of sugar, and even the sugar breaking the links in its chains, setting free atoms of carbon, oxygen and hydrogen.

Dad's got his reading glasses off, looking around wondering what that noise is. What noise, Mom's threading a long strand into a needle. Dad convinced something's rattling in the attic. Mom thinks it's the wind. He folds up the newspaper and peers out the darkened window. Is 12 times 13 a hundred and fifty-six, Gus doodles his pencil around in his scribbler. Shush, there it goes again.

Maybe it's a ghost.

Quiet I said.

Cora puts a jacket on.

Where're you going?

Checking outside for ghosts.

You stay here; it might be a prowler with a rifle.

I'm just going up to my attic.

Since when was it yours?

It's my laboratory.

Laboratory—don't give me that foll-de-roll. It's my attic, and I'm going up there to see if there's a prowler.

No. I don't want you up there.

He pulls out a drawer in the sideboard, retrieves the flashlight, and turns the switch. What the…He wants to know who's been fooling with it, why there's no bulb. Mom with the needle halfway through the sock, sure there's another one in the drawer. Well someone'd better find it quick. He dashes out the front door. Cora runs out the back arriving at the ladder first.

I told you to stay inside.

She blocks his way on the ladder.

I've got experiments laid out.

I'm gonna padlock that door.

There's no need for any padlock.

Out of my way.

No. I'm going up to check. She opens the door, crawls in and bangs it shut, latching it. The little filament attached to her potato battery glows in a tiny orange line. She pulls the light cord. Hunter's nowhere to be seen. Dad rattles the door and tells her to open up.

There's no one up here.

Then let me in.

She opens the latch and sits on the trunk. He clambers in, tromping over the blankets and coats on the floor—the scratched leather one of the boy. The armless shadow of the dressmaker's skeleton looms up the wall under the peaked roof. Her father rummages through her rock samples and library books, wanting to know what all this coal's doing up here, she could burn the house down. Fossils in coal—stuff and nonsense. He gathers up the coal and throws her fossils down in the yard. From her plank workbench, he snatches up the potato and pulls the flashlight bulb out of its wires. Goes on and on about how dangerous it is to leave them without a flashlight. How thoughtless and selfish she is. What if the power went out and they had to get around in the dark. He doesn't want any rotting food up here either, and the whole attic better be cleaned up by suppertime tomorrow.

Okay, I'll clean it up.

Fine. Now get back downstairs.

No. I'm staying up here and cleaning it up.

I don't want any more noise.

Okay no noise, I'll stay up here and study.

———— • ————

At last the door slams and the man's footsteps clump down the ladder. Hunter climbs down from the rafters, and shivers in the unheated room. His foot's numb.

He's so mean, wrecking everything, Cora whispers. He doesn't care one bit how good my marks are. Or what I do after high school.

Her boy-hair head's on her arms on top of her knees. Hunter

wonders how she made the light glow in the dark just using a potato. How did she figure out how to do that? But she probably doesn't want to talk to him now. She says she's going to show her father a thing or two, and that she's not doing that baptism on Sunday. But why would she have to baptize a baby, she can't be a priest.

He sits on the blankets, pulling out another piece of meat from the jar she gave him, and showing her the barrel of the shotgun, when she asks about his sack. Some men threw it away, he says.

Does it work?

I guess so.

Then she wants to know what if she got a horse and they rode back to his reserve?

He chews the last chunk of meat slowly, licking his fingers when it's gone. What horse?

I have a friend; he's got a big Clydesdale cross.

On the floor a book cover has pictures of teepees, a pipe and a moccasin—a drum with a buffalo on it, a man wearing a feather on his head—he's beating a drum but not a drum like the men held in their hands in the big teepee, more like a drum he saw worn around the waist by white men in a parade. A boy dressed in a white underwear suit, runs and punches his fists. His face is very red and his crazy long black hair streams out behind him. *Two Little Savages,* the book says.

When?

Tomorrow.

Opening another book, Hunter finds pictures of huge hairy animals with long noses dragging on the ground and curly horns coming out of their mouths. Inside another he finds jars and bottles holding liquid or powder, some of them bubbling up through narrow tops, some of them connected by pipes and wires, others cooking on flames that look like lamps without their chimneys.

Cora wants to know if he knows about Buffalo Lake, because

they'll have to go around it to get to the reserve. Hunter tells her what Grampa said: a long time ago there were lots of buffalo, but they drowned themselves when the white men came.

Drowned themselves?

She looks at him like Father Lafarge, like he's so stupid he'll never say anything right.

Grampa said the buffalo drowned themselves in the earth too, but he doesn't tell her that. Maybe they lived around the lake, he says.

I think they did, she says. She seems to know. But how would she know? How would she know where his reserve is? She tells him to take the blankets with him in the morning and go to the rowboat in the trees. She'll bring food and shells for the shotgun.

———◆———

Netty wants to know if Cora's wearing blush.

Of course not, why would I do that?

Mr. Black'll send you home in those dungarees and baggy old coat.

It's my costume for the pageant.

Whatcha got in your satchel?

My lunch.

Not going home.

Nope.

Hilda and Netty keep staring at her, saying she's up to something, her eyes look mischiev-i-ous (its mischivus, not mischeev-ee-us) and they're going to stick to her until she tells.

She searches for Gerard in the crowd of boys near the goal posts. Now they're accusing her of going on a picnic with Gerard.

Definitely not.

The boys' backs make a solid wall of cropped heads on jackets and trousers. Hands in pockets or holding a scribbler. All looking at the ground. They let out a whoop, as something hawk-like

—whizzing and buzzing—swoops up, then dives straight down a few yards away.

Cora skirts around the backs of Bunk and Gordie Wellman, and Izzie and Elmer Bond. Gus and Dougie are there too. In the centre, Gerard kneels on the ground turning the propeller of a model plane. It splutters to life, and tries to leap out of his hand. He launches it in the air, and it zooms up dipping and diving around, then into the crowd. The boys duck and scatter like a flock of crows.

The bell rings. You haven't seen me, she says to Netty and Hilda. Remember, you haven't seen me. She pushes them toward the school.

We'll be late for the Chem test. Gerard picks up the nose-dived plane.

I found the Cree boy again.

One blade of the propeller is bent toward the body of the plane. He tries to force it back.

You coming? He starts toward the school.

I need to ask a favour.

He holds up the plane and squints at the propeller.

That boy—he wants to get home to his Mom and Dad.

Gerard dusts off the wings of the plane with his handkerchief.

I don't think we should fight the Indian way, Dumont. He shows her what he's painted on the plane: Riel's flag.

I told him I'd try to get a horse and take him back to his reserve.

Where?

Past Buffalo Lake near Ponoka.

For a moment they're distracted by Judge Rupert's green and black Studebaker traveling along Hill Avenue towards Original Road. He's coming back from a farm near Botha, Gerard explains, they're shooting old horses and he's buying the meat.

You eat horses.

Not for us, for the foxes.

Oh.

She thought of the Maynards' team, Jock and Joe, with huge

red holes in their sides, no they shoot them in the head. They cut off their legs, chop their flanks and ribs and backbones into square pieces. They put their big round hooves into a pot and melt them down into glue.

What horse?

Could you...

You mean Arrow?

Could you...

Dad would have a fit...

What if I rode him?

He sits on the school gate, slowly shuffling it closed.

It'd take at least three days.

I think I can do it in two.

He unlatches the gate, swings it shut again.

What about at night?

We'll build a fire. I've got blankets.

He's not going to go fast with two of you.

She takes the back way to the barn while he sneaks into the house. The path leads through two rows of cages with walls high as her head, each one containing a wooden hutch and two or three foxes. Miniature cages for food and water are wired to the outside of the bigger cages. The foxes are white and grey. Or grey and sand. Their ears are large and pointed, their snouts narrow, their tails almost as thick as their bodies. They curl on the ground nose to paws. Or press their noses against the wire, their yellow eyes looking through her with scorn and disdain as though they see something she'll never see on the far side of her meaningless body.

Gerard gives her a road map from the glove compartment of the Studebaker and a compass he found in Judge Rupert's museum. Arrow snorts and nuzzles his nose into the saddlebag full of oats.

What if something happens—what're you going to do?

We'll go to a farm, get help.

Gerard strokes Arrow's nose. Combs his mane, adds a rub-down cloth and an apple to the saddlebag.

Cora's stomach bolts like when Dad was going to wallop her. Gerard doesn't have anyone like Netty or Hilda. She's taking away his best friend. And she doesn't even know if she can do this ride, but she must do it, cuz she said she would.

I'll take really good care of him, she promises, the best best care.

When you get back, maybe we could study Chem together, maybe go riding.

He looks her full in the face so she can't look away, and it isn't that horrible way Bunk looks at Netty.

Hey, I could even show you some drawing tricks.

———————

Hunter walks along the ditch of the road, away from town toward the lake, the wind so strong in his ears he can't hear his own footsteps. He crosses some tracks near the elevator he'd slept in. No one's working in the flat fields stretching away all around and beyond the lake. No cattle grazing. Nothing growing even, except brown stalks. No one's driving on the road that runs away in a straight line between the fields.

With blankets and his sack, he heads into the ditch on the road along the lake. The jacket's too hot in the full sun but it's easier to wear it than carry it. He makes his way through dusty weeds, his head level with the gravel on the road, till he hears someone shouting hey kid, hey. Too late to duck down. He climbs back onto the road edge. A man in his white-man, important-man hat sits in his car going toward town. Shiny car. Black on top, green on bottom. The man asks why he isn't in school. I'm going to school tomorrow he says. Today I'm doing something for my Dad. What school the man says. Indian school, he tells him. On the front of the man's car stands a little silver man holding out silver wings. Don't let me catch you again, he says, and drives away in his green and black car carrying a wheel on its side.

CHAPTER 18

The man in the car had a hat like that whiteman Mr. Mcdonald that Dad asked for a paper to go to Edmonton. Where'd
you get the money, the whiteman said. Getting a ride with friends,
Dad said. You should be working, the whiteman said. My brother's
dying, Dad said. Standing funny, all bowed down like a curled leaf.
Holding his black Stetson in his hands in front of the whiteman's
table. Maybe the man in the car wanted him to have a paper, like
Dad. You get back to work soon as you've seen him. Thank you
very much, Dad said. Dad shook the man's hand when he got the
paper. Thank you, yes, thank you. Why did Dad and Uncle Arthur
say thank you so much?

Hunter covers the sack and the blankets with dead branches
and leaves in the trees around the old rowboat. Sits in the rowboat. Raises its broken oars out of the mud.

Watch my hand Grampa said when they played the hand game,
don't talk, just watch. He moved his hands around the table
passing the shell back and forth, then held his fists behind his
back.

How can I watch if they're behind your back?

Watch my face. Watch my arms. Watch my shoulder. Watch every move. Don't talk. Watch. Then you see what to do.

Ducks swoop up from the bulrushes. Something spooked them. Hunter climbs the aspen growing out of the boat, pulls his feet up on a branch, wedges himself against the trunk. Sun's already high in the sky. Hunter's stomach growls. Woods here too small to catch anything. The girl with her boy-hair must have forgot him, just went to school, forgot about the horse. He should just take the blankets, head for the tracks when day's gone and town people go into their houses.

A crow lands in the next tree, steps sideways on his branch. Opens his beak. Crow-tongue tasting mouthfuls of wind. In Grannie's story Crow cawed at Wîsahkecâhk and his fire. Old days, crows were white. I gotta go take care of some things, Wîsahkecâhk told Crow, You watch this fire, Wait till the fire's just coals, then roast the meat. What things could Wîsahkecâhk have to do anyway, besides roast his own meat? Grannie just smiled, said he was busy. Crow watched the fire. Got hot and sleepy. Closed his eyes. Suddenly wind shook his branch. He woke up, the fire was out. Crow beat his wings. Ashes flew up and landed all over Crow's feathers. But the fire was out; he couldn't roast the meat. Wîsahkecâhk said, Crow, from now on you'll be all black, and the other birds will hate you.

◆

Call me Cora she says, but he thinks of her as boy-girl. She's even wearing pants like a boy. Why do girls wear skirts anyway? Maybe it's cuz they don't have a willy and they have to squat to pee. But then when they wear pants are they still girls or are they something else, something only half girl like the Wihtikiw is only half people? He shudders thinking what if boys then wore skirts—legs inside a circle of cloth, can't run fast—Fish-eyes screaming at him, Just like a silly girl, SSSSISSSSY, when he helped Grannie make bannock.

Cora gives him a cheese sandwich and a cookie. Then ties his sack and her satchel of bread and food to the saddle horn, and puts the blankets behind the saddle for him to ride on. Like Dad did on Kîyasiw when they went to a farm where a machine made bundles of wheat. They went along in a field piling bundles into stooks, till Hunter got too tired and Dad sent him back to the stream where Kîyasiw was tied. Hunter drank water, then untied the horse and climbed on saying Giddup like Dad did but Kîyasiw kept munching till Hunter pulled the reins, and dug in his heels. His feet didn't reach the stirrups. The horse walked into the field and neighed. Maybe he was calling for other horses, or maybe for Dad as he trotted down the field and Hunter bounced along. He pulled on the reins but the horse had his own ideas and Hunter was not part of these; he was just a little bump holding onto the horse's back. Next thing he knew he was looking at the sky, and Dad was saying, You don't even know how to ride. Laughing, You better get back on. Dad made Hunter ride around him in a circle learning to trot and canter. Then the whiteman got mad at Dad for fooling around when he was s'posed to be stooking.

But in school when he wrote out lines — every letter perfect — no ink blots — the nun still said what did you do it like that for?! and wouldn't give him his letter. How did you know what were the right words, the right way to say the words? Watch, Grampa said, but no matter how hard he watched, no matter what words he said, he knew he could never be like the white of the whiteman.

Cora gets into the saddle, then tells him to stand on the old boat, put his foot in the empty stirrup and climb up. Where to put his hands. Not to touch. Not to touch whiteness. A girl from white people who isn't even a girl, in her pants and boy-hair. She grabs his arm anyway and he gets his leg over the horse's rump. No stirrups for his feet dangling over the saddlebags. His face close to her back. It smells of soap and clean, like clothes Mom just brought in from the clothesline. He grabs the saddle skirt.

She shows him a piece of paper with lots of lines making boxes all over it, and a blue patch, Buffalo Lake, where there's no lines — the head and legs of a buffalo with a creek running out its tail. They ride the horse out of the woods into some fields, keeping away from grain elevators and railcars. Already little smokes of the town are swallowed in wide stretches of dirt and dead grass. Under the big bowl of sky, a train line runs away into the land until the land pushes its two shiny rails together.

That's the Canadian Northern line, she tells him, We still have to cross the Canadian Pacific. But he doesn't care. He wants to hold the reins, tell the horse to go fast and swing along in the saddle — fly over the fields like the crows.

———

The boy's almost not there behind her, except for a hint of warmth that wouldn't be there if she were alone. What's he holding onto? The blanket or the saddle skirt or maybe nothing at all. Maybe he's planning on running away even from her. She talks into his silence. She's got to show him she can do it, she's got a plan. We'll stay away from the Red Deer road, stay on the edge of town.

She doesn't know how much he understands or even cares. We'll go past the Nuisance Ground, she says (maybe he doesn't even know what this is), then take section roads and fields.

The Nuisance Ground's where people throw things away. See those heaps of bottles and that smashed buggy and the bedsprings. The boy taps her shoulder, Miss, Miss.

You can call me Cora — it's okay.

Maybe he has a Cree name, maybe he can even give her one, and she'll be different, not just a girl, she'll know something secret, she'll become someone town people don't even know. Do you have a Cree name, she calls over her shoulder.

What kind of name?

A name in your language — like... like... (she thinks of the drum-beat poem from school) Hiawatha.

Who was that?

A famous Indian I read about in school, but he was Mohawk or maybe Algonquin.

Never heard of him.

He wants her to steer Arrow away from the Nuisance Ground. Bad men live there. Crazy men.

Did you go here when you left the farm?

A clattering of tins makes the horse jolt. She clings to the horn and struggles to stay on the animal's bumping shoulders and haunches. The boy, thrown into her, grabs her waist then quickly lets go. A man with hair flying out around his head stands up behind the bathtub—his beard full of straw. The man's face is grey like a patch of dirty snow. His red eyes stare right past them. She turns the horse away from the dump.

That man Louis—he's okay, the boy tells her, just makes himself sick when he drinks.

Did you make friends with him?

Yeah, I guess so.

She steers the horse across the tracks, then the Camrose road.

That goes to Camrose, she tells his shifting silence behind her. We don't want to go there. We want to go to Buffalo Lake over there. (Her words seem to echo emptily). That's where we're going tonight. She points over a few brown and white steers standing in dust and pulling at clumps of dry hard grass. Yellow grass and dust that goes on till it reaches bits of greeny-black at the edge of sky. The steers are thin and covered with flies. Where are the wheat fields that used to be here, and the men tossing bales into the threshers?

They come to a narrow road that runs straight away on either side till the land pinches it to nothing. The town behind them's disappeared into dried fields and bunches of yellow trees.

A dot of red moves toward them.

A dot of red on a horse. Behind it a cloud of dust.

Men in red coats came on horses. From his spruce-tree look-out, he watched them go up to the house. Big flat hats on their heads. Later he found hoof marks and horse biscuits all around the front door. Red men that took Dad away.

They came to the assembly room at the school. Red-coated men with flat hats. If you run away, we'll find you, they said, we'll bring you back. You'll be punished by your school. Like the one they chained to his bed.

She turns the horse away from the red dot onto a narrow road. It's faster on the road and it'll be easier for Arrow.

Hunter looks behind. Now the red dot's hidden in their own cloud of dust.

He'll see our dust.

They head into another field toward a clump of brown trees. He swelters in the smelly jacket, legs sore and stiff splayed over the saddlebags. The trees get further away as they go toward them.

They find a small pond, and she lets the horse drink. I must drink too. She lets him get down. His legs, numb, throw him sideways. Down on his knees, with Arrow beside him sucking mouthfuls in easy-moving lips, he cups hands in the water. They don't have that long curved piece of wood carved to a ball at one end, scooped-out cup at the other that Grampa showed him — warriors carried these for drinking, they reached down from their horses, filled the cup from the stream, just kept on gallop-ing. He brings his cupped hands to his face, then stumbles toward the trees.

Where're you going?

Just quickly.

Oh.

He watches a beetle scurrying away from his river of pee, then starts another small lake to corral it.

None of your savagery, the father said, that first day at school when he went looking for a backhouse. Here we have running water and toilets. He pushed Hunter toward a white bowl.

It was good to pee again on the leaves, when he wanted, not just when the father said. Cora will have to pee too, out here with no toilets or toilet paper. But Cora has no willy to chase beetles with, she'll have to pull down her pants and squat. Sometimes there aren't many trees either and she might not like it if he sees her, but from the back girls are the same as boys; it's in front that they're different.

Back on Arrow, they follow an almost dried up stream making a snake path through some willows. On the left side the sky looks brighter at the edge, right side darker blue, the sun ahead of them starting down the side of the skybowl. On the far edge of the field, a black dot passes from one edge of sky to another— the dust behind it swirling into a squirrel-tail of bigger and bigger puffs. The dot stops, swallowed up in its tail. It turns a corner, sweeps along the next side of the box shooting its puffy tail up to clouds in the sky.

Squirrel-tail melts away. Nothing moves except them and the trickle of water.

It runs under a fence. Squares of wire on grey posts that look like the map she showed him—a fence of boxes all around a blue animal called Buffalo Lake. Boxes even running over the blue squiggly lines running into the lake. The blue lines didn't matter —only the black lines. She turns the horse to the darker sky. They reach a road, same as the other roads—straight till the ground pinches it to nothing—same dust, same pebbles, same pair of smoother tracks running through rougher bigger rocks spilled into weeds at the edges. A layer of rocks and dirt smeared over the prairie. She turns the horse along the road back toward the sun.

Maybe these roads would've helped Grannie when she followed the cow. Her father told her to follow the cow if she went into the willow bush. Make sure to catch her when she has her calf. Grannie was a girl then, like Rose-Berry. She even had the same name. She was coming back from school and saw that cow walking into the willow bush. Lots of milk. Grannie ran home, got her sister. She had only bare feet, nothing to eat that day. They followed the cow into the willow bush and found her with a calf sucking. Grannie tied up the calf with her belt, and milked the cow, squirting milk in her sister's mouth.

Cora stops the horse where dust and rocks and wheel tracks of their road cross the dust and rocks and wheel tracks of another road. If it was Rose-Berry in front of him on the horse, he'd know just how to be, but she's not Rose-Berry. He wonders how the plants got into the rock she showed him, that a scientist gave her. What was a scientist anyway?

Four empty roads stretch away. Four corners of four boxes. I wonder whether this is this road. She points to a line on the fence-map. We could be here. Her finger rests on one box which has longer sides than ends. Or here. A box with sides the same all around. Buffalo Lake should be over there. She turns the horse to the darker sky. And he knows this is right. This is the way home.

Grannie pulled the calf behind and whipped the cow to make her move along. She chased the cow into a creek when she wouldn't cross. She pushed the cow; it just stood in the creek. Grannie tied the calf to a tree, and went to find her father. They came to a grassy place where he'd cut willow and piled it. We're almost home, she told her sister. This is where Nohtâwiy made a meadow. They walked on. It started to rain. They crawled under some willows. Their clothes were torn. Her sister's feet were swollen and cut. It became dark, and Grannie put her arms around her sister to keep her warm—she was only six. They stayed under the willows all night. Grannie was freezing but she put her sweater around her sister.

Next morning Grannie tore off part of her dress and wrapped her sister's feet. They went on toward home, yelling and calling. They walked all day. Nothing to eat. Her sister wore away the cloths around her feet. Grannie tore out the rest of her skirt, and wrapped them up again. She wore out all these cloths too.

Night-time they crawled under a spruce tree. Her sister cried so much no sound came out. She couldn't walk. She was all scratched, and Grannie held her in her arms in her sweater.

Next morning Grannie heard an owl hooting. She carried her sister on her back. She had shoes so her feet were okay. Her sister was heavy, and she was very tired. The owl flew off and landed on a faraway tree. It beat its wings, Grannie said, like it was going to catch a mouse in the grass and carry it off in its claws. It circled around and flew on. Grannie wanted to follow the owl, but her sister said it would attack them. Grannie followed it anyway to three different trees. They heard someone yelling. All that came out when Grannie answered was a croak like a toad. Someone yelled again, and she saw him. He fired three shots in the air. If we had just stayed with the cow, Grannie said, they would have found us on the first day.

They come to another road going toward and away from the sun. No owls out here.

A cloud of dust comes toward them on the road. They cross it, quickly trotting into the opposite field, his seat bouncing on the horse's haunches. He pinches his legs together on the saddlebags trying to raise himself off the blankets. A buckle digs into his knee.

The field rolls up toward the sky, and the horse slows, its flanks wet with sweat. Its hooves kick through thin strips of cut stalks no one raked or stooked, just left them on the hard dusty ground to blow away with their few little grains.

Someone yells. A farmer on his tractor on the road behind them. He's waving his arms and shouting. Sounds mad. The horse reaches the crest of the hill. They drop down the other side toward aspens and cottonwoods. The farmer disappears.

Arrow must rest, she tells him in the cover of trees. We'll get down now and eat some food. He wonders whether she's going to be like the nuns at school — always bossing you around, telling you when to do things. Always knowing things that you were supposed to know but didn't.

She tells him to take Arrow to the pond and let him drink—take him down through the grey aspen trunks. Trunks like skinny legs with black knobbly knees, Grannie said.

He wonders if they're almost at Buffalo Lake, but she doesn't know. She disappears behind some bushes.

The pond has shrunk to a patch of water about as big as a house. He takes the reins and steps onto dry cracked ground once under water. Pisweskiwaka. Will he sink like the steer to his knees, his shoulders, then just his nose?

Halfway to the water, Arrow's hooves sink to his ankles. The horse snorts and waves his head up and down. I'll go first he tells Arrow. His shoes fill with dry powdery dirt. Not water, not like the steer's mudhole. The horse follows. Cora too follows their foot marks to the water. She fills her cupped hands and covers her face. Drinks. Arrow slaps and sucks. His swallows make a noise like scooping water with a bucket.

Cora tears off a chunk of bread for him and offers him meat in a jar. She talks about some spirit, she calls it gitchie manito, she read about in school. Fathers didn't teach us anything like that, he tells her.

She asks a lot of questions. So many questions. He chews meat. Wonders if she'll let him have another cookie. She wants to know if his tribe ever took white people captive and made them into Cree. He doesn't think Mom and Dad are part of a tribe. It sounds like something bigger than them and the other families. Sounds like the old days Grannie and Grampa knew about. Before they had to live on the Reserve. How would you make someone a Cree? Didn't Cree have to come out of Cree, like Rose-Berry said her babies would come out, between her legs? Then he remembers Grampa saying at the battle of Frog Lake, Cree women covered up a white man with their shawl and the warriors thought he was Cree.

Do your people have spirit dreams? He shrugs. Grannie knew about men with strong dreams who beat the Wihtikiw—how'd they do it? How'd they make dreams come to them? How'd they stay awake and dream? This is not something you talk about, Grannie told him, rocking in her chair, by her rusty stove. When he gets home, he'll go to her house first.

Does your reserve have a medicine man, does he see visions? He says nothing, thinking of that whiteman Mom took him to who came to the reserve sometimes, his belly hanging down to his chair between his legs. Fat fingers, brown stains on them, pressed a stick on his tongue and looked in his mouth. Gave Mom a bottle of red stuff. Medicine. Mom made him take spoonfuls. It smelled like harness oil. Made him want to throw up.

He takes a bite of bread. White people's bread has holes in it, kind of thin. Not like the fry-pan taste of bannock. The kind Mom roasted in the oven. You feel full with Mom's bread.

———

Cora wonders if Netty and Hilda said anything at school, Bunk probably pestered Netty — where's Four-eyes. Four-eyes on the rag?

She's not the same as them. She knows things they don't even think about. Dark things, mysterious things, like barylambdas and fossils and hydrogen atoms. She knows things the way Indians do that town people never think of — like all sorts of plants that can cure people — even Dad said that — they had secret knowledge — and she too has secrets — she knows she isn't just a girl, she can be anything. She could have a store like Mr. Wellman. Or a museum like Judge Rupert. She could pound horseshoes on the forge or run a grain elevator.

Hunter wants to know if her dad'll follow them, but she tells him no, because her dad won't care, and anyway her dad won't even know until sometime tomorrow.

I think he might be pretty mad when he finds out.

I don't know. He always says he's going to give me to the Indians. Maybe he will this time.

What Indians?

I don't know.

What would Indians do with you?

I think he just says that to make me smarten up.

What's that—smarten up?

Follow his rules, wear silly dresses, get baptized.

Hunter shrugs, looks at her funny.

Anyway I'd rather be an Indian than a girl, so it doesn't matter.

You? An Indian! How could you be that?

Maybe you could show me.

Show what?

How to make fire by rubbing sticks together, I read about it in a book by Ernest Thompson Seton.

I don't think so.

He bites into his bread and watches the horse nosing at grass.

———◆———

What's on the other side of his silence—she doesn't know. He goes over and pats Arrow's neck, runs his hands over the bridle and the saddle, then sits down again beside her satchel and hangs his arms over his knees.

She explains that baptizing means going completely under water and saying you believe in God; then you get welcomed into the church, otherwise you'll never be saved. Hunter says they didn't have that kind of baptizing at the school, they had to say glory bes and hail Marys and if they didn't the Fathers would make them burn in Hell. She tells him she's not going back to church, ever, and that from now on sky, sun and moon will be her church.

He shakes his head, watches the horse. So silent, like he's waiting for her to just do whatever she must do. She's starting to get that feeling she gets when Hilda and Netty think she's being wacky and she should just act like normal people. But if she's a booby and an oddball she's just going to darn well be that.

She asks whether Hunter's people have a different heaven and hell than what the fathers taught in school, but he says it's just the same — Father Clarence at home made them say Hail Marys too but he was nicer than the fathers at school, because he played baseball and made picnics for everyone. Then she asks if his Grannie and Grampa believe in the same heaven and hell, but he just looks sad and wishes he could see them.

Maybe before they took him away to school, he learned the tracks and signs of animals, but he just looks at her like she's cuckoo when she asks, so she asks if he knows where squirrels hide nuts, because maybe they could get nuts to eat on their ride. Like Dad did, she thinks, that time he climbed up to a nest to get the eggs and then just as he got there the owl got back and attacked him. Flying into his hat, till it fell off, then clawing at his arms and hair as he clung to the tree.

I followed a squirrel one time, he tells her, I looked in his tree trunk and found feathers.

Maybe that squirrel lived in a woodpecker hole. Did you take out the feathers?

No.

Maybe, she thinks, Hunter doesn't know any Indian secrets. Maybe Indians like that only live in books and she's a booby and should just shut up and quit pestering him, but at least he must know some words in his own language.

———————

She wants him to teach her a Cree word. The Cree word for Cree. Or the Cree word for whiteman. He doesn't know. Grannie would know. She'd say proudly pihew — that bird that walks under bushes and beats its wings thump thump thump — you catch it with your hands. But he can't talk proudly like Grannie. He stomps on a deadwood stick cracking it in two, then kicks away the pieces. She puts a hand on his shoulder. I'm sorry, I shouldn't have asked

—you don't have to. He brushes away her hand—Okay, I'll teach you a word.

Okay.

Takwahiminân.

Takwa him. Takwaham.

Takwahiminân.

That sounds like a lot of words, what does it mean?

That berry over there.

She looks at him like the Fathers did. Like he'd never be smart enough to learn anything.

So if I see a berry I say Takwa himi nan.

Not that.

What then.

It's the name of that kind of berry.

We call those chokecherries.

Nothing to do with choking.

Dry the leaves and make tea Grannie said, Good when you have a stomachache.

With Arrow's back under them again, they bump to a trot in gray dried grass and patches of dusty ground at the top of a little hill. Sun on their left, dropped halfway from the top to the edge of sky. Fields tilt down to a clump of cottonwoods, then up again to far-off lines of bushes, trees, maybe roads.

A cracking sounds—snap like rifle fire. Cora doesn't hear it. She carries on making Arrow follow the top of the hill. Thinks she saw Buffalo Lake over there. Over the up-and-down hills of fields. This field was once the bottom of a sea, she says, a sea of giant lizards. Like a huge lake of salty water. What's a lizard? A snake with legs. Big as a train—the ones that swam here. Trains with legs. And birds big as people swimming underwater.

Rifle cracks again. He points to a red dot in a line of scrub. Go down in the trees.

It'll be dark soon. We've got to get to the Lake.

They carry on through the field turning away from the red dot and toward a solitary spruce. The ground tilts up again.

More shots. Close now. Up ahead, he points. Arrow snorts, pricks his ears forward.

Up there.

On the next hill. A bright red man on his horse. Big hat. Must be a road along there. She turns back. A faraway red dot is moving toward the one on the hill.

Hunter swings around on his belly and pushes himself free of the horse.

Hey where're you going?

He runs to the spruce tree, into the dark arms and black shadows of its lower branches.

———————

She spurs Arrow to a trot, putting the spruce between her and the man on the rise. At the tree, she dismounts and pulls Arrow close to the lower branches, wedging herself into their prickly, sticky mass. No sign of Hunter. Gripping the reins, she presses further into the branches. Arrow stomps. Shh! She strokes his nose. The man canters down off the rise toward the other red man. She slides through scratching needles, keeping the tree between her and the men.

They sit on their horses. One points into the field with the spruce tree. The other holds his hand up to his eyes. Then points to a clump of cottonwoods. The other breaks his rifle, seems to be reloading. She can almost hear the snap as he closes the gun, then digs in his shoulder pouch. He hands something to his partner. The partner breaks his rifle, loads. The horses sidestep. The men slide their rifles into saddle holsters.

Go to the next trees.

She looks up through the tangle of boughs and needles. Can't see him.

Go.

They'll see me.

Go. Keep the tree in the middle.

Where?

Over there, not far, another road.

She can't see him. Where's over there.

The men spur their horses into the field.

She climbs back on Arrow, and edges him at a walk away from the prickly branches. Over her shoulder, the men disappear behind the field's rolling ground. She spurs Arrow toward a line of scrub. A flash of red catches the corner of her eye. She canters into the scrub and finds a farm lane. The men emerge from the cottonwoods toward the spruce tree. They halt and circle the tree. Then head toward the scrub. She dashes down the lane. A farmer comes toward her driving a solitary horse and wagon with a few bales of straw. The lane ends in a field of scrawny stalks flattened in dust. She veers into it—just rolling ground—no cover till small blobs of trees in the distance. She trots down into a dip and the land rises behind her making the lane and the wagon disappear. Stay in the hollow, she tells herself, snake along the hollow till she reaches the blobs—till she too is a dot on the edge. Go slowly, not to raise dust.

—◆—

She carries a rock with a shell in it toward the water. Dad it's a lizard. Dad! It's an old cow bone, he says. I'll prove it, she says, it'll swim in the water. But her hat keeps falling over her eyes, she can't see the water. The sandy rolling water that is not water, and her hat that is not a hat but Arrow's nose nuzzling into her face.

Her mouth tastes like dust.

How long has she been… Where's…

From a fence rail, she clambers onto Arrow and begins to retrace her path. Scrawny flattened stalks that never grew into grain cover the ground in the fields around them. The sun is low. Shadows of willow and chokecherry spread long black claws way out in the field. Even thistles cast a black row of sentinels three times their normal size over the ground. A chill slices the air.

She must go back and find him. How? The map's no use. Who knows where they are? Where he is. She must get to the lake before dark. Maybe she'll try the compass if she can find him. She must follow the line of chokecherry and willow, then back that way. The way of the shadows. Then find the lane. The pasture. The solitary spruce.

Last light almost gone. At the edge of a marsh, she can just see a dark strip of water further out. Her legs are wooden sticks, clumping through hummocks of grass. She stabs at the ground with her sticks searching out a path away from stumbling holes. Her hands behind her link to leather straps that link to horse that link to the boy following horse. Is he still there? She can't see past the animal.

Her back searches for traces of horse heat. Her cold fingers don't want to bend around the reins. Maybe they'll be cold all night. At Buffalo Lake summer camp they had a tent and a cookstove and kerosene lamps. Now in the dark she must start a fire with no paper, no kindling — so start with leaves and little twigs, find them somehow in the dark. Back in Stettler the front-room stove will be crackling — the house glowing with light bulbs and homework. Mom, Elaine, the boys thinking what? That she's out at Hilda's farm? Dad thinking rude, selfish, not letting them know. Or is he happy she's gone back to the Indians?

Where's the beach she remembers from summer? She leads them into a thicket, picking her way between spindly trunks, shuffling through fallen leaves — Arrow's hooves snap sticks of deadwood. She trips over a branch. The horse snorts and yanks the reins back. She coaxes. He takes another step. Dark things flit over their heads. Hunter on the other side of the horse coaxes too, holding his arm up against whapping branches. The lake's somewhere over there.

As soon as they reach the water, Arrow drops his head and takes huge gulps. She combs her hands through his mane. Rubs the rag Gerard gave her over his shoulders and flanks, keeping her face into his pulsing warmth. Hunter too stays close to horse-heat, away from the chill night that hangs over them in a vast bowl of faraway stars—just them, no houses, no cabins, no fishing shacks even. Just them with their tiny plan. Her voice feels thin and shaky, asking his shadow can he gather sticks and dry leaves. His shadow stumbles away and she hears him rustling leaves and snapping sticks, as she tethers Arrow in some trees. Her stomach's an empty cave bigger than her whole body.

Her hands shape some leaves into a pile, dump some sticks on top. Hands shivering, she drops the match. Strikes. Drops it again. Drops the little matchbox. Bugger. A spark catches a leaf. A little flame. A little whiff of smoke. But it snuffs to red edges around a hole.

Shivering hands strike another match. Drop it. Strike again, knocking the sticks off the pile. Bugger. Damn it.

Wait, he tells her, and makes a little teepee of sticks over a clump of dry grass and leaves.

She puts another match to it. This time, he lies flat out, belly to ground, and blows the sparks, each breath stroking the red edges of leaves, making them brighter and brighter till the sparks spread to other leaves and the smouldering leaves spread to smoulder-ing twigs and the twigs sprout little flames. She holds her hands over the tiny fire, then hugs her knees up to her chest. Thank you, she tells him, in her quaky voice. He scrambles away.

She wants to say thank you again when he returns with more sticks, but she doesn't. They must make beds with no pillows and sheets, no roof even, they must sleep wearing all their clothes, somehow keeping warm by the fire. She gives Hunter some bread and the rest of the cookies and they huddle over the heat. They finish the jar of meat, chewing in silence, licking their greasy fingers. The dinner table at home, with its forks and knives, glasses and china, please pass the salt, drifts away from her in the darkness. She could eat ten jars of meat. There's one left plus half a loaf of bread. She'll have to make it last.

I can shoot something, Hunter says as though reading her thoughts.

What?

Duck. Gopher.

At the farm, she and Hilda cut tails from gophers and left the brown furry bodies at the doors of their ground holes for the coyotes. They laid out rows of bloody stumps to get their bounty, a penny a tail. Or sometimes got another penny from Judge Rupert if they collected the bodies for fox food. Eating gophers would be like eating the mice Mom trapped in the kitchen.

He breaks the shotgun, and she makes him poke a stick through it pushing a bit of the grooming rag. He loads shells. Puts the loaded gun back in the sack.

Maybe they are safer now with the gun ready, against things in the vast night-bowl. Or maybe it's the fire that makes them safe, as they sit on their blankets and feed it sticks. The flames shoot sparks and the teepee of fat burning deadfall fills her with its red glow. Hunter too hunches into his jacket, and gazes into the burning wood — fire-glow on his face. Her voice doesn't feel so quavery.

She asks him if he ever heard about Chief Buffalo Child. He shakes his head. She read about him in a newspaper. It said the Chief was Canada's oldest Indian. He told the newspaper he was born in a camp of two hundred teepees. Everyone got sick. Everyone in the camp died. Only one man lived to crawl away. As he was leaving he heard a whimper and found a baby with his dead mother. The man took him to another camp. They fed the baby and he grew to be five years old. Then it was fall and the boy disappeared from the camp. They searched for him everywhere but he was gone. The snow came, still no sign of him. The people thought he was dead. That winter the ground froze hard and the snow was deeper than usual. Next spring they went out hunting. Along the trail they found an old buffalo cow pawing at the snow till she cleared a patch of grass. A little person ran out from between her legs and threw itself down in this patch. The boy ran away from the hunters, and the old cow ran at their horses with her head down. But in the end they captured him. They took him back to the camp and brought him up to be a chief.

CHAPTER 19

Sky pale grey, his body circles half the ash pile, hers the other half. Their breaths are small clouds. Beside them the lake stretches pale and choppy — way bigger than Bear Lake, bigger than any lake on the reserve. Sitting up, he feels the wind blowing through his clothes, blowing even through his bones. Far across the windy water a blue brown finger of land slides itself under the edge of sky. He pushes through ashes for a spark to catch some leaves and twigs and a stick of deadwood, and she too pokes at the fire trying to make it catch. He's forgotten how to talk to her. She seems almost as far away as that finger of land.

She wants to know whether they should eat some of the meat and bread now or save it till later. He doesn't know — probably save it, even though he's hungry.

We have to get around the tail of the buffalo. She shows him the blue animal on the map in its fence of boxes, and tells him about a man named Gabriel Dumont — he had a camp around there — a big summer camp, a hundred teepees. They came every summer to hunt buffalo.

I'm in a play about him, she tells him. I'm Gabriel Dumont.

What's a play? She gives him that Father Oxford look again—that you-stupid look. Then smiles a you-okay look.

A play is when everyone pretends to be someone else and acts like those people—it tells a story.

He thinks of men singing and beating drums in the big teepee, men and women dancing around the tree at the centre. One wore a hat of buffalo horns. He asks her how many days long the play is and whether she's allowed to eat when she's in it. But the play's less than an afternoon, though she can't eat unless the lines say so.

Dancers tied themselves to the centre tree with ropes until they sang their song, maybe plays have ropes. Maybe she's pretending to be Gabriel Dumont right now and he's somehow in this play, but she says she only does that in school.

We'll go along this road till we cross over Tail Creek, she tells him, then through the fields again. It's Saturday. We don't have to be in school. No one'll notice us.

The redcoats are looking.

We have to get all the way from here to here.

I'll hunt something to eat. He takes the gun out of the sack.

No wait—there's no time to hunt. We must go twice as far as yesterday. She opens a small leather box, a red and black needle jiggles in a circle inside. Keeps pointing in the same direction when she turns the box. She says it will tell them which way to go.

But we don't know where we are until we get to Tail Creek. She closes the box.

We need food, he says, it will not take long. He walks off the sand into long grass and tangled dead weeds, carrying the gun.

She says something, but her words disappear in the wind cutting across the lake.

A hawk swoops over him, circling the marsh for mice. He walks toward clumps and islands of reeds and rushes where he might find birds.

Only once Dad took him duck hunting. Don't shoot way overhead. Just when the bird is landing or taking off. He raises the gun and scans the marsh through the sights. No birds. Hold the gun level, Dad said. Point just in front of it. Go along with the gun in front of the bird pulling it by the nose. Then pull the trigger. His shot thundered out, jolting his arm. The birds flew up in a great cloud and were gone. He walked a long way with Dad through soggy marsh to find another flock.

He drops now onto hands and knees in the long grass, and crawls toward the water. He'll only have one chance.

———

She folds the blankets and re-saddles Arrow. Huddling into her father's old coat against the chill gust off the lake, she leads the horse along where the long grass meets a thicket of chokecherries. Dare you to eat those, Netty and Hilda taunted her on the CPR track walking out to the Maynard farm. Dare you, you'll choke to death. No you won't, Dad says Indians eat them all the time. My Dad says his brother almost died after eating one. Netty crossed her arms. Eat those, Hilda said, and your tongue'll swell up till your mouth is plugged, and you'll die of asphyxiation. Don't be silly, you're not going to die from just eating one. So eat one then —dare ya. She put one in her mouth. Spit out the pit. Her friends watched, horrified. Nothing wrong, just sour. So eat another one then. You eat one. Uh-uh, not me. She ate another and another. They walked along. Her teeth felt all furry. Her tongue scraped against her mouth like an old stick. What if she. Hilda looked at her. Are you all right? I'm fine. Are you sure? Course I am, I'm fine.

But what if she? It'd be all her fault if. She could've died. And it'd be all her fault.

Clusters of purple chokecherries dangle above her head. No, it would've been Dad's fault. But he would've blamed it on her, even though she was dead.

Takwa takwa—what does he call them? She can't get the word right, it must've sounded idiotic to him, like she probably sounds idiotic to Mme Lumière when she says French words. Maybe they taste different if you call them takwahimium. She puts some chokecherries in her mouth. Takwahmum. Only if you eat the pits do they choke you, Netty said the next day, guess that's why you didn't croak, gosh you sure looked scared. No I didn't. White as a sheet, Hilda laughed.

The berries make her teeth furry, just as sour as she remembers. Even the birds are leaving them on the bushes.

Why's Hunter out in the long grass? No time to hunt she told him. Just his head pokes out above the marshy edge of the lake.

Not the way Dad went hunting when she picked up his hip-waders from the porch while Dr. Armstrong and Mr. Iver of Iver Motors were loading shotguns and decoys into the back of the mayor's Pontiac pick-up. I'll take those, he grabbed them from her. He glared and jerked his head toward the house. Hey, Hodge, Mr. Ivers chuckled, let's take her along—she can set decoys. Dad marched silently over to the truck, dumped his waders beside the wooden mallards. Mr. Ivers winked at Cora. She slung the shotgun into her shoulder and sighted a knothole on the woodshed. Your mother needs help with the baking.

I want to shoot something moving. Gophers are too easy. She trained the gun on a passing gull.

Your mother needs help.

Behind Dad's back Mr. Ivers shrugged his shoulders and held his hands out, palms up.

Give me the gun please.

She sighted the moon in the old backhouse.

Let me learn to shoot ducks.

Dad gathered up his binoculars and the carrying case for his shells.

Out of sight of the other men, he pointed his hand sharply from her to himself. Give me the gun.

Mr. Ritchie, the mayor, started his truck. Mr. Ivers and Dr. Armstrong got in.

What if you got sick and couldn't hunt?

Don't make me cross.

Someone should be able to hunt food and I'm the oldest.

Give me that. He glanced over his shoulder at the truck — the backs of the men's heads in the cab — then grasped the barrel. She held the butt.

You took Gus last time and he's only twelve.

You know perfectly well why. He pushed her away and yanked the gun out of her hands.

Hunter's gone now, submerged in grass and bulrushes. A solitary duck and then two more land a stone's throw in front of his spot. Something else moves further along the shore. A black Stetson and a red plaid cap — the men are close enough to make out the dark sticks of their shotguns, walking toward the inlet staked out by the boy. Cora mounts the horse and scans the marsh.

No point in calling him. The wind would swallow up her voice no matter how loud she yelled. The horse stamps, shakes his bridle. Pricks his ears toward the oncoming hunters.

Suddenly Hunter stands up, raises the gun. A shot rings out, or was it several shots, scaring up a cloud of birds.

He runs along the shore of the inlet. Maybe he got one.

———————

He got one, he knows it. He saw it fall. He drops the gun and runs toward the clump of bulrushes where the bird should be. Splashes into the water. To crumpled rushes pressed open by a blue wing, a green head, a curled yellow foot. He reaches for the soft dead feathers. Something black and low gets there first, scoops the duck out of the rushes, head dangling from its black jaws.

He throws himself on the dog pushing it down in the mud — dirt in his face, dog kicking his ribs. Riding the black squirming body, he tugs at the bird. The black snout tightens its grip, eyes rolled back at him. He grabs the back legs and flips it on its side.

The dog growls and dashes into the grass. He falls on it, hands into neck fur as he wraps his legs around its ribs, grabs an ear and slaps fur on skull. He tries to pry the jaws apart. The dog lets out long angry snarls.

Hey get off my dog! Someone grabs him from behind, yanks him around, and throws him on the ground.

You're nuthin but an Indian. Whaddaya think you're doin?

Two men with guns stand over him. Rubber pants up to their waists ballooning off suspenders. One wears a battered Stetson, the other a plaid cap. Their faces stubbly like the men at the dump. He starts up. Plaid cap puts his foot on his chest.

You hurt my dog. Stetson bends over it, patting and stroking its head.

He pats the dog all over, feeling its ribs and legs. Drop, he tells it, Drop. The dog lays the bird at his feet. Good boy. That's a good boy.

That dog stole my bird, Hunter grabs the rubbery leg pinning him and heaves the man off balance. He rolls away, scrambles to his feet.

You little shit, I shot that bird, my dog marked it.

Where's your gun then, plaid hat snaps.

What's a kid like you doin with a gun anyway?

It's mine, Hunter says.

Where is it then?

Back there.

How come you're not in school?

Sir, please give me back my bird.

All polite, ain't ya now.

He keeps his distance from the men in their rubber sacks. The dog snuffs weeds, and limps off toward a bush, stops — front paw off the ground.

Stetson bounds over to the dog and kneels on the ground. Hey buddy, you gotta sore paw? The dog sits on its haunches, tongue hanging out. Stetson holds its paw.

You hurt my dog you little shit. The man's face like something clawed it.

You little cunt-face.

Hunter backs away. Stetson clumps toward him wallowing in his rubber pants.

Let's go, Sam, we didn't come out here ta chase kids.

He hurt my dog.

Hunter glances over his shoulder. Cora on horseback strides through the long grass. He dashes toward a white berry bush where he thinks he dropped the shotgun, the man clumping along behind him. Hunter veers toward Cora, then back toward the water. Stetson's between him and the berry bush. Hunter circles toward the dead mallard lying in the grass. Stetson follows.

He's goin fer the bird, the man shouts. Now both men follow him, calling him cunt-face and redskin, their rubber pants slapping as they run.

Hunter scoops up the floppy carcass by its feet, then circles back toward willow bush and trees — the girl and horse between him and the men, calling to him, Let's get out of here. He circles past her toward the white berry bush. Leave my brother alone, he hears behind him.

The hell he's your brother.

He's my adopted brother.

He's a runaway.

Hunter grabs the shotgun, heads for the bush. Pushes through a thicket of whipping, scratching branches, further and further. Till behind him he can see only a tangle of black stems, and a wall of yellow-brown leaves.

————

Cora trots Arrow back and forth between the men and the choke-cherry scrub, each time getting a little further away. The dog sits in the long grass watching ducks land on the lake. In their rubber pants, the men stand in the middle of the grass, staring at her. She stops at the edge of the scrub. The men have turned to the dog. Stupid little bitch, Stetson shouts over his shoulder.

She waits till they're out of sight, then heads back to the charred sticks of her camp on the beach. Arrow dips his head to the lake.

Up a hill behind the beach, she comes to a trail cutting into a thicket so dense it closes into a tunnel over the path. Hunter doesn't answer her calls. Ahead of her, the tunnel walls swirl around a hole into murk.

Did Gerard tell his dad, and did Judge Rupert in his tall white courthouse with its flagpole and brown banisters tell the police to get the horse back? Is she a delinquent? — like Bunk when he drove Mr. Maynard's car all over the golf course? Or Mugsy when he shot Mrs. McKickly's cat?

What if she and Hunter never came back? Just lived out here, like Gabriel Dumont? If they went hobo? If they became buffalo children? She carries on into the darkening tunnel, pushing branches out of her way. The saddle creaks against its leather skirt, her feet snug into the stirrups. She calls out, stops to listen. Why doesn't he come out of this brush — this blur of leaves and crisscrossing sticks? She retraces her steps on the trail. She mustn't go too far or she'll lose him. Maybe he's watching her now from the tangle, like he did at the spruce tree. Sitting with his gun and duck. Watching the horse standing on the trail, her on top of the horse, the horse nibbling a clump of dandelions, then raising its head, pricking its ears, turning to look back at her, moving one ear back then forward.

We could get to your house today, she says to the tangled thicket, why don't you come out?! She listens for a rustle or a snapped branch. How can anyone be silent for so long? Gus and Dougie always sniggered or whistled giving away their hiding places. Trying to lure her in so they could run back to base and free the captives.

She dismounts and tethers the horse to an aspen sapling, then pushes her way into the thicket, ankle deep in fallen leaves. The branches close behind her. She can't even see the horse. So neither could he.

Could he be in that dark clump? A stick cracks under her foot. A magpie scolds. She mustn't rustle leaves, mustn't make even a mark in the leaves. She must roll from heel to toe silently.

The clump is nothing — a cross-hatch of twisty black stems tufted with leaves. She heads for another that looks like Judge Rupert's bear on all fours. Twigs stick in her hair, and claw her jacket and trousers. The bush-bear melts to a tangle of branches. She stops, listens. Something cracks deadwood. Something not her. Maybe there are bears out here. What if the hunters are following them? She heads for another dark buffalo-clump where the boy could be hiding; it dissolves into empty twigs.

Off the horse in this brown black jumble, she feels tiny-legged, like a squirrel or a mouse. She should call out but she can't. There's too much silence, pressing in from all sides. The silence goes right to the sky and spreads out across the lake, across the miles of prairie all the way to Hudson's Bay. She's nothing but a gnat in all this silence that listens, bush that listens, its dark knots and sandy shafts of light filtering down through dead leaves — every twig, every berry, every weedseed with its ears perked. What's her gnat-voice in all this listening?

Another crack of deadwood sounds, maybe it's Arrow. What if the hunters find Arrow? Which way is he? She must get back. Which way is back — which way is Hunter wandering leaving no footprints? What if they never? They couldn't find? And she brought them here. She made them. And they.

She must get out. Now. Wherever out is. Down the hill, she must find the trail. Find him.

She crashes into brush, snatching at branches, yanking them away. Stomping dead wood. Kicking through leaves, at least leaving a mark of where she's been. She plunges down. Down is toward the lake, unless she went over a hill. Leaves and twigs cling to her jacket and hair as she bursts onto the path. Then hangs back in the shadows looking one way and the other. The horse is gone. She runs along past some purple asters, past a silvery clump of wolf willow, winding left then right. She's back at the beach. She runs back up the trail till she comes to an aspen trunk. Hoofprints mark the ground. Or is it further along, another aspen? A dim circle in the dust seems to go back, not forward. She runs along the tunnel looking for faint circles.

A thickish sapling near a soapberry bush — this is where she left Arrow. And Arrow's gone. Ran home probably. Think — she must think. She must look for Hunter. They'll have to walk to the nearest farm, and turn themselves in. But Hunter won't, he'll run again. And she, what'll she say to Gerard? God great spirit. God. God. God. Let Arrow. God please. Arrow.

———•———

She's kneeling on the ground by the aspen where he found the horse. He'd tied his gun and bird back in the sack on the horn. Stood with his palm on the great neck, smelling sweat, fur, seedheads of grasses. Dad, the mostos — will he be there when Hunter gets home? Huge brown eye under long lashes looked at him. Soft nostrils nuzzled his back. Jingled the bridle.

He freed the horse from the aspen. Climbed into the saddle, its smooth leather. Now he was really part of the horse, not bouncing along like something tied on. He clucked to Arrow, nudged heels in his ribs. Rode into a tunnel of bushes till it closed to a deer path — the horse stopped in a thicket of branches. He turned around, let the horse carry him back down the path.

Hands over her face, she curls forward, pressing fingers into her forehead. Sticks and leaves cover her coat. The horse nickers. She takes her hands away. Mouth a round oh. Then springs up and throws her arms around the horse's neck. Calls his name.

Strokes his cheek, strokes his long white nose. Puts her face into the soft brown hair of the neck.

He's my friend too, he says.

She looks up at him in the saddle — a twig of brown leaves caught in her glasses. Her cheeks are wet. She looks away. Takes the reins under Arrow's chin. Tugging at the ends in his hands. He pats the horse, holds tight to the reins.

Let me ride in the saddle.

You can't. She doesn't look at him. He's not my horse, I have to take care of him.

She keeps looking at the horse's neck.

This boy-girl doesn't like him. She can have her horse and he'll walk.

He unties the sack and gets down from the saddle.

Where're you going?

I'll go by myself. He drops the reins on the ground.

We're in the middle of nowhere, you'll die. She picks up the reins.

I'll find a train.

Police'll get you just like that.

He slings the sack over his shoulder and walks down the path. Hooves clump along behind. Her hand on his shoulder yanks him back. He shrugs her off.

I'm not mad at you, you know.

He pushes on. She grabs the sack and the gun, pulling him backwards. He swings around pushing her off.

Don't be stupid. I'm trying to help you.

She pushes him onto the ground. Plants her foot on the sack. He lifts her foot tipping her backwards. Seizes the sack but she throws herself on his back and sits on him before he can get up.

You can't just take a horse when it's not yours.

He likes me just as much as he likes you.

He heaves up on all fours wrestling her off. She snatches his arm and twists till he loses his grip on the gun. Okay you wanta fight, we'll fight, he whirls around crouching — fists up. She chucks the sack into the bushes. Then comes at him, arms stretched in front to push him down.

We've got to get out of here before those hunters get back to town.

He punches her face, knocking off her glasses.

You're not my sister. You could never be an Indian.

She stumbles, clutching her cheek, then slaps him hard on the ear.

On hands and knees, she puts her face close to the ground, and feels around under bushes. Like Wîsahkecâhk looking for his eyeballs. Why did he hit her? He never hit Rose-Berry. He picks up the glasses and hands them to her. One eye's cracked. She sits on the edge of the path fitting the curled arms over her ears, then rolls and unrolls the leather straps of Arrow's reins in her palm. The horse waits, watching them with his huge brown eyes.

I'll let you ride in the saddle when we're in the fields after Tail Creek. She looks at the ground. Rolls and unrolls the reins.

How come you act like a boy?

She shrugs, says she doesn't know. Her eyes look at him now but she's not there in her eyes.

He hands her the sack.

———◆———

Out of the thicket, she turns Arrow west through range land along the lake shore. No Trespassing, says a sign in red letters on a worn plank. They pass it into a field, staying off the road till the crossing at Tail Creek. *Forgive us our trespasses as we forgive those who trespass against us.* Is it trespassing to hit someone when they've hit you?

She keeps her distance from a farmhouse and barn but there's something wrong with them — their doors and windows empty like wide-open blind eyes; she sees right through them to sky and dust and dead weeds on the other side. Arrow jolts at something white and twisted — the ribs and backbone of a steer lying in the dust, then another skeleton with its pelvis and legs and a patch of hide still attached. A hay rake and tractor stand as silently as the skeletons, half buried in drifts of dried weeds and dirt.

At Tail Creek they search for pools in the dwindled flow. Hunter scoops mouthfuls, then splashes his shoes and feet. She washes her face and dips her glasses, carefully drying the cracked lens. The map says they must get across Highway 21 and avoid Alix and Mirror.

Past the creek a dark oblong blocks the road, something twirling on top of it. Arrow whinnies and perks his ears at a spotted mare standing in tangled shafts and harness — a wagon on its side, the twirling thing its wheels. The lank sides of the mare show her ribs.

Aylmer Soup and Swift's Lard crates make the sides of the wagon, its tent roof of canvas scraps held on by bits of wood. Clothes and dishes spill onto the road. A man in too-big overalls bends over the mess, telling his son to pull a shaft out of a loop.

Beside the wagon, a woman stands with a baby in her arms and a boy hiding in her apron. Tryin to turn around'n go to Stettler instead of Mirror and she went over, the man says, You couldn't give us a hand could ya? Amy kin hold your horse and we getter righted agin. Bind up the shafts somehow.

Do unto others as you would . . .

The kind daughter always helps others, said the brown book with gold lettering. Even when her cruel mother sent her three miles to haul water while the lazy selfish daughter stayed home. An old crone at the well begged her for a drink. The kind daughter rinsed the pitcher and held it to the old woman's lips. After that diamonds and pearls fell from the kind daughter's mouth every time she spoke. The cruel mother told her other daughter to fetch water too, beating the lazy girl till she went. A fine lady at the well asked her for water but the girl haughtily refused to be her servant. After that snakes and frogs fell from her mouth every time she spoke.

Whirlwinds of dust skitter toward them across the open, tree-less land bringing its blind emptiness of skeletons and abandoned houses — emptiness silting in the whole of Canada — swallowing up tractors and farms and Dad's job in the store — swallowing up Edmonton and Toronto, and even Aunt Beulah and university.

Mister, we've got a long way to go today. Behind her Hunter shifts his legs off the saddlebags.

Only take five minutes with you and your brother there.

The child in his mother's apron wants bread and jam. Not till we get to Stettler. He lies down in the dust, rolling and wailing. His mother lets him roll, and shushes the baby.

This's all we got, now the bank took everything — this here wagon, and a few pots and pans.

He tells his son to pull again, no not the traces, pull that. Where're you going in such a hurry if it's not too much to ask.

Out towards Ponoka. (How many hours and it's already almost noon. How many miles?)

Riding double all the way to Ponoka — that's a helluva ways from here.

They've gone fifteen miles maybe — going as the crow flies they've got at least another twenty.

They're hungry, Hunter whispers in her ear.

They'll get food in Stettler. She clucks to the horse. Arrow balks, doesn't want to go off the road to get around the wagon. She urges him on with her heels, but he dances sideways at the horns and empty eyeholes of a skull.

We could give them half the duck.

No we can't. We need all the food we can get.

Her stomach jumps like Arrow jumping away from the skull. Crazy-jumping at this emptiness swallowing everything, she and the boy drifting along like tumbleweeds on Judge Rupert's map, the horse snorting and pulling, the dizziness of her own oddball world with its patchwork of knowing, not knowing and boobiness.

Without stirrups, she bumps along on Arrow's haunches, letting Hunter have his turn in the saddle. Ahead of them along the horizon, black dots move from one edge of sky straight into the other edge. The black dots become a truck with a chopped-off cab and oily black tank, followed by another with hay in its slatted rack. Then going the other way a roadster with its top down, and a truck towing a car on a hook. Engine-grind and the drone of tires on blacktop fill the air.

Giddup. Hunter digs in his heels. They canter toward the highway — too fast — way too fast.

She grabs the reins and pulls them in. The horse careens, as Hunter pushes her arm away and slides to the ground.

Where're you going?

Keep outa sight.

She shifts from the blankets to the saddle. Vehicles grind toward them out of the hazy distance and rumble past on their spoked wheels. A slatted truck with a load of pigs. Then a red pickup like the mayor's that her father went hunting in. Same black running board, same visor over the windscreen, like the truck is wearing a cap, same headlamps bulging up like frog eyes. The men in the cab wave at her. Arrow spooks at Hunter's crouching shadow.

A truck with a high roaring cab, barrels toward them pulling a long box on lots of wheels. Dyson's Pickles. They dash across the tarred surface.

She feels weightless, timeless, as though Arrow started a leap and never landed, his lost hoof-beats stuck inside her, waiting to come down — circling around, turning her insides to jelly because they can't come down; there's no more ground to land on, only another highway running into the one they just crossed.

A truck with a big box pulls another big box. McNabb Transport on the side. Then a fire engine goes past. Get back on, Cora mutters, pulling Arrow up beside a pile of old fenceposts, we're gonna have to run. Foot in the stirrup, he reaches up. Grabs her coat and the saddle. A red truck's stopped at the edge of the road, three men coming toward them. She swings the horse away, galloping further down the road and across.

———◆———

Arrow's head's down—his back one solid muscle bolting forward. His hooves hit the ground, fly, hit the ground, fly. Hunter grabs the saddle seat and braces for the hits. They pound through his butt and back, toss him from the saddle blanket. Let him land, toss him away again. Soon his bones'll fly apart and drift away on the wind. His hair'll blow off, his eyeballs bounce away.

They rise up on a hump of ground, then plunge down, then up again. Highway and men getting smaller and smaller. They canter along a valley, till they cross a range road. The sun on their left. Woods ahead, a straight path cutting into them. More green, not so much dust. Then trunks of trees on either side, and leaves like a roof over their heads. He changes his grip to the saddlebag. The horse slows to a trot. Bounce bounce bounce. His stomach growls. No food today. His head almost falls forward onto her back. Maybe he could just lie down on the horse's rump with his head hanging over his ass. His whole body flipflopping like a fish on a line. And the line pulling him over the fields and ponds and trees, the farms and skeletons and fences, reeling him in to Grannie and Dad and Mom, Auntie Marge and Uncle Jack.

They walk through grassland and clumps of aspen and spruce till they find a small pond and two cottonwood trees. Stumbling behind a tree, his legs feel light and useless. She doesn't get the food out. Just sits on the edge of the pond looking into the water and holding the rope tied to Arrow's bridle. Then she lies back on the grass staring up into the sky. He curves his body over a sun-warm rock, lets the pounding ride slowly sink into it. Queg queg queg goes a magpie.

After awhile, she ties Arrow to a tree, and they eat the rest of the bread and canned meat. No more food except the duck. Just enough oats for Arrow for one more day. Get vegetables from gardens. But she's afraid to go too close to the farmhouses.

He goes back to his rock. A blackbird lands in the pond rushes. Grannie ate blackbirds. You're lucky to get farm chicken, she told him. I used to nail boards together and prop them up with sticks. Then when the blackbirds came under I pulled out the sticks and the boards killed the birds. I skinned them and cut them up and made soup.

Grannie said they ate skunk, too, and it tasted really good.

My grandmother ate skunk, he tells Cora.

She's washing her face in the pond. She looks at him like he might be a skunk.

She ate snake too and mice and frogs.

So how did she cook snake then?

She ate it raw.

If I catch a snake, will you eat it raw?

Just joking.

I just saw one, I'm going to catch it. She scrambles up the bank and onto the grass, searching for the snake.

Only kinda chicken I had as a girl was prairie chicken, Grannie said. I used to watch where those prairie chickens danced. Then bend sticks over, all over that place. I tied little snares to each stick. Those prairie chickens danced with their heads down. Right into my snares.

She's coming toward him, a small snake wriggling in her hands.

I brought you a snake for dinner.

Just joking. Even before she dumps it down his neck he can feel its cold oily skin worming into his back. He throws off his jacket and flaps out his shirt tails till the snake zigzags away in the water. Then steps into the pond, makes his hands into a scoop and heaves water in her face.

You rascal.

He's out of the water and running round the other side. She's chasing him, scooping up water in the empty meat jar and heaving it down his back. He dashes off toward the next clump of trees.

I'll get you. She's right behind him. Her eye where he hit her is turning black. She's laughing.

A fence blocks his way. She tosses the meat jar and grabs his arm, twisting it behind his back, pushing him into the wire squares.

Say uncle.

He's laughing.

She twists harder. Laughing. Say uncle.

Aunt.

She lets him go.

Sorry about your eye.

She touches it. Does it look bad?

Turning black.

Black as those Holsteins?

On the other side of the fence two cows pull at grass and a feather-leaf plant Grannie makes into tea. Put the root on your tooth if you have toothache, she says. Another cow stares at them and sniffs.

Milk cows. Like the one they had, that Dad used to milk before he sold it. Squeeze closed at the top and then squeeze the rest of your fingers Dad showed him. One hand, then the other. Out it comes. He grabbed the pink skinny teat and squeezed, got nothing. Takes practice, Dad said.

He asks Cora has she ever milked a cow. She hasn't. She's seen her friend. It doesn't look that hard. He puts a foot into the wire fence, grabs the post.

You're not going to...

Why not.

For starts, you don't have a bucket.

Squirt it in my mouth.

He straddles the top of the fence, jumps down on the other

side. The cows take a few steps away. Three sets of black eyes stare above their blackish-pink noses.

Cora lands beside him. Wants to know if he's planning to lie down under the cow for the squirts. He grabs a handful of dandelion leaves, holds them out and walks toward the animals. They back away, eyes wide, black ears twitching toward them. He bends forward and reaches out his handful of greens as far in front of him as he can toward the one with the black nose patch. The cow sniffs and tosses her head.

In the corner of his eye Cora skirts out into the field way around the cows. Make them come this way, he whispers.

Okay. She points along the fence. There's more down there.

She holds her arms out on either side like a giant scary thing, corralling cows toward him. One of them slides past her, lifting its tail. Oh for Pete's sake. She leaps across the splat and lunges at black-nose. The cow trots off, and Cora lands on her knees. The cow sees him and heads to the fence. He springs toward her, arms around the splotchy neck. Face into cowshit and cowhair. She lets out a long moo, dragging him into some bushes. Other moos sound further out in the field. The cow heaves herself away from him, hoof grazing his leg. He pushes the solid hulk of her, making his arms into a collar and wedging her between him and the fence, then strokes her neck, and pets the swirls of thick hair on the hard ridge between her ears. She bellows again.

Cora breaks off a branch from the bushes. You're supposed to give them something to eat, she says. You lock their heads in a manger. She offers the cow the branch. The animal blows steamy breath and turns her head back to the others staring at them from a little way away. Don't worry, we'll be really gentle, Cora tells the cow — I'll hold her, you milk her.

You do it.

Why me!

You saw your friend, you said it looked easy.

You said you knew how. She snatches the meat jar through the wire squares. Here.

They switch places and he squats down near the back of the cow. Teats are what girls have, Eagle said. Girls don't have things that hang down. Good thing girls only have two instead of four, Eagle laughed.

Tiny jar on a dried cow pat. He reaches toward the milk bag, face into cow belly. Puts his fingers around two teats. Pinches at the top. Squeezes. Nothing comes out. The cow sidesteps. Its tail whaps the back of his head. He crawls up to her again, places the jar between the four hooves. Getting anything, Cora wants to know.

Shhhhh!

He tries two hands, one at the top to hold shut, the other one to squeeze. A thin stream hits the cow pat. The cow lifts her hind leg and drives her hoof into Hunter's ribs pushing him over. He crams his shoulder into cow-belly, his back against leg. Gets a big squirt of milk. Aims the teat at his mouth. Closes. Squeezes. Milk tastes warm, buttery. The cow bellows again. Cora shushes her.

He gets some in the jar, but the cow stamps her feet, knocking it over. He wipes off the dirt on his pants. Holds the jar with one hand, grabs the teat, squeezes, squeezes, squeezes. Milk foams. Cora tastes it, says she wants more, says he's good at it.

You try.

Uh uh, not me. She keeps her arm around the cow's neck, holding her to the fence.

He drinks a cup, squeezes more into the jar. Warm cow-skin on his face. Other cow-faces closer now. Warm animal bodies moving around him. Animal sniffs and snorts, chomping of cuds. Cora says they all want milking. One of them has horns.

Cora says they should go now, look how long the shadows are, she can't see Arrow on the other side of the fence, we've got to find a good place to camp. He gives her another jar. She drinks it. Okay next one's the last one. He squirts froth into the glass.

Downs the melting buttery milk, holds the jar under the teat for another.

The cow walks. Cora's let her go. Disappeared. A collie dog's barking at his heels. He clambers over the fence. Hears voices, blends himself into the bushes. Just out riding. What happened to your eye. I walked into a tree. Not from around here are you. Yes I am. Runaway ain'tya, with an Indian boy. No sir, I'm from Tristram. Tristram — helluva ways from here — whatcher name? Mcdonald, sir, Liza Mcdonald. Whattaya doing mucking with my cows. Just stopped to pet them sir. She's backing away from him toward the fence. Where's your horse then? Over there, I really must be going, it's getting late. She's at the fence. Not so fast. Someone's with you. No sir, I'm by myself. My dog's barking at him. She's over the fence. Must be my horse sir, I really must go. Stay outa my fields. Yes, sir.

———

His turn to ride in the saddle. He stands in the stirrups firm and ready, feeling the weight of his body creak the leather. She points to her fence of lines over lakes and rivers. Like boys in school, roads have numbers — such as 53 that goes to Ponoka. But where are they now? She chucks the map away. Then picks it up and stuffs it in her satchel. Climbs on behind him. Let's go that way — pointing a little toward the sun but mainly to the darkest sky ahead. Shadows of trees already stretch over the meadows between islands of cottonwood and aspen. Sun red and low.

He clucks to Arrow. Digs in his heels. If Arrow were an arrow, they could shoot from a bow. They could fly like Wîsahkecâhk to any line or town they wanted. They cross a dirt road into an open field. He spurs the horse to a canter. Then turns Arrow in a circle, Cora slides sideways, clutching at the saddlebags. Hey what're you doing?

Seeing how fast he can turn.

Save that for barrel racing.

He turns Arrow the other way, makes him go round again — his body the horse's body, his legs the horse's leg's, his feet pounding the ground like thunder. Circling and snaking across the field. She's silent behind him holding on to the back of the saddle, weighing down the boy-horse like a sack of potatoes. Or maybe keeping him from flying to the moon and then falling into a mudhole like Wîsahkecâhk.

———

In the growing dusk, they can't ride. They walk, watching for holes where Arrow might put his foot. She leads them across a road — maybe it's 53, who knows? Dark tree-shapes lie ahead. Lakes have trees around them. Please let this be a lake. Somehow they will have to cut up the duck and cook it. Hunter wants to put rocks around it and make the fire heat the rocks. She's so hungry now she could eat a horse. What if they were lost in winter and they had to eat Arrow?

She shivers. The horse snorts and leaps backward. Something's moving on the ground ahead. Hunter runs toward it — a row of furry hummocks on long hind legs, with bushy tails — a mother raccoon and two yearlings. He grabs one of the yearlings by the tail. What're you doing? The animal whimpers clawing the ground toward the others. The mother growls.

Kill it and eat it.

He holds it by the scruff.

We've got the duck. She calms Arrow.

The mother raccoon snarls and runs at Hunter. He kicks her away. The yearling shrieks.

Stop. Let it go.

No.

He grabs it by the hind legs, raises it over his head and brings it down hard on the ground breaking its neck.

Oh my god. She presses her face into Arrow's neck, holding close to the puffs of the horse's breath, listening to his hoof stamping the ground.

Hunter stands on the other side of Arrow, untying the sack from the saddlehorn.

I'll carry it, he says, and walks on ahead. (Why's she so scared of him killing a raccoon?)

———◆———

He pushes into trees, tromping down deadfall, breaking off branches, chucking them away, whacking white ghosts of aspen trunks, whacking at their black knobbly knees in the almost dark till they reach the lake.

I'll get firewood, he tosses the sack down on the stones by the water. Leaves her black breathing shape with the horse sucking up water.

Branches hit him in the face. He yanks at them. Can't break them off. He tears off peeling bark. Brings handfuls back to shore, then handfuls of leaves, heaping them in a pile and pulling a circle of large pebbles around them.

His hand hits fur and feathers of limp bodies when he digs for the knife in the sack and tromps back to the trees to hack with it at bark and branches. Then lug deadfall to the lake. Jump on it, break it up. More bark, more branches—a bigger and bigger pile —burn the whole place down—she still standing with the horse by the water. Not tying him up like she usually does, and rubbing him with the cloth and giving him oats. Just standing there holding his reins and pushing pebbles around with her foot. The matches are in her satchel.

We're turning into animals, she says.

We need a fire.

Wolves—just grabbing anything like that and killing it.

Arrow's wet—we should rub him.

He takes her hand and puts it on the satchel, and she opens it and gives him the matches. She remembers the horse then and spreads blankets, crouching there, with her cracked glasses, white face in the firelight, white hands over flames — saying nothing, feeding sticks to the fire.

When she looks at him her eyes are like the government man looking across his table at Dad.

She puts her hands over her face. Then pushes a bigger stick into the flames. I still want us to be friends, she says crawling over to his blanket and holding out her hand.

Girls hold hands with you. That's what Shorty said. You hold hands, that's how it starts, and then you kiss them and feel their titties. And then you put your dick inside them.

He shakes her hand, like Dad did with the government-man.

Gonna cut up the duck and the raccoon. Don't watch.

He hacks at the duck's neck. Why's it alright to shoot a duck and bad to kill a raccoon? He flips over the bird, hacks from the other side. Blood mashes into pebbles. He thinks of Wîsah-kecâhk's little brother when they were the only two children in the world living by themselves on the prairie. A hairy man carried Wîsahkecâhk away in a canoe that moved without paddles. His little brother, left all alone, turned himself into a wolf and howled.

Hunter's knife sticks in neck bones. Cora pushes her fists into her chin, watching. A long time later, Wîsahkecâhk came back and found his brother. The wolf piled the bones of his kills neatly; only people would do that. Hunter squishes the duck bill and green head on the ground. Yanks against the dull knife till bone snaps. Her eyes shift away, somewhere in her thoughts. He digs the knife into body feathers.

I'll make you into a person again, Wîsahkecâhk said, but wolf brother was afraid of everything people do. What things Hunter asked, but Grannie just said everything people do that makes them people. Wîsahkecâhk took his wolf brother into a sweat-tent and burned sweetgrass over him. He sweated out the wolf part, happy to be a person again.

Hunter digs a hole where the wing joins on. Twists. Grabs it. The wing stretches out fanning the feathers. Hands around the wing-bone snap feathers and yank. He chucks the wing on the beach.

We did that with chickens, Cora says (face out to the lake), we put the chicken in boiling water and pulled out all the feathers. But I guess we can't do that out here. No pot for water. She hunches around her knees next to the fire.

His knife points into the top of the leg, he grabs the foot, twists and turns, and at last holds out a skinned leg. She stares at him.

It still has a foot on.

So. (If she's a boy-girl, she's not much of a boy.)

She takes the foot. Then drops it on the stony beach, pushing it away from her leg.

Hold it in the fire, cook it.

She balances it on two stones so the meat sticks in the flames.

Coals're better, doesn't burn.

He hands her the other foot, then tears off the rest of the skin and feathers from the body. Builds a nest of stones around it, like they did in the woods at school. But she wants to put a stick through it like her Mom and Dad did when they went camping.

He shrugs. Yanks a branch from his firewood, rams it through the duck.

With the tips of her fingers she turns the curled, webbed feet.

Let me see it, she says when he pulls out the raccoon. He lays out the limp body on the blanket. She runs her fingers over its ears and the rings on its tail. Then puts her palms together, and closes her eyes. Like she's in church and she wants the raccoon to go to heaven, not burn in hell like the flames around the duck.

She opens her eyes.

Did you say, Our Father who art in heaven?

No, nothing really. She looks into the fire. Just hope that we find your house tomorrow.

I'm gonna cut its head off, you better not watch.

She watches anyway, like before. Clasping her hands and pushing her fists into her chin.

She tells him she's got a book all about two boys who lived like Indians — a man teaches them how to stuff an owl. The book shows you the pictures of how to do it. There's this man in Stettler who stuffs animals, she says.

You wanna stuff this?

Oh no, I guess not.

He slits open the raccoon belly, dumps the insides into the duck skin. Stabs and scrapes — the knife doesn't fit inside the little body. He hacks off the paws and tail. Cora turns the duck on its stick. Pokes at the curled duck feet.

Just duck feet in the fire after Wîsahkecâhk told Fox where his birds were roasting. Wîsahkecâhk got mad at Fox, set a fire all around Fox's nest. But Fox jumped over the fire. Only his fur got a little burnt.

He walks to the shore, swishes the skinned body in cold water. Puts it in his nest of stones, piles stones and burning wood on top. Scoops guts into the two skins, washes the knife.

Where're you going?

Into the woods. Throw these far away.

Don't go too far.

She's looking into the fire through her round cracked eyeglasses — holding on to her knees like they're that rock Father Clarence talks about in church.

He pushes into the dark, kicking rotten deadwood, following bits of firelight on tree-trunks, shouldering off bushes that claw his jacket. Just faint glints now on the trees. Almost nothing. His eyes see in the dark. Raccoon eyes. Raccoon becoming him, searching for shadow trunks in patches of night. This far enough? No. He pushes on. Looks back along the shore to a tiny glow of fire under night sky, tiny ripples of light on black water. Tiny shadow of Cora.

Now he can't see when he turns back to the woods.

Little brother lived with Wîsahkecâhk and his wife, but she noticed he sat alone a lot with his head drooping. He told Wîsahkecâhk his wolf wife and wolf son were in trouble and he must go back and help them. Good luck, said Wîsahkecâhk, Just remember one thing: never wade into any kind of water. He turns back into a wolf. Wolverine had already killed his wife, but he saved his son and taught him how to hunt. On the way back to Wîsahkecâhk, he chased a deer just for the fun of it — chased it right into a lake where something big dragged him under. Wîsahkecâhk must rescue him again, Hunter thinks, but how?

————•————

Hunter's footsteps sound along the beach. A patch of light catches his face. Her nose is full of sizzling bird. She holds out one of the duck legs. Let's cut a piece off with your knife. Test it.

Yeah, good, he says biting into it. He crouches close to the fire.

She bites into her piece. The outside's dry and hard. Kind of muddy tasting. But food. She takes another huge bite of the leg, not like thin pieces Dad cuts. She chews hard, takes another bite. Tries not to look at the webbed thing in her hand.

Least no foxes stole our duck.

Why would foxes do that?

Cuz Wîsahkecâhk was stupid. He had all these ducks roasting, then he told Fox they were going to have a race and then eat the ducks.

Who's Wîsahkecâhk?

Him and his brother were the first children. He talks to animals, makes them the way they are. Animals play tricks on him. Fox pretended he had a hurt leg and couldn't run, so Wîsahkecâhk got way ahead. Fox ran straight to the fire and ate all the ducks. Wîsahkecâhk came back — all he found were duck feet.

He chews his leg down to the bone. She, too, scrapes her teeth on bone. Then wishes they had soap to wash hands.

What's your sister like?

She likes to make things.

Like clothes?

No. She builds bridges.

Where?

Wherever she is. With string and wood and newspaper. Bridge hangs on the string. She piles stones on. Sees if it breaks.

He hacks apart the rest of the duck. She tears flesh off the bones, swallowing without even chewing. Don't gobble, Mom's voice says.

He wants to know if she knows any stories about animals.

I know one about a bear.

So. Tell.

Okay. A king was so afraid his daughter would be harmed he locked her in her room. But a witch helped the daughter escape in a wheelbarrow.

What's a witch?

An old woman with special powers to make things happen.

Oh.

She covered the daughter in a bear skin. A prince saw the bear and started to shoot her. No no, don't shoot, she said. He was very surprised by a talking bear and he took her home to his house. He left her in the kitchen while he went to a ball. Let me come too the bear said. But he pushed her back in the kitchen and told her to do the housework. At the ball he met a beautiful princess.

The prince tried to follow the beautiful princess but she disappeared. Each night for three nights the same thing happened. On the fourth night he put a ring on her finger. But still she disappeared. I gave my ring to a beautiful princess he told his mother, and the bear started to laugh. Go back to your kitchen, the prince told the bear. He told his mother to bring him some soup. The bear dropped the ring into it. I am the princess, the bear said. And the prince married her. And they lived happily. Ever after.

Small sparks fly up into black sky speckled with stars. The night is cold on her back. She adds more wood to the fire.

He married a bear.

No, she turned back into a princess.

What happened to the witch?

I don't know.

I know one about a bear-woman.

Okay.

A man hunted buffalo every day. Then he came home at night and saw lots of firewood piled up. He thought someone else did that. But no one was there. Next day he came back and found his house all clean. He thought a woman came but he didn't see her anywhere. Next day he found some moccasins just in his size. Who made them? She wasn't there. So next day he got up very early, finished hunting and came home early and there she was sitting in his house. She made him hunt lots and lots of buffalo. She dried meat. Stacked it up for winter. She said we have to go to my people; they're hungry, they need food. She made him go ahead of her, put sticks in the ground at their night camp. She flew through the air to their camp with all their stored meat. After three days they got to her people. Her mother and father were happy, they welcomed the hunter and he stayed with them all winter. Then in spring he found out the woman was really a bear, and her father and mother were bears too. He was sad but he had to leave them.

The fire crackles. Its sticks glow and dance from white to black to red.

Were they really bears, Cora asks, or were they really people who looked strange to the hunter and just seemed like bears.

He stares at the tangle of burning wood, the mound of stones cooking the raccoon.

I think they were really bears.

CHAPTER 20

In the morning she blows on the grey sticks of the night fire, adding bits of leaves and twigs. It smoulders, doesn't catch. She's got five more matches for the trip back. Back where? Stuffing herself in Dad's trunk in the attic, like trying to cram in the sky — her bread-dough body swelling till it bursts the trunk apart, fills up the attic, pushes the roof off and oozes over the whole town.

She pulls her knees up to her chest and wraps her coat around them. The raccoon's mostly bones. Half to herself, half to Hunter. Back home Judge Rupert's raccoons are safe in their cages, looking out their masks. Back home Dad's mad at her and Mom's probably worried too. But she's outside everything they are now.

A bird lands on a dead tree over their camp — red head and black body — big as an eagle — but it has the hunched shoulders of a turkey vulture. They eat dead things, Dad said, animals that've died of disease, or been hit by automobiles, or killed by wolves and coyotes. It smells the insides of their raccoon and bird where Hunter threw them in the bush. Or maybe it smells them.

Drifting in this big outside, at least she isn't getting baptized today. Maybe they won't even go to church. No, Dad'll make everyone go. Even when Mom had pneumonia, Dad made them all go to church and let the fire go out. People'll ask where she is, and he'll have to say something, he'll have to think of this outside.

Maybe if she were an Indian, she'd know what the vulture meant. If she were an Indian, she'd run away like Hunter and stay outside Mom and Dad's world forever. She'd ride horses and kill raccoons. She wouldn't just be a girl. She'd know what to do to roam around like Gabriel Dumont, living out on the prairie, but she doesn't know. Even Indians like Hunter's dad don't know how to make fire without matches, and, thanks to white people, they have to stay on their reserve unless they get permission to leave. As though they're in school, and can never get out. Only Indians in books by white people roam wild and free with their buffalo, that Mme Lumière said were mainly killed by white men shooting guns from trains.

Hunter takes the saddle. It's his last chance to ride Arrow before he gets home. She shows him the map, shows him to stay away from roads—for sure people will be looking today. Where's the road? Back that way I think—we should follow near it but out of sight. I know where to go, he says, my people live over there. He points somewhere she thinks is northwest of where they think the road is but the sky is solid grey with high clouds and the sun could be anywhere. I think we should try to follow this, she pulls the compass out, and lines up its pointer with the N on the dial, Don't go where it's pointing but a little that way instead.

He takes the horse across some open fields and heads into patchy meadows between clumps of aspens and thickets of dogwood and Saskatoons.

Keep going away from where it's pointing, she tells him.

I know where to go, he says, I know.

He turns Arrow to avoid some trees. A farmhouse with a red roof and red barn comes into view. He turns back the other way around the trees. They come to a small lake parched back from its old shoreline and ringed with salt-coated dirt. They head around it, going toward the N on the dial, and then toward the E, passing between dying birch trees and cottonwoods, to follow a long strip of dried grass and dust to another dried up lake. The way round is blocked by rose bushes and wolf willow, they skirt it toward the S, but come to some farm buildings with tin roofs. They turn back and follow the lake shore the other way toward the N and sometimes toward the E. The lake is bigger than the other lakes, after a long time they still haven't got around it. Then they see farm buildings with tin roofs. Is it the same farm with white buildings or did the other one have brown buildings? Which way is toward Ponoka? She doesn't know.

They put some trees between them and the farm. Then she takes the reins from his hands, from her seat behind the saddle, and tells him, We have to stop now and rest, figure out which way to go.

We have to go that way, he points across the lake.

But we've got to get around the lake before we can.

Why don't you look at your map, use your needle box.

We don't know where we are on the map — we've got to get around that farm.

We're lost then. He slides off the horse and walks away.

No. We are not lost.

Why don't we go back to that 53 road?

Because — you know why.

You say you know things, and then you don't know them. He wanders along the lake shore, gazing across it, as though he were thinking of swimming toward his reserve.

She takes Arrow to the shore to suck at the lake, then lets him rest and chomp at dead grass. If only she'd made the bread and the jars of meat last longer; if only, but she didn't. She and Hunter drink handfuls of water. He squats on the shore poking a stick into the mud and flicking dollops of muck to plop into deeper water. Cora rests her head on her arms across her knees and follows some ants moving back and forth through a forest of grass stems, a little bit that way, then a little bit the other way — did they know where they were going? She looks up to see the vulture circling overhead.

A flock of ducks flies out of the reeds further along the shore. They need food, they don't know how long they'll be out here. This time, *she's* going to shoot one. She unties the sack and digs in the saddlebags for shells.

What're you doing?

I'm going to shoot a duck so we'll have something to eat.

We've gotta get going.

We need food, and the ducks're right here.

Why're you so bossy, always saying when we stop and go?

Can't you see — Arrow's tired — he's got to rest or he'll stumble or get sick — he belongs to my friend and he's very important to him.

She stands beside Arrow resting her hand on his great shoulder. Maybe he could find his way out of here, if they just let him, find his way home but they're not going home yet.

So. I'm your friend too, and that's my gun.

Listen — if anything bad happens to Arrow, or you, or me, it'll be my fault and if anything bad happened I could never — I could never ever...

She can't finish the sentence. She rests her head on the saddle, tries to stop silly girl tears in Arrow's chomping.

He grabs the sack, but she snatches his hand and spills the shells.

Your horse, my gun.

It's not yours, you stole it didn't you?

From a crazy man — shooting everyone. No one wanted him to have it.

He drops the sack and kicks the ground scattering shells and stones, then runs straight at Arrow with hands out to push him. The horse jolts, sidesteps, stands alert, ears perked forward.

What're you doing?

You go back to your town — your school. What do I have?

I don't know.

She picks up the sack with the gun, then gathers up the rest of the shells from the ground.

A girl can't shoot anything.

I've shot lots of things.

Like what.

Gophers.

Not the same as birds.

He flops down and rolls over, head on his arms, face into dust and dead grass.

She plunges into the bushes along the shore towards where they saw the ducks, calling to Hunter to come along and watch where the bird falls. He keeps his face to the ground, doesn't move. She carries on, looking for mallards and pintails like she'd seen so many times on Sunday walks, like she and Elaine fed breadcrumbs at Cold Lake — the birds would come right up to you, and then how would you shoot them? But there's no breadcrumbs here and anyway, past the bushes, the drying shore reaches a long way out to the water — nothing like bulrushes to hide in.

Pictures show hunters pointing up into the air at flying birds. Only ninnies shoot at ducks in water Dad'd probably say. But she's not going to think about Dad now, she's going to do it her way cuz they'll be easier to hit. She finds a quacking and whistling flock just off shore and gets as close as she can, though it's still farther away than her targets at the coal mine. She crouches down and pushes to the very edge of the bush cover, lines up the shotgun's V and crosshairs with the closest mallard. The bird swims out of line. The gun seems heavier than Dad's. She pulls it closer to her shoulder. Sights another bird. Her cracked glasses make it dance in and out of line. Then use the other eye, she tells herself, lining up with another bird. She pulls the trigger, stumbling off balance onto her elbow. The flock of squawking birds lifts off the lake and away. She got one, she can see a lump floating. She puts down the shotgun and runs across the shore into the water not even bothering to take off her shoes. But where is it? She walks about, getting muddy and wet up to her thighs. There's a hummock of floating grass, that couldn't have been it, could it? Searching for the bird, she's almost back where she left Hunter.

Didja get one.

He's still lying on the ground face down.

No. Well—I got one but I couldn't find it.

Now all the birds are gone.

Yeah.

He rolls over, his eyes black and smouldering, looking at her the way the sportsmen did back at Buffalo Lake.

So where's the gun?

It takes them till almost dark, crashing through bushes up and down the shore, to find it.

She gathers sticks and leaves for a fire, thinking what a complete booby she's been, worse than the most useless thing in the world. If she'd just been a normal girl...

He doesn't help her. He sits beside his sack and his gun, arms crossed on his knees looking into the dusk closing around them. She builds a little teepee of twigs and leaves, puts a match to it and blows the way he does, then carefully feeds in dry bark off deadfall. It catches and she feeds in bigger sticks. Holds her shivering hands over it. At least they have a fire to dry her clothes. Could they eat leaves and grass? Chew and chew and chew the way Arrow does?

She lays out his sack and blanket on the ground and then her blanket. He's still sitting, looking out at the last hint of light on the other side of the dark lake.

She walks over, puts a hand on his shoulder. Come and get warm.

He says nothing. Doesn't turn his head.

She goes back to the fire and piles up as many sticks and branches beside it as she can, then sits on her blanket. She can't go on any longer with Gerard's horse. There's only a handful of oats left, and no grass, just dust and yellow leaves. How could anyone live out here just roaming around? Who does she think she is?

———◆———

The whitish trunks of trees announce first light, day come back to her — smoke on her hands and face — stiff pantlegs from yesterday's walk in the lake — his sleeping hill curved around the fire, lying on his sack with the blanket over him. She blows on the coals, adds sticks, blows till it crackles up again. Then shakes his shoulder till his eyes open.

I'm going back to that farm — see if I can sneak some eggs, maybe a chicken too. Need your sack.

He closes his eyes, turns back to the crook of his arm. Stumbling stiff legged, she takes Arrow to a place among the trees where there's a tiny bit of grass, and gives him the last of the oats. Hunter slowly folds his blanket, shuffles past some bushes. His pee hits the ground.

They're like Gerard in Judge Rupert's blank-eyed gas-mask, clawing his thick leather fingers at the air. They move around the fire like farm machines with no one driving — Hunter hiding his gun in the bushes, then dragging his sack behind him — she stomping her feet that feel nothing, her stomach a giant empty pit.

Away from the fire, Dad's too-big jacket lets cold seep up underneath. She scrunches her hands up into its sleeves and heads back through some cottonwoods toward the tin-roofed buildings, trying not to crack the dead branches under the fallen leaves, but they crack anyway, keep tripping her. How to wake up, not be a mindless farm machine. Is he behind her?

After the cottonwoods, there's a wagon track along a row of willow trees. The eighth commandment, Pastor Crawford drilled her. Thou shalt not steal. What's required in the eighth commandment? That we pursue lawful and useful work to provide for our needs and for those unable to provide for themselves. Breaking a commandment, she's sinning against God. Her evil and darkness deserve Dad's belt, Mom's cold shoulder, the Pastor's moulding prodding fingers.

She stops, looks behind. Hunter's pulling carrots. Stuffing them in his sack. He doesn't care about this evil, just takes what he needs. He looks at her waiting, pulls more carrots, adding them to his stash. Then catches up to her, dragging his sack of carrots. Can farm machines talk? She whispers to him which one does he think's the chicken house.

Maybe the one with the stovepipe.

Another small building has a flat roof — it could be that one — and it's farther away from the house. He shrugs, looks back through the cottonwoods.

She picks the flat-roofed one. Okay, let's go get some eggs.

Chickens'll wake everyone up.

Inside the chicken-house. No-one'll hear them.

As soon as they open the flat-roofed building she remembers the smell of the boar in the Maynard barn. She pushes Hunter back but it's too late and the pig's rubbing up against them like the Maynard's boar did to the gilt — rubbing its nose over their calves, nudging it up between their legs until they slam the door on the shoving animal.

He was right. It's the other hut. For sure it'll have eggs — clean and white like the ones in square compartments from Wellman's store, on the lids of the cartons a kneeling woman tossing handfuls of grain to plump birds. Once a week they could eat one of the white perfect eggs.

But where do the birds wandering around the floor or clinging to long poles spattered with chicken poop lay their eggs? Hand over her nose she crosses the mucky floor, almost bumping her head on the low ceiling with its drooping cobwebs, toward a shelf divided into sections. To put eggs in her pockets, she has to let go of her nose. Hunter beside her reaches into a box, puts an egg in his sack. Don't put them in there, they'll get broken, she tells him, Put them in our pockets. A hen turns its red fleshy crown the colour of lips this way and that, wandering over to a hanging bucket.

A bigger bird runs out from behind the stove scratching up more dust, straw and feathers. Ouch. What. Then she knows what. It's clawing at her legs as she kicks at it, grabbing as many eggs as she can. It's on the stove now shrieking.

She bends over a bird on the poles, closing her arms around flapping wings, then empty air — Hunter saying let's get out before someone comes.

We can put it in your sack.

She reaches for another hen, and the rooster lands on her back pecking her head and neck, but Hunter pushes it off. She gets a bird squirming and flapping under her, pinning it down to the pole, the bird mashing its rubbery lip-red comb into her face. He's already at the door, telling her, get the feet. What then? Swing it against the ground like he did with the raccoon? The poles, the chicken feeder — she can't anyway, she can't. It opens its beak, making little gasps as she holds it upsidedown.

I guess we should kill it. (Its eye watching her, raspy breaths going in and out of its beak.)

Kill it later.

Hunter pulls his sack over it, and they run back down the wagon track and through the cottonwoods — the rooster shrieking its morning call behind them.

Arrow rumbles at them. She throws more branches on the fire. Unloads eggs. How to cook them with no pot. She puts them into the coals at the edge of the fire. Hunter cracks two and eats them raw. He opens the sack.

Let me do it. She grabs at the bird. (She's got to make up for yesterday.)

Okay, hurry up.

How?

He shrugs.

She snatches at its back pulling out feathers as the bird flaps half out of the sack.

Twist its head.

Its eye and the red fleshy lobes around its throat squish into her palm.

Hold it down with your other hand.

Warm brown feathers struggle against her, its heart pulses at its throat under her fingers, as the bird squawks and gasps and claws her knee. She tightens her hand around the head and turns, mashing the open beak, the lobes, the eye and even the tongue of it.

Turn harder.

The head's facing backward — and still it gasps, groans and kicks, till she wants to jump on it and smash it with stones. She gets both knees on it, cracking its ribs, both hands around its panting head, and twists till something breaks, and she falls back from the heap of feathers, the head all lolled over, the eye still looking at her. It's dead. It's finally dead. And she killed it.

Hunter wrenches it out of the sack, rips open the ribs, hacks off the head, then yanks off skin and feathers. They throw the carcass with the feet still on it onto the coals and heap other coals on top, stirring and poking at it till they can tear off half-cooked meat. An egg explodes gushing liquid into fire. She cracks one, douses it in the water, and downs it in two bites.

His foot nudges her leg and she looks up.

Least we did better than Wîsahkecâhk and got chicken meat on our bird feet. He smiles.

And then they hear dogs. She throws the carcass and half-cooked eggs into her satchel, ties blankets, gun and sack on Arrow, pulls Hunter up behind, and urges the horse away from the camp. The dogs seem closer. Men shout back and forth to each other. She urges the horse, but they run into another lake maybe it's the first one they came to yesterday, they head around it, and through some scraggly trees. At the bottom of a slope, they come to a road. Cora gallops Arrow along it, risking in the early morning they won't be seen, then veers off into fields to stop in a small clump of aspens. They rest and listen for shouts and dogs.

The sky coats their faces with its dense pink. She hasn't told him that she's got to turn back. That she knows she and Arrow can't live in the fields and woods any longer. But how can he walk?

I know this road, Hunter, says, It's not far from here.

You mean Ponoka?

Yeah. My house too — not far. That way there's a trail. (He waves north.)

Can you walk? I've got to get back to town now.

You don't want to go to my house?

It's not that I don't want to.

He slides off the horse and stands with his back to her, staring out toward the road.

I want to but I can't — I've got to get Arrow back to town, and let Dad and Mom know I'm okay.

He shrugs.

She gets down, and starts untying her satchel. I want you to have this.

She puts in all the matches and shells. Take the blankets too.

How will you make a fire, he asks.

I'm not going to, I'm going back up the road and getting help from a farm. Arrow can't go any farther without proper food.

She stuffs the blankets into the satchel. Hunter leans into Arrow's neck and strokes the horse's nose.

If anyone asks I'll tell them you hopped a train to Edmonton, she says.

Are we still friends?

I sure hope so. She waits till he's finished saying goodbye to Arrow.

Don't let them catch you — okay, she says as he heads away from the morning light and out across the field carrying the bulging satchel on his back.

CHAPTER 21

She sits in her bedroom, holding her stinging and puffing hands in her lap. He switched her so many times, Mom asked him to stop. A hundred times wouldn't be too much, he growled. I dunno how any of us can ever face Judge Rupert again. A whole search party out looking, and you run off again. Lucky if that horse doesn't have to be put down too, and I'll have ta pay for that. She watches him in the garden, digging up potato plants, scooping the shovel deeper, clawing through the dirt with his hands. She's to stay in her room till she's ready to talk to the Pastor. No school. Nothing.

She places her hands on the cool glass but the pain doesn't go down much. Aspens have welts on them, Hunter told her, because Wîsahkecâhk beat them with a chokecherry stick. The trees didn't like how he'd tricked the buffalo, and they told the birds where his meat was roasting.

Dad's stopped digging and instead rams the spade along the edge of the grass, slicing off chunks of lawn that have pushed their way into the garden plot, banging the clods against the spade and chucking the roots and grass into a bucket. He scowls at her window.

Does he see her hands against the glass?

Just apologize, Mom said, just go see the Pastor and things'll right themselves. But it's bigger than any little word like sorry, she doesn't know how big it is. She doesn't even know where it is — this bigger thing. It was inside her but now it's gone, and she's as empty as the tin jug on the communion table.

She pulls out the letter she wrote before Dad came home from work.

Dear Aunt Beulah,

I hope you ~~are well~~ and Uncle Bob are well. ~~I don't know how~~ We are all well here. Mom is over her cold. ~~I helped her~~ We canned 20 pounds of beef today. ~~Dad is fine too.~~ Dad is leading a Bible study class twice a week. Gus is doing better in school ~~but he hates~~ doesn't like it and Dougie loves school. ~~Like me. The way I like school.~~ Elaine is getting good grades too, ~~though she's still a real circus acrobat~~ when she isn't walking along the tops of fences.

~~I've always admired~~ ~~I missed school today.~~ Over the weekend, I had a little adventure. ~~I ran away~~ It was in a good cause. ~~Dad's pretty mad at~~ I was trying to help an Indian boy. I've always admired the work you do ~~helping others~~ for the Red Cross. ~~I'd like to follow~~ ~~I was trying to do something along these lines~~ I'd like to work on food for the poor, like you do.

~~I borrowed a horse and tried to~~ My adventure involved taking the boy on horseback across country. ~~He was running away~~ ~~Perhaps this will seem odd~~ He wanted to ~~help his sister at their boarding school~~ get home to his reserve. You might think this wrong, but Mr. Maynard in our church says the boarding schools ~~beat the children~~

~~and a lot of them die from tuberculosis~~ treat Indian children very badly, and they should never be forced to go there.

~~I know that to do the work you~~ I want to go to the University of Toronto the way you and Aunt Faith and Aunt Judith did. ~~Marie Curie discovered~~ ~~I want to do experiments in Chemistry~~ ~~I want to~~ and study science that will help people, maybe the science of nutrition. ~~I read about it in Good Housekeeping.~~

~~Dad doesn't think he can afford to~~ I'm hoping to get a scholarship ~~My friend Netty got me a job cleaning rooms~~ ~~I'm wondering whether I could~~ but I'll need somewhere to stay. ~~Mom doesn't know I'm asking~~ Do you think I might board with you and Uncle Bob? ~~I can cook and clean.~~ I could help out quite a bit around the house, and help Marcie and Dwight with homework.

— ◆ —

Her messy scratches on the white sheet of paper blur into sticks and bumps and squiggles. Her thickened fingers rip the sheet in half, then quarters, then eighths. On her way out to the garden, she dumps it in the kitchen stove. She tells Dad she's ready. He gets his jacket and hat and they walk to the church, and the Pastor asks her if she's ready to profess repentance toward God, to have faith in, and obedience to our Lord Jesus Christ; and to no other. And she says yes.

For now.

— ◆ —

Hunter wanders around the house, spinning one of Grampa's empty shells and poking his hand in the sock Auntie Marge is knitting for him. Library—what's that, he asked Cora. It's a room full of books you can borrow and read—that's how I found out about the lizards as big as trains. Books that told her how a potato can make a light glow.

He finds one of Rose-Berry's bridges on the window ledge and adds a few pebbles to its load. Rose-Berry far away at that school. No one to visit her when the brothers and sisters meet on the benches in the green room. Mom and Dad can't go. No money for the trip. They can't take her out of that school anyway. They could go to jail if they did that. They could go to jail if he stays here.

Everyone is over at the church now for the funeral of Shorty's sister Baby Mary—she died of what Ernie had. Stay inside, out of sight, Dad told him. But he's not going to. He's going out. He's going over to the government man, Mr. McDonald, tell him he's ready to go back.

Three more years till he's fifteen—then he'll be free.

Glossary
(generally from the *Alberta Elders' Cree Dictionary;*
* marks a word from *Cree: Words*)

apistikakes	magpie
kîyasiw	she/he runs swiftly
kokôm	your grandmother
kwâskohcisîs	grasshopper
mihkosiw	he/she is red
misâskwatômin	Saskatoon berry
*môniyâhkâso**	act/be like a whiteman
mônîyâw	white people
mostos	buffalo
namewak	sturgeon
namoya	no
natonam	she/he searches for it
nehiyaw	Cree people
nikâwiy	my mother
nikosis	my son
nimosôm	my grandfather
nimosôminan	our grandfather
nîstâw	my brother-in-law (my sister's husband)
nistes	my cousin
nitikwatim	my brother's son
nîtisân	my sister/my brother
nitosis	my aunt
nohkôm	my grandmother
nohkomnan	our grandmother
nohtâwiy	my father
nôsisim	my grandson
okiniy	rosehip
onocayikowiw	hawk
pakesîwin	playing the Cree hand game
pihew	grouse
*pisweskiwaka**	quicksand
sihta	spruce tree
takwahiminân	chokecherry
wâpos	rabbit
wihtikiw	person who goes insane and turns to cannibalism, legendary in Cree tradition
Wîsahkecâhk	legendary figure in Cree tales
wîsakimin	low-bush cranberry

Family Relationships on the Reserve

Most families in bands on reserves are related in some way, so that for a boy like Hunter almost everyone outside his immediate family is his grannie, grandpa, auntie, uncle or cousin. Housing on reserves, especially in the 1930s, was limited and many members of extended families shared small quarters. Three interrelated households are imagined here described from Hunter's point of view: (1) Daniel and Mary George, their children Hunter and Rose-Berry, Uncle Jack (Mary's cousin), Auntie Marge (Hunter's great aunt, Daniel's aunt) and Grampa/Nimosôm (Hunter's grandfather, Daniel's father); (2) Uncle Lenny (Daniel's cousin) and Auntie May, their children Lizzie, Tom and Fish-eyes, Uncle Norman (May's brother), Lena (Norman's wife), their children Eagle and a new baby, and Uncle Joe (Lenny's brother); (3) Auntie Ethel (Mary's sister) and Uncle Arthur, their children Shorty and baby Mary, Grannie/Nohkôm (Hunter's grandmother, Mary's mother living in a cabin next to the main house), Uncle Alex (Arthur's cousin) and his son Ernie.

A Historical Note on Rupert's Land

In 1670 Charles II, King of England, granted all of the Hudson's Bay watershed to the Hudson's Bay Company. This area was called Rupert's Land in honour of the king's cousin, Prince Rupert, who was the first governor of the Company. This huge expanse of North America included what later became northern Quebec, northern Ontario, all of Manitoba, most of Saskatchewan and Alberta and a large part of the Northwest Territories. The Company had complete control of the territory until 1870, when it surrendered it under the *British North America Act* in exchange for £300,000, land around its posts and 2.8 million hectares of farmland in what became the prairie provinces (*Canadian Encyclopedia*).

Acknowledgements

I am very much indebted to the Cree tales and legends. Some of my sources for these include *Sacred Stories of the Sweet Grass Cree* (Bulletin No. 60, Anthropological Series No. 11, National Museum of Canada, 1930); *Cree Trickster Tales* by Edward Ahenakew (*Journal of American Folk-lore* 42 (1929)); *Medicine Boy and Other Cree Tales* by Eleanor Brass (Glenbow-Alberta Institute, 1979); and "6-009: Translation From Cree To English As Told By Harry Harris Of Pelican Reserve" (http://www.calverley.ca/Part06-Legends/6-009.html).

Other sources consulted for this project include *Indian School Days* by Basil H. Johnston; *Kôhkominawak Otâcimowiniwâwa Our Grandmothers' Lives As Told in Their Own Words*, edited and translated by Freda Ahenakew and H. C. Wolfart; "...And They Told Us Their Stories," edited by Jack Funk and Gordon Lobe; *Voices of the Plains Cree* by Edward Ahenakew; *Alberta Elders' Cree Dictionary*, edited by Nancy LeClaire and George Cardinal / *alperta ohci kehtehayak nehiyaw otwestamâkewasinahikan*, edited by Earle Waugh; *nehiyawewin: itwewina / Cree: Words*, compiled by Arok Wolvengrey; *Indian Residential Schools in Canada: the Painful Legacy* by Mudhooks (YouTube); *"A National Crime"* by John S. Milloy; "Notes on a History of Indian Residential Schools in Canada" by George Erasmus (2004); "Natives died in droves as Ottawa ignored warnings" by Bill Curry and Karen Howlett, *Globe and Mail* online (2007); *Spurgeon's Sermons* (http://www.spurgeon.org/spsrmns.htm); *Cree Narrative Memory* by Neal McLeod; *A Baptist Catechism* adapted by John Piper, online; *History of Canada* by I. Gammell (1922); and *History of Canada* by W. L. Grant (1924).

I would especially like to thank Melanie Fahlman-Reid and Stephen Reid for their valuable comments on and insights into the manuscript. Melanie's knowledge of Cree ways of life and Catholic schools and her detailed editorial suggestions helped enormously in the final revisions of this narrative.

I'm also very grateful to the many people in Stettler who helped with my research there, especially Deborah Cryderman and her colleagues at the Public Library, Stan Eichhorn of the P&H Elevator Preservation Society, Graham Scott and staff of the Town Office, and Karen Wahlund and Wilda Gibbon of the Stettler Town and Country Museum. Let me emphasize again, however, that none of the people in my imagined Stettler are to be identified as real people.

I would also like to thank the Banff Centre for granting me a scholarship which enabled me to participate with this manuscript in the Writing Studio of 2011. In particular I thank Greg Hollingshead for his inspiring leadership of that program and his insights into writing fiction. I am enormously grateful for the editing of this novel at Banff by both Michael Crummey and Daphne Marlatt, whose attentive responses and cogent suggestions enabled me to find its proper shape. Thanks too to Jacqueline Turner and Nicole Markotić for their advice on early drafts.

Suggestions and responses from my editor Doug Barbour and the other readers at NeWest were very helpful in preparing the manuscript for production, and I thank you all most gratefully.

In addition to being a wonderful traveling companion, my sister, Karen Yearsley, provided invaluable advice on flora and fauna in the Stettler area. And to Peter Quartermain, I can never give enough thanks for his comments, proofreading, encouragement and support.

Thanks too to *West Coast Line* 65 (Spring 2010) and 72 (Winter 2012) for printing sections of this novel.

Growing up in Cobourg, Toronto, Iqaluit, Midland and then remote British Columbia, **Meredith Quartermain** developed a strong sense of landscape and place which has influenced her writing. One place that especially intrigued her was her mother's hometown of Stettler, A B, and she recorded her mother's stories about growing up there. Then, years later, she visited the town, and found the magic of walking on her mother's girlhood street and exploring the country around Buffalo Lake where her mother had hiked and learned to swim.

History and the ghosts of past events surrounding places have been defining currents in Quartermain's poetry about Vancouver. Her previous books include BC Book Prize winner *Vancouver Walking,* Vancouver Book Prize finalist *Nightmarker,* and BC Book Prize finalist *Recipes from the Red Planet*. She is also co-founder of Nomados, a small literary press in Vancouver.